Handlers of Dragons

KIM CORMACK

Mythomedia Press 2754 10th Ave V9Y2N9 Port Alberni BC

While writing Handlers Of Dragons, our family suffered the heartbreaking loss of its guiding light. Nana Scott was a truly special woman with a feisty spirit, a spectacular sense of humour and a heart of gold. For us, most days began with an early morning visit to Nana's house where we'd have coffee and make her breakfast before Cam went to school. There's an empty space in our lives now. With a steady ache in our hearts, we bring everything she taught us along on our journey. Till we meet again, Nana.

ACKNOWLEDGMENTS

I have been truly blessed to have incredible friends and family in my life. To my parents and children, thank you for your unwavering support of my dreams.

Love to Haley McGee and Leanne Ruissen for being my awesome, talented editing support system. You ladies always find everything I miss. Love you both. Auntie Faye, thank you for always being my biggest fan. Your journey with cancer shows us all what true strength of spirit is. You are an inspiration to us all.

A Message To My Readers

Thank you for being super patient with me. Stress and M.S do not mix. This year has been the stress Olympics. I'm busy writing book three in Lexy's series. I hope you enjoy the fourth book in Kayn's series. Love to you all.

Happy Reading XO

1
CONTINENTAL DIVIDE

The musical symphony of exotic birds had Kayn mesmerised. Each step she took through overgrown brush brought her closer to the next chapter of her story. She ducked under a low-hanging branch. The colourful Toucan perched there didn't flutter a wing. *It remained in place as a steadfast reminder of a love that had dissolved into nothing but memories. Thoughts of the jungle in the Testing instantly brought her back to purple flowers, heartbreaking goodbyes and the devastating events thereafter. Even a momentary thought of her mortal ties still made her want to succumb to the hollow numbness of her Dragon ability.* She felt the pressure of Zach's hand squeezing hers. *He'd probably been listening to her thoughts.* Kayn returned her Handler's gesture and swallowed her emotions down as she always did. He didn't want her to make his day more difficult. She closed her eyes, allowing her Handler to lead her blindly into the unknown. Zach yanked on her hand. Kayn was instantly brought back to the here and now. Markus was brushing away the foliage on what appeared to be a small animal's burrow. The ground opened, revealing stairs descending into darkness, much like the Ankh Crypt in British Columbia. As they followed their leader into the shadows, it felt like a symbolic representation of her life. Zach took her hand again as they reached the bottom of the stairs and she felt the strength of their spiritual tether. *It had taken a while, but it was now a certainty.* Markus was fumbling around cursing. *He was probably regretting leaving their Fire Starter Grey behind.* Markus swore again, searching for something to light the torches. *She'd absorbed Grey's gift back in that town full of demons but hadn't attempted to use it since and didn't know if she could.* Just when she was about to offer it up as an option, the light began flickering from a torch, and the five newest Ankh got their first look at the Crypt. It was identical to the last one she'd been in, with ornate tapestries on the walls representing the story of their Clan.

Pausing by one with the Brothers of Prophecy and the girl they all knew was Lily, Zach nudged her, teasing, "Your boyfriend is super old… absolutely ancient."

While fighting the urge to touch the carving, Kayn commented, "He is, isn't he?"

Markus marched down the corridor ahead of the group, lighting each torch with the flames of the first. Leaving inconsequential things behind, they caught up with the rest just as Markus placed his hands against the stone. He stepped through the solid wall at the end of the hall without saying a word. They'd done this before. None of them gave it a second thought as they followed their leader into the unknown and stepped out into a minimalistic white room. *This was different.*

Markus commanded, "Quickly, please."

They followed his lead as he strolled right through another wall into a lab, startling the people working there. A statuesque Asian lady wearing a lab coat embraced Markus like an old friend. Animatedly chatting, she led the Ankh down a dimly lit corridor and up an unusually steep flight of stairs into another sparsely decorated room.

Where were they? The large plaque they'd passed on the stairs had read, 'The Aries Group.' It made sense, but she still had questions. She heard the faint hustle of a busy street and easily identifiable music outside of the walls. *Were they in the Middle East?*

The five Testing survivors were ushered through the kitchen of a busy restaurant. The employees barely gave six strangers a second look as they were led out a door into the sweltering heat to black jeeps with tinted windows.

The lady who hadn't acknowledged their presence paused her chat with Markus long enough to say, "What are you waiting for? Get in. Three per vehicle."

Kayn and Zach climbed into one with Astrid. Mel and Haley got into the other. Zach leaned in and whispered, "We're not in Kansas anymore."

No, they definitely weren't. The front door of their vehicle slammed. *She couldn't see the driver through the barrier.* The engine started and they took off like they were in the Indy 500. Their surroundings whirled by in a blur as they weaved through traffic. *Obviously, road safety was not a thing here.*

They'd been driving in awkward silence for a while when the barrier rolled down. The driver announced with an accent, "Do what you are told."

Alrighty then. They slowed as they pulled into a luxurious walled desert compound with flourishing vegetation. Stifling nervous energy with humour, Kayn glanced at Zach and remarked, "I've already been the virgin sacrifice once this year, it's your turn."

Her Handler sparred, "I'm quite confident there are no virgins left in this group."

They got out of the vehicles and were quickly escorted into the building. *Markus didn't come. Once again, their leader had tossed them into the deep end with no idea what they were doing.*

A dark-featured, gorgeous man with an inviting smile addressed the new Ankh in perfect English, "My name is Amar. I'm not sure how much Markus has explained, but we have a group of four set to go into the Testing. We were hoping you would join the festivities this evening to represent your continent."

Wasn't the Testing every five years?

Answering Kayn's thoughts, Amar disclosed, "Your continent's Testing is every five years. Our Testing is every two. We have a much larger, more disciplined population to work with. Tomorrow, our elders head out to the Summit, and our untested Ankh will be left alone in this compound for the next week. Don't panic, Markus and others you know will be in attendance this evening. We have issues that need to be dealt with beforehand."

Wearing a tank top with a bikini underneath, Kayn felt naked as she caught on to the mortified expressions. *Markus could have told them to put on more clothing.*

Guiding the group down a long, ornate hallway, Amar announced, "First things first, you can't be walking around dressed as you are." He escorted each of them to a suite and politely urged them to remain there until they were brought something appropriate to wear.

The room reminded her of the King's suite from virgin sacrifice night. She felt like she was in a safe place but suspected she'd always feel that way now, knowing she was part Guardian. She didn't feel a speck stronger. Truth be told, she hadn't had the time to figure out how she A blonde woman in a business suit barged into the room, pushing a rolling rack of dresses. She asked her to pick her poison with a classy British accent. *If this continent had a separate Testing, why had Leanne from Trinity gone in with their group? She was British.*

Responding to her thoughts, the lady remarked, "Maybe her family was on a vacation? It happens." She snatched a dress off the rack, passed it to her and declared, "This one will look gorgeous on you. Change quickly."

It took a minute to figure out how to put the dress on with its multiple floating layers of lavender silk. Like the princess from a fairy tale, Kayn wandered onto a balcony overlooking a flourishing courtyard. Over the walls was endless untouched desert. Sweat moistened her brow. She wiped it off. In the heat, the modest layers of floating lavender silk clung sensually to her curves. Aware of the seductive power of subtle femininity, she felt more beautiful, than she had in gowns that left far less to the imagination. *Everything about this place was foreign, yet amazing. Hopefully, her boyfriend would be joining her in this luxurious suite. He'd taken her paternity announcement in stride. She'd been blissfully sleeping in his arms when she was awoken in the wee hours by Markus's light rapping on the bungalow door. They were assured the others would be joining them. She'd left Frost this morning without a word. They'd been having so much fun together. It was going to suck if they were separated again for months with no warning.* She heard footsteps and turned. *It was their host.*

Amar grinned his approval as he asked, "We were told of the training Lexy put you through before entering the Testing. Would you be willing to go on a quick pre-dinner jaunt to the In-between to give my group the Dragon experience?"

In theory, a Dragon was a part of a fairy tale. The Dragon in her always took precedence. Kayn shrugged and answered, "Why not?" She followed Amar out and down a long, extravagantly decorated hallway. They met up with the others in front of a door with a large Ankh symbol carved into the stone. *Fancy.*

Amar pressed his hand against the door. It magically opened. He directed, "After you."

The five strolled past their host into the room with three large Ankh Tombs similar to the Crypts on North American soil. *It hadn't occurred to her that there was more going on with her Clan than what she'd already seen. Why hadn't she assumed there would be Clan on other continents?* They wandered over to the Tombs.

Mesmerised by the ornate engravings, Zach touched a Crypt and it opened. He abruptly stepped away and apologised.

Amar laughed, "Touch anything you want son."

Zach's body language suggested he wasn't a hundred percent on board, but she was rather stoked at the prospect of going full Lexy on the group of international Newbies she had no emotional attachment to. It was freeing to allow her inner Dragon out to play. Murder was always a lovely distraction.

"Well? What are you waiting for?" Amar urged.

This was going to be fun. Kayn got into a tomb. Zach climbed in with her. Astrid, Melody and Haley joined them. As the stone ground shut above her, Kayn grinned, eagerly anticipating what came next.

Their eyes met, and Zach whispered, "You are always totally ready to rumble, aren't you?"

Chuckling, she answered, "So ready." Their Tomb shifted. As it locked to the one next to it, brilliant light began rhythmically strobing. She squinted in the blinding glare of Rose Quartz before closing her eyes. They'd travelled to the In-between on countless occasions, but she was always excited in the moments before they left the land of the living. The Tomb began to strobe at an even pace and then came the familiar humming. In her mind, Kayn counted down, *3, 2, 1.* They were catapulted up at a stomach-churning velocity.

Zach released his inner Grey by hooting as the they spun like a vomit-inducing carnival ride. It paused for a second.

She knew what came next. Her stomach lurched, spiralling downwards, descending into the In-between. In what felt like moments, they were free of their Rose Quartz Tombs, falling with the moist, cool wind against their flesh. Her senses soared as she plummeted through the clouds and caught sight of the clean slate desert below. They landed side by side like gods in the inviting warmth of the sand. Kayn looked up at the multihued blue sky. *The beauty of this place never ceased to be anything short of miraculous.*

Mel ran her fingers through her hair while mumbling under her breath, "It would have been nice to meet these people before going on the offensive."

As they began debating what they were going to do, Kayn wandered away. *This place held the answers to so many questions. She was part Guardian, but what did that mean?* While standing in her barely there, goddess-like attire, she felt different. *Had her role changed? She didn't want that. She hadn't had enough time with her surprise sibling before they'd parted ways.*

Catching up, Zach enquired, "Where do you think you're going?"

Kayn stopped walking. *She wasn't supposed to leave his side but it felt like the rules of old might be irrelevant now.* Facing her Handler, she confessed, "I was thinking about everything that happened yesterday."

"You definitely had a few bombshells dropped on you," Zach acknowledged as they casually strolled away from the others.

This had all gone down the night before. She needed a moment. She recalled Seth's speech. He'd said, the rules no longer applied to them without explaining what he meant. Squatting, Kayn and placed her hands in the luxuriously tactile sand. *He'd told her to come find him in the In-between. Could she? What was she capable of? He'd left her with a million unanswered questions.* When she peered up, they were all gathered around. *Were they waiting for her to give them direction? She didn't know anything more than she did yesterday, besides her paternity. Any one of them would be a better leader. She didn't want to lead anyone. She wanted to cease to think and succumb to the Dragon within. The Testing had only been four months ago. She was still a hot mess of emotions or lack thereof. It was like she was two sides of a coin and each day the universe flipped her to see what it was going to get. Last night, her Handler had taken the news of her paternity in stride but they hadn't had the opportunity to speak privately.*

Astrid broke the silence, announcing, "There's no point in just standing here. Let's go."

As they wandered away from her, Kayn leapt up and jogged to Zach's side. She took her Handler's hand, hoping her paternity didn't change anything. *Their bond had become second nature, but it hadn't always been this way.* He gave her hand a reassuring squeeze and she knew everything was good. *Here, in this place of peace and eternal calm, she usually felt at ease but not now. Not this time.*

Mel nudged Kayn, enquiring, "Well? How do we find them?"

How was she supposed to know? She didn't have a clue how her abilities worked or even what she was capable of. She might as well attempt to do something. Gazing at the symbol of Ankh on the palm of her hand, she curiously massaging it with her thumb. *The last time, they'd known who they were looking for, but this time, they were strangers. The only thing they shared was the brand on their palms.* She glanced at Zach and grinned as he caught on to what she was trying to do. He placed his hand with the mark of Ankh on his heart. She did the same... *Nothing. It was worth a try.*

Continuing their stroll, Astrid teased, "It's a shame your abilities didn't come with instructions."

"Sadly, no," Kayn countered, smiling at the tall blonde with the pixie cut. *She had no idea what she was doing. She could find the people she cared about, but strangers... How were they supposed to find four complete strangers?*

"Are we just going to continue to walk around in the sand all day?" Haley questioned. "Does anyone have any ideas on where they might be?"

She had an idea, but it required separating from the others. She might as well do it. Wandering through the desert wasn't getting them anywhere.

Gently squeezing her hand, Zach clarified their bond still worked by quietly scolding, "Don't you dare take off on me."

"I need to do this alone. I won't be long. I promise," she assured, releasing his hand. Kayn stepped away from her Handler's disapproval and closed her eyes as she thought of the man, she could barely stomach to call her father. With her eyes shut, she disappeared in a flash of light

When Kayn opened her eyes, she was standing before an ominous castle-like structure. Instinct alone led her movements as she scaled the stairs to the entrance. The door appeared to have no knob or handle. She shoved it but it wouldn't budge. There was, however, a large ornate knocker. She knocked three times and waited. She quickly stepped away from the door as it opened.

For a second, Tiberius was shocked to see her. He teased, "Was killing you not enough to solidify your breakup with my grandson? It really seems quite self-explanatory."

Hilarious. Kayn countered, "I'm not here to see Kevin, I'm looking for Seth."

"Now young lady, why would you possibly need to see Triad's Guardian?" He enquired almost flirtatiously.

She choked over her words, "He's my father."

Taken aback by her admission, Tiberius said, "Well, that's one hell of a plot twist, gorgeous. Come in. Make yourself at home."

Kayn strolled past Tiberius, knowing there was a distinct possibility she'd be coming face-to-face with Kevin. *They'd talked things out but that was before she'd stolen his cell.*

"Don't worry, he's not here," Tiberius confided as he led her down the hallway that opened into a luxurious emerald and gold-flecked marble room. He motioned to the pile of pillows on the floor and directed, "Wait here, I'll go see if he's available." He left her there.

She was too nervous to sit on the floor. This wasn't like her. Not anymore. Feeling more powerful on her feet, she remained standing. Glancing around at the place it seemed empty. Echoing footsteps from the hall announced his return. She mentally prepared herself to see her genetic sire.

Strolling towards her, Tiberius slyly disclosed, "He's otherwise occupied. He has a casual thing going on with our friend Stephanie. He says he'll find you when he's finished."

Gross. She hadn't needed that visual. She'd gone out of her way to speak to her immortal douche of a father and she'd been blown off. With a fake smile, Kayn politely excused herself as she shimmied past Tiberius and quickly made her escape. She'd almost reached the door when Tiberius situated himself between her and the exit. *He obviously wanted to say something.*

Breaking the silence, he enquired, "How's Lexy?"

She bit the hook he'd dangled, by replying, "Why do you ask?" Eavesdropping on Tiberius' inner dialogue as he struggled to come up with a reason other than the obvious, she pressed her lips together to stop herself from smiling.

Aware she was on to him, he replied honestly, "She's been kind of stuck in my head."

He had feelings for her. Interesting, it wasn't just an attraction for him. Feeling defensive for various reasons, she shut down his fantasies the same way he'd tried to snuff out hers, "She's been seeing Orin."

Visibly stricken, Tiberius moved out of her way.

Lexy was her sister. She didn't have the right to stand between her and anything she wanted, even if the thought of it turned her stomach. She confessed, "It's nothing serious."

"Did I hear that right?" Triad's leader questioned while holding the door open.

Shit. He'd heard her thoughts. Kayn strolled by without a response. *Why did she come here? She should have known better.* Rushing down uneven stone stairs, she missed one and tumbled awkwardly, landing on her rear. *Of course! She was such a klutz. Some things never change.*

Laughing, Tiberius called out, "Break anything kid?"

Kid. Right. I'm dating your brother you ignorant tool. Shaking her head as she got up and brushed herself off, she met his Cheshire cat grin with an overly curt, "I'm fine."

"Have a nice day kitten!" he obnoxiously teased as he closed the door.

Kitten, cute. She was going to adorably kick his ass the next time they crossed paths. With her ego eloquently stomped on, she vanished in a flash of white light and reappeared in the desert where she'd left her Clan. *She was alone. They obviously went looking for her.* Instinct prompted her to place her hand on her heart. She thought of her Handler. With another burst of light, she was in the forest. The rest of her Clan were off in the distance. *She'd found them easily.* Kayn sat on a fallen log, requiring a moment. *It was interesting that Seth had a physical place in the In-between and that Triad hung out there. If Stephanie was here, he was. The idea that she could run into Kevin at any time, made her uneasy. She was in a good place with Frost. She had Zach and a surprise sister. She even knew who her father was. Father was a mortal word that obviously meant something completely different in Seth's mind. She'd gone out of her way to seek him out and he couldn't even cut his booty call short to speak to her.* She cringed again. *Stephanie. She'd been able to begin the road to forgiveness with Kevin but for some reason, when it came to Stephanie, she couldn't.* Sensing her Handler approaching, Kayn peered up.

Zach sat beside her, saying, "We need to set ground rules. Where you go, I go. No exceptions. Especially now when you're dealing with added stress."

She saw his point. She disclosed, "I needed to speak to my absentee father. I wasn't sure I could bring anyone with me."

"How'd that go?" Zach enquired, picking at bark on the log.

"He couldn't be bothered," Kayn admitted, leaving out the details.

He placed his arm around her, whispering, "Seth is a horrible person. Being your father doesn't change that. I wouldn't expect much. Azariah is our Clan's Guardian, and as fate would have it, your Aunt. If you have questions, isn't she the logical choice?"

Her feelings were difficult to interpret so there was no point in trying. Kayn met her Handler's eyes as she whispered, "Lesson learned. Forget about it. I plan to." She turned her attention to the Newbie Ankh approaching with her friends.

She nudged Zach and questioned, "How did you find them?"

"It was Haley," Zach whispered.

Kayn grinned as she watched Astrid and Haley chatting with the Ankh they'd never met. There were three boys and a girl. It was different dynamics. Observing their body language, filled in the blanks. Zach left her side as she remained on a log, listening as a bystander. *They were furious a one of the boys. Was this an isolated incident or did they all despise him? It would be best if she didn't identify with the people she was about to torture. If they were nameless, faceless individuals, it would be easier to shut her emotions down.* The boy the other's appeared to loath introduced himself as Amar's son.

Zach politely extended his hand, "Nice to meet you Amar's son."

The boy smirked and responded, "There's no point in shaking hands with the inconsequential."

Was this guy serious? Offending her Handler was a bad idea.

She might need to get up and smack this idiot.

Zach knit his brow as he clarified, "I'm Kayn's Handler.

Are you really sure you want to act like this?"

Amar's son quipped, "And that means what to me?" He looked directly at Kayn as he provoked, "So, she's the new Dragon? The blonde girl over there who looks like she couldn't hurt a fly. I'm terrified."

A lovely girl with waist length midnight black hair in a braid and deep olive toned skin apologized profusely while shaking Zach's hand, "I'm so sorry. He hasn't been training with us. I'm not even sure why he's here."

Mel stepped in and clarified, "He hasn't been training with you? Why not?"

"He feels he's above us," an attractive red-haired boy with a British accent announced.

Amar's offspring ignorantly rolled his eyes as he muttered under his breath, "I shouldn't have to train with the riff raff."

This kid's ignorance was annoying.

Astrid coldly addressed the entitled teen, "When we die, we go to the same place regardless of our station. Nobody cares about the size of your bank account in the Testing."

The insolent youth shrugged as he replied, "My father oversees this continent. Why would I have to go into the Testing?"

The group gathered where she was seated so Kayn reluctantly got up.

"How does Amar expect him to blend with the others?" Astrid whispered.

This whole group stood no chance in the Testing. Haley, their Clan's resident intuitionist gave Kayn a look. *That was her cue.* Kayn thought of a knife, and it appeared in her hand. She marched over, met Amar's son's eyes and baited, "Interesting theory you have there. My father happens to be Seth. You know, the Guardian in charge of Triad. That makes my Aunt Azariah, the Guardian in charge of Ankh. My boyfriend is Frost, you know the guy in charge of your father, and in a surprising plot twist, Lexy is my sister. I just finished Immortal Testing. I find it odd that you don't think you have to go."

The defiant teen met Kayn's gaze as he scoffed, "Sure you are. Why hasn't anyone heard of this?"

"We have," Zach clarified. "It's true. It all just came out."

She'd had enough of this idiot. Ominously, clutching her weapon, Kayn stepped forward and commanded, "Run!" The group hesitated just as they had when Lexy and Grey ordered them to flee. *The spoiled brat didn't flinch.* Intrigued by the teen's insolence, she grasped Amar's son's arm, asking, "And your name is?"

"Samid," he stated, trying to look like he wasn't buying her dominance.

Either this kid was incredibly brave or a fool. On the fence as to which he was, Kayn impatiently blurted, "We don't have time for this." With a swift slash of a serrated edged blade, she slit Samid's throat. Shocked, the boy clutched his gushing neck wound, staggered backwards and slumped to the ground. Weapons appeared in the Newbie Ankh's hands. *Interesting, they were prepared to stand their ground. Perhaps this situation wasn't as hopeless as she'd originally thought.*

"This kid is such a dick," Haley commented, poking Samid's body with her foot.

The others knew their place in the immortal food chain. Even with weapons brandished, their fear was obvious. Kayn inched closer, enquiring, "Do you know what a Dragon does?" They practically tripped over each other as they fled into the woods.

Samid's body twitched. Kayn grinned as the boy scrambled to his feet.

Still clutching his throat, Samid insolently raged, "My father will have you Entombed for this!"

The five immortals doubled over laughing as Kayn revealed, "Your father set up this training exercise."

"I don't believe you," Samid stubbornly retaliated, brushing off his immortal attire like appearance mattered. He noticed the rest of his group had fled.

"I'd run away now," Zach suggested.

Amar's son didn't move a muscle, defiantly standing his ground. A blade appeared in his quivering hands.

He was going to make her kill him again before their twisted game of hide and seek even started. Kayn grinned and cocked her head as she menacingly directed, "Run."

Samid raised his chin, insolently maintaining his stance.

Kayn glanced at her Handler, knowing she had to at least make him appear to play a part in her decisions while she was of reasonably sound mind. *If she didn't, she'd never hear the end of it.*

Zach shrugged as he gave her the green light, "Go for it."

That's all she needed. With a rapid slash of her blade, Samid clutched his throat and crumpling to the ground. As she stood by his corpse, waiting for him to awaken, she glanced over at her friends and said, "Go after the others. This may take a while." Astrid, Haley and Mel wandered into the woods.

Zach remained by her side. Once again Samid awoke after being taken out in the same way. He struggled to get up, and attacked her, swinging his weapon with skill most impressive yet not nearly good enough to cause her any concern. Kayn easily took him down again. *This guy was ridiculously stubborn.* Five more times, Samid awakened and came at her, showing he had half-decent skills but nowhere close to what he'd need to have a shot.

Deciding it was time to stop the insanity, Zach stepped in, declaring, "This guy has a stunted ego. We'll be here all day."

This time as Samid got up, wielding his knife, Kayn tossed hers aside, provoking, "I won't even use a weapon. Do your best." With each skilled swing of his blade, Kayn easily manoeuvered out of the way. When she was done playing around, she decided to allow him to have his moment. She stood there, held both of her arms up and goaded him into stabbing her. He did. Moderately shocked by her lack of response, Samid released the hilt of his knife, leaving the blade within her as he stepped away. Kayn casually removed the blade from her midriff. Her wound warmed as it rapidly healed. Cocky as hell, Kayn lifted her short, blood-stained white sarong to show him, she'd healed. *He'd accomplished nothing.* Zach cleared his throat. *Oh, shit. She wasn't wearing anything under her sarong. Why did she always forget about that?* Amar's son winked and responded to her impromptu flash in Arabic. Kayn understood what he'd said like he'd spoken English.

'*Go ahead, take it all off.*' She darted forward and snapped his neck, silencing the testosterone show.

"This guy just isn't getting it. He's also not the least bit concerned about the others," Zach pointed out.

Meeting her Handler's frustrated expression, she nodded. *She understood what he was saying. It was time to allow the thought that always took her mortal empathy away. The sensation of Kevin's blade on her throat and the sight of him walking away. She started there, but their last conversation had defused the betrayal she felt, and it wasn't enough. This was new.* Her mind scrolled through the highlights of the Testing until she found a torturous brutality that unlocked the monster within. The girl who understood ration sunk into the emotionless abyss of her Dragon self.

This time as Samid rose, he was met by ruthless torture until his only instinct was to flee. For weeks, she relentlessly pursued the untested immortals through various landscapes of the In-between, adapting to each as though she'd always been there. Sensing their fear led her to their location, as a scent would in the air. After proving there was no escape, she made them jump from cliffs and come at her just as Lexy had before their Testing, until they had no will for either fight or flight. Her Handler stayed with her. She was aware of his incessant presence but unconcerned. When it was time to leave the youths to lick their wounds, Zach grabbed her arms and asserted, "It's time to wake up. Come back to me."

Somehow his words reached the sliver of her that remained. She wanted to stop him from bringing her back but as his eye's boar deep into her soul, she could do nothing but stare into them. He lured her from the abyss with sheer force of will as his touch extinguished the fire of her vengeance driven ability. The weight on her heart lifted and a sense of calm sedated her.

"There you are," her Handler whispered, grinning.

The scenery flashed as they were transported to an endless sea of transparent water. It was calf high where she was standing. Colourful starfish were scattered across on the white sand of the ocean floor. *It was like standing on a beach as the tide was coming in.* Kayn didn't move as dazzling orbs of energy sped past her legs making her heart dance and she smiled.

Zach chuckled as he admitted, "This is not where I meant to bring you.

This wasn't bad. She wiggled her feet beneath the surface of the now thigh high water. *It was rising but which way was the shore?*

"Let's try again," Zach suggested as he clutched her shoulders and squeezed his eyes shut.

Nothing happened. It was awkward. The water was up to her waist. How long was he going to stand there trying to think them out of the precarious situation he'd placed them in?

"Give me a minute. Have a little faith in my abilities," Zach mumbled as he shut his eyes again.

Besides Dragon Whisperer, what were his abilities again? Waiting for him to figure this out felt like a bad idea. The water was up to their chests. Across the still surface of the water, she saw something. Oh, come on! Dozens of shark fins. Nobody ever had to wait too long to watch Karma smack her down. She wasn't in the mood for this. Had she been left in her sociopathic state a dozen sharks coming at her would have been as concerning as flatulence during afternoon tea. Tick Tock buddy. He had ten seconds to think their asses out of here before she took over.

Noticing the sharks Zach changed his mind, "Do it!

Grinning widely, she teased, "But I have faith in you."

"Do it!" he urged in a pitch reserved solely for blind panic.

She thought about the first thing that came to mind and they ended up back at Triad's creepy castle like domicile. *No, no, no! Anywhere but here! She'd rather be devoured by sharks.*

"What is this place?" Zach questioned as he wandered closer in awe.

She grabbed his shoulders and ordered, "Forget you've ever seen it." She thought about the white sandy beaches where they'd once had slushy drinks while sprawling in the sand and reappeared there. *This was more like it.*

"That's my girl," Zach laughed as he thought of a Pina Colada and one appeared in his hand.

They found a cozy spot and sprawled on their stomachs with their drinks. Kayn sipped from her curly straw, reminiscing about the murderous time spent with Amar's four. *It was like someone else had done it and she'd been a fly on the wall. She'd succeeded in breaking their spirits, but the attachment needed to survive the Testing couldn't be taught. Amar's son's soul would never mesh with the others. It was more than that. She sensed Samid was meant to be Triad.*

He broke the lull in conversation by responding to her thoughts, "Maybe he is supposed to be Triad? I could definitely see it."

21

A crab tickled her foot and slowly made its way up her leg. Zach placed his hand in its path and it crawled onto his palm. *It was bothering her. She'd been contemplating tearing its tiny legs off. He was so in tune with her that he was handling situations before they even happened now.* She leaned in to take another sip. The sanctity of their special place was violated as the scenery flashed. They were back at their clean-slate desert.

Marching over to the others, Zach complained, "This better be good. We were having cocktails on the beach."

Astrid laughed, "We didn't summon you. It must be time to go."

Amar's partially immortal teens couldn't even look at her. *Her brutality would always be remembered. If they survived the Testing, it would be appreciated. They weren't going to survive.* She recalled Lexy's words... *They rarely do.*

Astrid nudged her and whispered, "Do you want me to speak to Amar?"

"I'll do it," Kayn coolly replied. It felt like she'd failed. *He'd been looking for a miracle, and she didn't have one to give. The trio had a slim chance of survival, but only without Amar's son.* Zach took her hand. *He would always care for her. He didn't have a choice, but then again, neither did she.* Without warning, their bodies violently lurched upwards. In a heartbeat, they were in strobing Tombs plummeting out of control into oblivion. *She recalled the last time this happened. Oh shit! She offed them too many times and killed the Healer operating the Tombs, just as Lexy had while training them not so long ago.* Kayn placed both palms flush on the lid above her as Lexy had, fighting to regain control of the rapidly descending, sickeningly spinning Rose Quartz Tombs.

Mel hollered through steady whooshing, "I'm with you, Kayn!"

Kayn felt her lifeforce draining into the Rose Quartz encasing her body as she willed the Tomb to stop with every inch of her being. She sensed the other Healer with each breath as though they were one entity struggling to control the uncontrollable. In her mind, Mel whispered, *'I'm done... I can't.'* Lightheaded, nauseous, and utterly exhausted, Kayn fought to keep her palms in place until the last ounce of her energy was absorbed into the Tomb encasing her. Her final thought was of Zach as the spinning slowed and the lights went out.

2

MORTAL BONDS

Kayn gasped as she came to. *It took a few seconds to realise where she was.* She called out, "Are you guys alright?"

Zach's irritated voice grumbled beside her, "Yes… Just frigging peachy. Now, let us out."

Kayn was grinning as she placed her palm in the print on the lid and it slowly ground open. As she climbed out, Grey took her hand with undisguised disapproval. *When had they arrived? Whoops.* Lexy and Orin's lifeless bodies were sprawled on the marble floor. *She'd killed Lexy and Orin. Lexy was divine justice. Killing Orin was just funny.*

"Feeling better?" Grey enquired as Kayn placed her hands on one of the Tombs, starting a chain reaction. They opened, and as the Ankh crawled out, Grey glared at Zach and scolded, "You quite obviously let this training exercise get out of hand." When Zach noticed the bodies on the floor, he chuckled. "What was I supposed to do? She was completely psychotic."

Their humorous commentary was interrupted as Lexy groaned, "Colour me impressed, you took out both of us." She got up, stretched and cracked her neck. "I've got Orin if you've got Mel."

Whoops, Melody was still in one of the Tombs. Kayn peeked into a Tomb and found Mel's lifeless body. Her eyes were wide open staring into the unknown. *She wasn't certain she could do this so soon after resurrecting herself. Using other people's abilities was still new.* She placed her hands against Melody's chest and willed the Healing ability to surface.

Mel's eyes fluttered open, she mumbled, "Hope that week-long murder spree was worth it."

"Just like going to the spa," Kayn sparred as she helped her up. She stifled her laughter as the new Ankh shimmied by her without speaking. *She hadn't made any friends in this group.*

Lexy wandered over and asked, "So, it went well?"

Kayn slowly shook her head as she explained, "It was fun for me but this group isn't attached to each other like we were. I don't know why but I feel like Amar's son is supposed to be Triad."

"He's not going to be happy about that," Orin declared as Lexy helped him up.

"He has to know," Astrid remarked.

As they strolled into the hall, Zach commented, "He was probably hoping a few weeks pursued by a Dragon would give his kid a much-needed attitude adjustment."

"A few weeks isn't long enough for that ass. Maybe with more time, and if lobotomies were legal?" Mel countered.

"Is it even worth telling Amar this? That's what we need to ask ourselves," Orin added.

"I'll speak to him," Kayn volunteered as they made their way down the marble passageway to their rooms, parted ways at their doors without bothering with pleasantries. As Kayn reached for her doorknob, sensing someone inside. Frost, he was lounging on her bed eating grapes. Her heart soared. *She'd needed him to be here tonight for various reasons. The number one reason being, the way he made her feel. Just the sight of him made her know with all certainty that her heart was still capable of experiencing joy. He was only a few feet away.*

Frost got up, all sexy and shirtless and flirtatiously welcomed her, "Hey stranger."

She raced across the room, leapt into his arms and buried her face in the nape of his neck, inhaling his insanely intoxicating scent. *He always smelled so incredible. Addictive…That's what he was.* He gathered her in his embrace and spun her around, nipping at her neck. *It tick-led.* She laughed as he carried her to the luxurious king-sized bed. "Time out!" Kayn giggled. "I was just coming back to the room for a quick breather. I told Orin I'd talk to Amar."

He tossed her onto the bed and crawled across the satin sheets after her, seductively coaxing, "But baby, I know you have energy to burn off before the banquet."

She did. He was sexy as hell. If she didn't go right now, she was going to lose this argument with her libido. Placing her palm on his chest, she asserted, "Hold this thought, I'll be right back."

Lounging on her bed, he groaned and taunted, "That's right, keep me waiting."

Contemplating Orin's, is it worth telling him statement, she reluctantly got up, glanced back at temptation and admitted, "I'm glad you're here."

With a knowing twinkle in his eye, he flirtatiously baited, "I bet you are."

She just needed to keep her head on straight for a few more minutes. Escaping the room, she hurried down the hall into the large foyer. It took her all of five seconds to track down Amar. Her host greeted her kindly, but his woeful expression revealed his hand. *The situation was as she suspected. He knew his son had no chance.* Her unsinkable soul began taking on water. She met Amar's melancholy with resolve, "You already know what I'm going to say."

"I do, but I was hoping there was a deal to be made," Amar countered, trying to appear unaffected by grief. He tore a cluster of grapes from a platter before him and moved it closer to her.

Suspecting she knew where he was going with the conversation, she took some grapes and beat him to the punch, "It's not my place to make a deal with you."

Inching closer so they wouldn't be overheard, he whispered, "I know that, but you're an anomaly that's not supposed to exist. Hope lives in grey areas. Seth is your father. You are Azariah's niece. You are the only person that can't be Entombed for making it."

Don't say it. Do not say it. Kayn slowly shook her head as she explained, "I have no relationship at all with my father. Nothing."

"But you could," Amar implored. "I need my son to have more time. If he's on your continent at the time of our Testing, he becomes yours."

They didn't want him. "Listen, for lack of a better way to say this, Samid isn't compatible with Ankh on any continent. A few more years won't change that. Maybe if he goes with Tiberius?"

"Not Triad," Amar pleaded. "If I must give him up, I want it to be to friends. People I know will care for him."

"I can't agree to this," Kayn countered. "You need to speak to Markus or Frost. You're basically asking us to sacrifice the next group that goes into the Testing. If we try to place him with who we already have, there's just no way they'll have a bond strong enough to make it out. He's more than a little difficult to deal with."

"People change, under the right circumstances with the proper guidance," he rebutted.

No, they don't. Not really. Triad strolled in with ironic timing. As her eyes met with Kevin's, she realised her argument was invalid. *Kevin had become a different person under Triad's guidance.* Even though she was trying to shut down her reaction to his presence, it tugged at her soul.

Tiberius shook hands with Amar and purposely irked her by saying, "Have you met my grandson, Kevin?"

Amar shook Kevin's hand, teasing, "I heard they let your grandfather breed."

Tiberius winked at Kayn as he snatched the rest of Amar's grapes off his tray, sparring, "It's a dangerous thing messing with perfection. We have catching up to do. Drink later?"

"Looking forward to it," Amar answered as Triad's group walked away.

Kevin turned back, looked directly at her and mouthed the words, "We need to talk."

They shouldn't. Kayn nodded as she appreciatively watched his rear-view leave. *This was going to be awkward. Seeing him brought her back to the carefree girl that laid in fields watching bumble bees. For a moment, she recalled the games they used to play as children and the way he made her feel as they became something more. Their run-ins were few and far between. The last one had left her feeling like their friendship was salvageable. They'd recently had the opportunity to tie up loose ends by saying what they needed to say to each other. She'd only been there as a distraction while Astrid and Haley stole someone from Triad, but it had turned into so much more.* She steered her thoughts back to Frost and shoved the sentimentality of who Kevin had been to her away. *He's your enemy. He's Triad. You can't be friends. Not really.*

"I'll speak to Markus and Frost. Please, don't stand in my way," Amar whispered.

She snapped back to reality. *That much she could give him.* "I won't," she promised as Amar took off after Triad. *Her ex and her boyfriend at the same event. What could go wrong?* Kayn remained there, knowing she needed a moment before going back to Frost. *How long had it been since their Testing, four or five months? She wasn't even sure. The last six months had sped by in a blur of violence and mediocre life choices. Well, all but one of those choices... Frost.*

Melody's voice interrupted her thoughts, "I just saw Triad, they're already here."

"Kevin needs to speak to me about something," Kayn revealed as she got up. They strolled back down the hall together.

"So, Trinity will be here for the festivities too," Mel determined as they reached Kayn's door.

Meaning Thorne. Melody also had rather heavy baggage.

Kayn looked at her friend and whispered, "You've got this." "You too," Mel answered. As they embraced, she whispered in Kayn's ear, "Don't concentrate on what you've lost. Think about what you've gained. He's in there, isn't he?"

Grinning, Kayn replied, "Of course he is." *Frost was in that room waiting for her and being with him made her deliriously happy. Why was she complicating her afterlife by allowing any part of herself to continue dwelling in the past? She needed to keep Kevin's role as her adversary straight in her head. Diluting her anger towards him by having that chat in Alaska had messed with her resolve.*

As Mel wandered away, she called out, "Stop over-thinking it!"

That was going to be easier said than done. Kayn took a deep breath as she opened the door. Her heart swelled as she saw him. *He'd fallen asleep, waiting for her.* Fully intending to just watch him sleep, she climbed into bed next to him. A smile crept across his face. *He was only pretending.*

He playfully towed her on top of him and teased, "Do you ladies have drama going on?"

Straddling him with her flowing lavender dress hiked up around her hips, she countered, "No more than usual." There was a pause in their conversation as they gazed into each others' eyes. She confessed, "I was afraid they were going to randomly split us up again."

"They will...You need to work on that pesky bond with your Handler. I'm just glad they're giving us time together now," Frost replied with a mischievous grin. While aggressively clutching her hips, he seduced, "You look insanely beautiful in that dress. Leave it on."

He was turned on. It felt like an invitation. Logic disintegrated as she gave him a peck on the lips. As their lips parted, she provoked, "How much time do we have?"

Sliding his fingers through her curls until his palm cupped the back of her head, he aggressively pulled her lips to his as he promised, "More than enough."

Their lips met in a breathless seductive dance as he slid a hand between her thighs. She whimpered as the feverish pace of his fingers made her squirm.

Chuckling, he roughly flipped her, pinned her to the mattress and coaxed, "We could just stay here all night, Amar would understand."

Reality was a buzz kill. They had to go. For various reasons. Amar had to talk to him. Kevin needed to speak to her about something. Frost abruptly got up and left her lying on the bed so turned on she could scream. Without saying a word, he started getting dressed *He didn't have to. She knew why he was pissed.* "You can't be mad at me for having thoughts," Kayn complained as she followed him to the door.

"Thinking about him while you're in bed with me is a bit much. You could at least try to be considerate of my feelings," he aloofly sparred.

Blocking his escape route, she refuted, "Don't be like this, I want you. I'm with you."

Gazing into her eyes, Frost caressed her cheek and said, "I know you do. I want you too. I'm not being unreasonable. You'd react the same way if I was in bed with you and Lily crossed my mind."

This was true. She'd have a damn meltdown if they were in the middle of something and Lily popped into his head. She tried to justify her thoughts, "I'm sorry. Listen, you don't know what's going on with Amar's son. I was talking to Amar when Triad showed up."

"You should be grateful I'm still here, when everything inside of me is screaming at me to run before you stomp on my heart," he retaliated.

She countered, "You can't just walk out every time we have a disagreement."

"I can this time," Frost sparred as he did just that.

What just happened? She flung herself on the bed. *Come on! Did he really think Kevin wasn't going to cross her mind? She understood this was a touchy subject, but seriously?* Someone knocked on the door. *Maybe he'd already realised he was being ridiculous?* Kayn opened the door and it was Lexy. *Her sister.* She stepped aside and ushered her in with a wave of her hand and a grin.

"Your room is better than ours," her newfound sibling remarked, scrutinizing the rich tapestries on the walls. "Did you and Frost have a fight?" Lexy asked as she wandered over to check out the view from their balcony.

That was fast. It had been all of five seconds since he'd stormed out.

Lexy responded to her inner commentary, "I bumped into him in the hall."

"If he's going to be pissed off whenever he hears a thought he doesn't like, we're going to have a lot of ridiculous arguments," Kayn exclaimed as she leaned on the shiny marble railing and gazed at the hauntingly beautiful desert scenery.

"If it makes you feel better, I'm fighting with Grey too," Lexy disclosed as her crimson hair shifted like flickering flames of a fire in the warm breeze.

She could guess what happened. "You thought about Tiberius, didn't you?" Kayn teased.

Lexy gave her the truth, "He's in the room next to ours.

Grey wasn't impressed."

"Forget about Grey for a second. How do you feel?" Kayn probed as she looked at her sister.

"Truthfully? Excited, nervous, on edge," Lexy divulged with a sly smile.

Kayn grinned. *She knew exactly what she was talking about. This was nice.* She piped in, "Mel's having the same day. Thorne's going to be here tonight."

"Where's Zach?" Lexy enquired.

"No idea, he was probably giving us some time alone," Kayn responded.

Smiling, Lexy remarked, "He's also going to be in an awkward situation tonight. The four of us should stick together."

Did she know? "Stephanie?" Kayn questioned.

"Her too," Lexy answered as she wandered away from the balcony.

She was talking about Patrick. Kayn didn't bite but found it peculiar. *Lexy wasn't there for that conversation, was she?*

Her sister snatched a flawless red apple off the tray of fruit on the decorative table by the door as she curtly said, "Ignore Frost. He has no right to judge anyone... ever. Neither does Grey for that matter."

This was true. They had both been a little liberal with their bed mates.

As Lexy grabbed for the doorknob, she paused, looked back and blurted, "I deserve to have some fun too, don't I?"

"Of course, you do," Kayn agreed, pressing her lips together so she didn't smile. *She wanted a second opinion. Permission to want who she shouldn't.*

"Good talk," Lexy declared as she walked out, closing the door behind her.

Kayn smiled at the back of the door, knowing that was probably Lexy's attempt at sister bonding. *She'd have to save the Stephanie bombshell for later.* She started giggling. *That little venting visit had come out of nowhere.* Standing by a tray of fruit scrutinizing its contents, she noticed a tasty looking banana. *She was too frustrated with Frost to eat something phallic. There was fruit she'd never seen before.* She picked up the mystery fruit and sniffed it. *How was she supposed to eat this? Was it supposed to be peeled? Did she have to just bite into it?* With little time to waste so she bit into it. *The skin tasted nasty. She needed to spit it out but where? The bathroom. She'd put it in the garbage.* Kayn wandered across the room into the washroom with the yucky fruit peel still in her mouth and spat it into a wad of toilet paper. *There was no garbage can. Weird? It was just a tiny chunk.* She flushed it. *She couldn't put the fruit back on the tray with a bite out of it; that was kind of gross.* She marched over to the deck and pitched it into the garden below. Someone cursed in the shrubbery beneath her balcony. *Oh crap!* She dove back inside with her hand clasped over her mouth to stifle her laughter. *Whoops. She hadn't thought that out.* Kayn wandered back to the fruit tray and ate a bunch of grapes to get rid of the bitter taste. She flopped on her bed and sighed dramatically. *Apparently, immortals could still be awkward and dorky. Good to know.* She'd been lying there for a while when she began overthinking their little spat. *Should she go and find Frost? She'd never been in a relationship before, but this didn't feel like her fault.* Kayn got up to grab more grapes while continuing to beat their disagreement to death in her head. *He knew how unfiltered her thoughts were.* He was going to have to get used to random things and people crossing her mind. Kevin still crossed her mind a lot even though she was one hundred and ten percent committed to Frost. He was a link to her past. A reminder of her mortality. A beautiful life that was no longer. Someone knocked and without waiting for her to answer, they entered. It was Frost.

He sheepishly strolled over, stopping in front of her, he implored, "Can we just agree I'm an idiot and move on?"

She smiled and ribbed, "A jealous idiot."

Chuckling as he inched closer, he took her hands and sort of repeated her words, "A ridiculously idiotic jealous fool. I was really trying to act like the idea of you two seeing each other didn't matter to me, but it does and that's not your fault. It's my issue. I'll deal with it."

She lovingly squeezed his hands as she explained, "You just gave me a big speech about our abilities and how we're going to need to be understanding of each other because our relationship needs to be a little more open concept, especially if they keep separating us for long spurts of time. I should have spoken to you about what happened in Alaska with Kevin. I didn't want to spend what little time we have together talking about him."

Frost led her over to the bed, sat down and tugged her with him. "I'm sorry," he whispered.

Straddling his lap, Kayn confessed, "Nothing happened but heartfelt apologies. We spoke for a while, shared appetisers, drank wine, and I stole his phone. Yes, there's emotional baggage, but we were best friends long before we were anything else. A part of me will always care. If Kevin needs to speak to me about something, I intend to honour our mortal connection and allow him to say whatever he needs to say. I'm with you, though." She used Zach's words from earlier, "Have some faith in me."

As they embraced, Frost whispered against her hair, "I am trying. I'll do better. I'm not used to caring. It's messing with my mind. Feeling this way about you is out of my comfort zone. I know what I said and I know what your job description was in Alaska. You were supposed to do whatever you had to do to keep him away from the hospital so they could get away. Can we start over? I promise I'll suck up my jealousy issues as far as the Smith kid is concerned if you promise me one thing."

"What's that?" she probed, affectionately nuzzling his neck.

"Promise you'll always be honest with me about anything that happens while we're apart," he whispered. "I don't ever want to be caught off guard. If I know about it, I can work through it in my mind and try to get past it. Logically, you have an in with Triad for various reasons. You'll be ordered to use it."

She knew that much. This was going to be complicated. If he wanted honesty, she'd give it to him, "Just so we're clear, I was friends with him before all of this and if there's a way to continue to be friends, I'd want that." Frost showed her he understood her logic by silently nodding. She was going to need more than a nod after this drama. She clarified, "I promise I'll tell you if anything happens but I want the same thing from you."

Chuckling, he pledged, "If unforeseen circumstances cause me to sleep with your ex-boyfriend, I'll let you know." Someone barged into the room, pushing along a rack full of dresses. A second person followed with one full of suits. They abruptly left. Kayn hadn't bothered jumping off Frost's lap. Still sitting with her arms around his neck, curiosity got the best of her as she dashed over to check out the selection. She scoped out the suits and said, "I'll pick for you if you choose for me?" Grinning, he got up and wandered over to view their garment choices for the banquet. He placed a hand seductively on her waist as he used the other to move each dress aside until he found a few for her to try on. As he removed his hand from the small off her waist, she felt the heat it was creating within her. He passed a dress to her. Funny. The dress had complete and total coverage. She passed him a classy suit and vetoed with his selection, "It's too hot here to wear that."

"It was worth a try," he chuckled. "Give me a second." He pensively searched through the dresses and passed her a revealing green silky spaghetti strapped one. "This one will bring out your eyes."

Loving his choice, Kayn slipped out of the dress she had on and allowed it to drop down her legs into a pile of lavender material on the marble floor.

His eyes appreciatively travelled her nearly nude curves as he hung his suit back up and said, "First things first."

Kayn smiled as she walked into his open arms. Being with him felt so right. With his hands possessively clutching her rear, he carried her back to the bed whispering his naughty intentions. She gasped as his hands warmed her backside. *He was going to use his ability to end their disagreement.* Her response was undeniably raw as the aching urgency turned to waves of pleasure, blissfully washing through her. She overexuberantly cried out his name as euphoria imploded within her, triggering her mirrored ability. Intoxicating pheromones exploded into the air, causing his to become more potent. The desire they felt became instinct driven urgency. There were no more sentimental declarations just deep throaty lustful promises.

His sleepy seductive voice whispered, "I think we outdid ourselves."

"What time is it?" Kayn asked because it was dark outside. They heard the music.

"Oh, shit!" Frost stammered as he jumped up, tossed her the dress he'd picked out and laughed, "Time to get up beautiful. We're late." He quickly put on the suit she'd selected and helped her do up her dress.

She exclaimed, "I need to have a shower! I don't have any makeup!"

With admiration in his voice, he stated the obvious, "You look sexy as hell right now, with your messy hair and kiss swollen lips. Just go with it."

"It'll be obvious," she sparred, laughing.

"One second." He dashed into the bathroom and called out, "There's makeup, a brush and hair product in here, even perfume. I prefer the scent you were wearing earlier though."

A pheromone joke, cute. Oh crap, their pheromones. She panicked, "Wait! We've set ourselves off!"

"It's been hours, we're only potent enough to loosen inhibitions," he explained. He remained in the doorway, leaning against the frame, watching her put product in her hair and opt to leave it as a mane of sexy curls.

She'd might as well leave it loose. Tiberius would undoubtedly spend all evening taking out her bobby pins. Kayn sprayed perfume and wandered through the mist.

Frost opened the door, appreciatively taking her in as she strutted past, he confessed, "I wish we didn't have to go."

She laced her fingers behind his neck and planted a kiss on his lips as she whispered, "Ditto."

He lifted her feet off the floor, put her down and prompted, "We'd better run. Markus is going to be pissed."

The couple raced down the hall to the tune of her clicking heels through the maze-like compound in the direction of the music. As they entered the banquet hall, Markus, Thorne, Tiberius and Amar were greeting the end of the line of immortals. *Oh, they might really be in trouble.* After a quick peck on the lips, they parted. Frost took his place with his brothers and a visibly frustrated Markus as Kayn started to walk away.

Frost called after her, "Save me a seat!"

She was so happy he was here. She smiled as their afternoon rendezvous replayed in her mind. Now, she had something to look forward too at the end of an evening that promised to be full of drama. As Kayn entered the luxurious banquet hall, all eyes turned to her. *Crap. It was like showing up late for class.* She took a step and the heel snapped off her shoe. *Oh, you've got to be frigging kidding me.* She removed her shoes as everyone watched, versus staggering the rest of the way with one on and slinked into a chair at the table, thankful Zach saved seats.

Zach leaned over and whispered, "Kick your shoes under the table and forget about it."

Sheepishly grinning, Kayn barefoot booted her heels further under the table.

Touching her leg under the table, Zach assured, "I know the centre of attention thing is a touchy subject but you look like a gorgeous Cinderella who lost her shoe."

She appreciated Zach. She'd neglected the hell out of her Handler today. She didn't even know how he was dealing with seeing Stephanie or Patrick? Where was Triad Sitting? She hadn't seen them as she came in. She'd missed the fun exchanges between the Brothers of Prophecy. She searched out Mel and gave her an apologetic look. *She was supposed to have her back while she bumped into Thorne.*

Mischievously nudging her, Zach teased, "Obviously you two made up?"

Everyone knew about their fight. She apologized, "Sorry I wasn't here for you earlier. I'm here now though, all night. I'm your back up, distraction, whatever you need me to be." She met Mel's eyes across the table and mouthed the words, "You too."

Lexy placed her hand on Kayn's shoulder and handed her a drink, "Do try to catch up."

She accepted the glass of red wine and casually took a sip as she scanned the room. The Clans were segregated at this banquet and the dance floor was enormous. Triad was sitting clear across the room. Her eyes searched for Kevin as per usual. Trinity was seated closest to Ankh. Kayn glanced at her Handler. Zach was gapped out, staring at Triad's table. She had the ammo to snuff out a hook up with Stephanie. As Kayn followed her Handler's line of sight, she wasn't entirely certain it was Stephanie catching his attention. She nudged her Handler and whispered, "Why don't you just go over there and say hi?"

Zach abruptly got up and asked Haley to dance. She watched him leading Haley to the dance floor and smiled as she looked over to where Triad was seated. Patrick was watching him too. The whole situation was fascinating. If she ever found herself attracted to another woman, certain she'd be able to own it. Kayn snagged a piece of rye bread from a wicker bowl on the table and buttered it. She enjoyed people watching. Even though Zach had Haley in his arms, his eyes kept travelling to Triad's table as though they were being drawn by an unseen force. He'd figure it out. Orin was talking to Melody, but she wasn't paying attention. She was watching Thorne as he sat down with his Clan. When Orin was sidetracked with another conversation, she met Mel's eyes and whispered, "I'm sorry I wasn't there when you had to shake hands with him at the door."

"It would have been just as awkward with you standing beside me," Mel assured as she sipped from her glass, staring at Trinity's table.

Astrid's voice piped in from across their table, "So, you've obviously made up."

Nice. It sure didn't take long for the rumour mill to run its course. Hope she wasn't hearing this same sentence all night from everyone? Kayn opted out of an explanation and grinned as she took a sip of wine. *Markus, Amar and Frost hadn't come back. They were probably talking about Samid. She'd promised Amar she wouldn't do anything to sway their decision but she was feeling guilty. She liked Dean and she'd been hoping they'd find a way to get Molly back. She didn't know the other new guy yet.*

Astrid responded to Kayn's thoughts by casually stating, "I made no promise to hold my tongue."

As Zach scooted back into his seat, he declared, "I've already put in my two cents. I feel like we have the time to assimilate him to our lifestyle. We have a couple of years until our continent's Testing. I told Markus I was all for him coming with us but if Triad steals him, we won't go out of our way to get him back. At least this way we can give his group a chance."

Zach had the best heart. She understood what he was saying. The group Amar was training stood no chance if Samid went into Testing with them but they had time on their side. Kayn kept peering up at the entrance. *She wanted to find out what Kevin had to say but Frost was being overly sensitive.* She glanced over at Triad's table and their eyes met. He motioned her over and she nudged Zach, "Kevin has something he needs to talk to me about. Come with me?"

He chuckled, "You're totally using me as a buffer so your boyfriend doesn't get jealous when he walks in and finds you talking to your ex."

That's exactly what she was doing. Smiling, she got up, grabbed Zach's arm, towed him to his feet and taunted, "Come on, you know you want to go over there." They manoeuvred around the tables until they reached Triad's seating. Kevin got up and motioned for her to follow him. Zach remained behind chatting with Patrick and Stephanie as she followed Kevin onto the balcony. *She hadn't succeeded in buffering anything. Frost was going to come back and she was going to be gone, with Kevin. Oh, well. He was going to have to learn to trust her.* She leaned over the balcony to view the garden below.

Casually leaning against the railing, he taunted, "You guys were late. Trouble in paradise?"

Deciding to be honest, she confessed, "I thought of you at an inopportune time."

Grinning, he teased, "How inopportune are we talking about here?"

She wasn't going there with him. Kayn impatiently urged, "You had something you needed to say?"

Fully aware she was dodging his flirtation, he whispered, "Try being a little more discreet."

With Frost? He didn't have any right to address her inappropriate behaviour.

"Speaking as your friend, until you know how to use your abilities keep a lid on the, I'm part Guardian' speeches," he asserted as his eyes met hers.

A waiter carrying a tray of wine wandered out onto the balcony and offered them a drink. They each took a glass and placed it on the railing.

"Is your psychic ability a secret or does Tiberius know?" she countered, effectively switching the subject.

"Let's just say I haven't been entirely honest with my Clan about the strength of my abilities for obvious reasons," he explained. Leaning closer, Kevin whispered, "Your relationship with Zach won't be strong enough to give him any real pull once you figure out how to operate your abilities. They'll need to find a way to control you. They're going to separate you from Frost so be prepared for an extended period away from each other while they foster your relationship with your Handler. If you or Zach ever need to get a hold of me, for any reason, send a message to my old email address. I was the original choice for your Handler. I'm sure you've already figured that out. We didn't end up in the same Clan but I may have pull when push comes to shove where Zach doesn't."

This could be a trap. His way of getting back at her for playing him in Alaska.

Kevin took something out of his pocket and prompted, "Open your hand." He placed a rough looking purple clover in her palm. She stared at it, lost in the sentiment. He lovingly closed her fingers around it as he whispered, "It's good to see you happy."

He walked away and left her, lost in the confusing sentiment the tiny crushed purple clover dredged up. For a while, Kayn continued staring at the dark endless sand beyond the walls of the compound as visions of her child-hood flickered through her mind. *He'd offered his services as Zach's back up if she inevitably went off the rails. That had to be against the rules. She'd known they would try to keep the reins on her relationship with Frost. That wasn't a surprise. It probably hadn't helped their cause when they'd shown up late for the banquet tonight. He'd missed the receiving line. She needed to go back inside.* She thought about tossing the flower over the balcony but as she made the action, she couldn't bring herself to let it go. *How much did he remember?* As Kayn looked at the clover, she knew the answer. *He'd remembered everything. Somewhere under all the Triad bravado, he was still the boy who gave her purple clovers.* She didn't have pockets so she tucked the flower into her bra. *She'd find somewhere to put it later.* With a hand over her secret clover, she swallowed back the emotions he'd dredged up. *It didn't matter. He was her enemy. It didn't matter what he remembered now. She'd moved on. She was happy.* Kayn grabbed her glass of wine and downed it as she went back inside, taking her seat at their table just as the meals were being served. *She was relieved Frost wasn't already there. She needed a second to rid her mind of Kevin.* Kayn peered up as a waiter came by with a tray of wine and took another. Her eyes were drawn to Triad's table. She took a sip, inconspicuously watching her ex best friend's relaxed interactions with his Clan.

Zach nudged her and asked, "Are you alright? What did he have to say?"

She answered truthfully, "We need to spend more time working on our bond. Remind me to give you an email address later."

Her Handler ribbed, "I could have told you that much and whose email address? You weren't out there conspiring to hook me up with anyone, were you?"

Grinning, she sparred, "Yes. How did you know?" She smiled as a roast beef dinner was placed in front of her. *She'd been craving something spicy. It was more than that, her body required something with a kick to it now. It would probably be offensive to the chef if she asked for hot sauce.*

"Yes, it would," Zach commented on her inner dialogue. "Come on, you can go one meal without slathering it in that stuff. They've gone out of their way to appease us."

She was starving after her extracurricular activities that afternoon. Their table chatted as they ate through the speeches until crazy loud music and strobe lights turned on. Lexy was sitting too far down the table to talk to her without yelling so she spent her time joking around with Astrid, Haley, Mel and Zach. *They were having a great time.* She barely noticed as her empty glass was taken away and a full one was placed before her.

"We're missing people, where are Frost and Markus?"

Astrid questioned as their plates were gathered and taken away.

"I'm assuming they're still with Amar discussing creative ways to save his son," Zach answered.

Kevin's words resurfaced in her wine giddy mind. *They weren't really going to separate them already, were they? They'd never get the opportunity to feel secure with each other if they were never given the time they needed to get there.*

3

INCONVENIENT EMOTIONS

She needed to make sure Frost was still here. Kayn excused herself from the table and made her way through the smoky, rowdy dance floor. *There was even a smoke machine. This continent was serious about their partying.* She bumped into her inebriated Uncle Frey, jumping up and down with both of his arms in the air like a prepubescent in a mosh pit.

"You're here!" Her Uncle flamboyantly sang, excitedly clutching her arms, making her leap up and down with him.

She had to laugh. *He'd greeted her nonchalantly every other time, they'd crossed paths. He'd been happy she made it out of the Testing but disinterested. She'd only ever been in his presence on three occasions. The first, was at their continent's banquet before her Testing and he'd only been interested in where her birthmark was. The second, was at a diner and all he wanted was details on her virgin sacrifice.*

"How have you been?" he yelled over the music. She hollered back, "Good! And you?"

"Good!" he bellowed back as a handsome guy butted in and stole him away.

That was short but sweet. Chuckling, Kayn fought her way through the strobe-lit smoke show of writhing bodies. She felt like dancing, but first, she needed to find Frost and touch base. As she wandered out into the foyer, they were sitting at a table eating. *Oh, shoot. She didn't want to interrupt anything.*

Peering up from his meal, Frost addressed her, "We won't be much longer. We're working out the details."

"I was looking for the washroom," she fibbed. Markus pointed down the hall. Kayn waved politely and took off giggly drunk. She ducked into the bathroom. *Was anyone else in here? She didn't see any legs under the stalls. She gave one of the doors a gentle shove and the door swung open but there was something blocking it.*

Kevin's voice exclaimed, "This one is taken!"

Abort! Wrong washroom! Oh, I'm such an idiot. She dove out into the hall and tried to get into the restroom next door. *It was locked! Come on! She could hear him washing his hands. She had nowhere to go! Damn it!* Panicking, she aggressively knocked. Just as Kevin stepped out into the hall, someone opened the door. Utterly relieved, she dove in. *Her saviour was her favourite Triad.*

"You do know you're in the men's washroom," Patrick chuckled.

"They can't all be men's washrooms," She sighed.

Laughing, he suggested, "Look at the door."

"I can't, I'm hiding," she explained. Kayn sat on the counter.

"Well, now I'm intrigued," Patrick teased as he joined her. Once perched beside her, he questioned, "You're not trying to avoid Kevin, are you?"

Something about Patrick always made her feel relatively safe confiding in him, so she did, "We were late. Frost missed the receiving line. They are always separating us. I wanted to make sure he was still here. They were busy so I told them I was looking for the bathroom. When I shoved on a stall it was Kevin. The rest were locked. I couldn't escape."

Entertained by her weird confession, Patrick teased, "You're adorable tipsy and for the record, Kevin was in the wrong bathroom." They sat in humorous silence for a minute before he enquired, "How have you been since the Testing?"

"I'm not sure I came back out," Kayn answered.

"I understand. I didn't come back out either. None of us did," he admitted, meeting her eyes.

Tears swelled so she looked away. He touched her shoulder, reassuring, "He's never stopped caring about you."

She knew that. She felt the same way. She couldn't admit it though. It wasn't right to admit it when she was in a relationship with somebody else.

"How's Frost?" Patrick changed the subject, "That boy is inhumanly sexy."

Smiling at the endearing Triad, Kayn replied, "It's complicated."

He playfully nudged her and teased, "Don't you dare use that cliché as an answer. You're better than that."

With a warm smile, she asked, "How did you end up in Triad? It's just never made sense to me, you're far too nice."

Patrick whispered, "I think Tiberius was trying to make sure Kevin would mesh with his group and survive the Testing. I've always been quite certain it had nothing to do with me."

There was a knock on the door. Kayn called, "We'll be right out!"

Frost's voice answered, "You know you're in the men's washroom, right?"

Patrick winked as he animatedly whispered, "Speak of the devil."

She gave Patrick's shoulder an uncoordinated friendly pat and slid off the counter. Her legs were unsteady and she nearly toppled over into one of the stalls, but he caught her. Kayn steadied herself as she declared, "I'm good. I've got this."

The sweet Triad quietly cautioned, "Slow your roll, my wasted friend, you do not have this. Never binge drink around an ex. I don't have a shitload of life experience but that, I know." Patrick opened the door. He manoeuvered past Frost while coyly commenting, "Your sexiness."

Smiling, Frost playfully shoved her back into the bathroom, locked the door and asserted, "It's confession time."

Shit… Really? Oh no. "There are too many things to confess, you're going to have to be more specific," she sparred as he backed her against the counter.

"You did their training. Tell me about Amar's son. Did we just make a mistake by taking him?"

Intuition was a funny thing. She responded, "If you had to ask, you already have your answer. I promised Amar I'd keep my mouth shut and let the choice be yours."

"Off the record," Frost flirtatiously probed as he seductively lowered her strap and tenderly kissed her shoulder.

She was too smart to be played. Kayn urged his chin up with a finger. His eyes connected with hers. She moved in and aggressively kissed him until he forgot what he was trying to get out of her. She reached for his zipper and he swatted her away.

"Trust me sweetheart, there's nothing in this world I want more than to take you right here, but this is not the place," he whispered against her lips.

"Why? The doors locked and I'm not wearing any underwear," she innocently tempted.

He smirked as he stepped away and roguishly promised, "When I get you back to our room you are in so much trouble."

She slid off the counter, willing her tipsy self a cool moment. She strutted by him and provoked, "Promises, promises."

Laughing, he chased her down the hall, caught her before she made it back into the banquet hall and scolded, "I should throw you over my shoulder and carry you back to our room right now."

Kayn laced her fingers behind his neck and pressed her body against his as they began swaying to the music. She changed the subject, "Have you eaten anything?"

"We were served while debating young Samid's future," he answered.

"He is coming with us then?" Kayn enquired.

"We owe Amar's son a chance at survival even if he is a pompous little shit," Frost confirmed. "Did you get the chance to find out what Kevin wanted?"

"I did, he basically told me to watch my ego. He also said I wasn't attached enough to Zach and that they were going to separate us."

"He's hit the nail on the head there. We have a week apart coming up while I attend the Summit with this group, then we only get two weeks together before a month-long stint apart," Frost disclosed. "Your group has to stay here for a few days. We need the other Clans to be long gone before you come back through the Crypt with Samid into Mexico. Dean is with Arianna and Jenna, that's why they're not here. We'll all be meeting up after the Summit."

The smoke had drifted out into the hall, creating a mystically sensual ambiance. *This smoke show was going to hide a lot of sins this evening. She could feel it.* He tenderly kissed her. As they parted, curiosity won the battle being waged within her as she enquired, "Where are you guys off too for a month?"

"We're heading into South America to clean up someone else's mess," Frost explained.

Gazing into his eyes, she confessed, "A month apart is going to be rough."

We can discuss this tomorrow. It's time to cut loose and have fun," he proclaimed.

That sounded like an excellent idea. He twirled her in a circle. She was laughing as he tugged her against him. He ran his fingers through her curls. She thought he was about to say something deep and meaningful as he tossed a verbal curveball, "Your sexiness. What was that about?"

Patrick said that as he walked away. She laughed and prodded, "Like people don't say stuff like that to you all of the time."

"They do, but it was the random timing of it that threw me off. You were in there talking about me, weren't you?" He baited as he led her further onto the dance floor.

"Maybe," she giggled as they gyrated to club beats under the privacy enhancing veil of smoke. Before they had a chance to get carried away, they were joined by the rest of their Clan. Like the stinker he was, drunk Grey stole her away. Over Grey's shoulder she saw Frost dancing with Astrid, Haley and Zach. *It was cute. Right now, it felt like he was just a guy on the dance floor and she was just a girl. They were strangers in a club amidst strobe lights and smoke. It made her wish they'd had the opportunity to meet this way.*

Grey snapped his fingers a few inches from her face and loudly said, "Earth to Kayn!"

She scowled as she fought the urge to dropkick him in the balls. *Who snaps their fingers to get someone's attention?*

"Zach's turn!" Grey announced as he grabbed her immortal babysitter and shoved him at her.

"He just snapped his fingers in my face," Kayn hissed while seething with irrational rage.

"Nope. We're not doing this tonight. Ignore him. Happy place. Grey's hammered. He's being a jealous tool. Tiberius has been relentlessly hitting on Lexy. Did you hear he got the room next door?"

She had heard that from her sister's lips. Her sister. That was still a crazy thought. Zach started dancing goofily because she was standing still, going through the list of funny dances to make her laugh. She slowly shook her head as he did the sprinkler. When he began fishing, she laughed, "Don't make me do the lawn mower."

"Oh, like this?" Zach joshed as he began mowing his imaginary lawn.

Through the billowing cloud of smoke, she saw Patrick watching the show, laughing. The Clans remained separate for longer than usual but as everyone's inhibitions loosened, so did the seating arrangements. She ended up back in Frost's arms as the dance floor became a hedonistic free-for-all. They did shots and dirty danced the night away concealed by the smoke and pulsating light show. Eventually, duty called. Frost had to leave because he'd missed greeting everyone as they arrived. She chose to take a break. Exhausted and tipsy, Kayn stumbled back to her seat at the table with Zach. She felt like people watching as Frost shook hands and chatted his way through the attendees. *Lily was sitting with Amar. Interesting, they appeared to know each other well.* Kayn took a sip of her wine as the waiter offered her dessert. Normally, she would have passed, but after all those shots, she'd be sick if she didn't eat. Grey strolled past her and laughed as he messed up her hair. She mischievously swatted his rear *He really did have a nice ass. It occurred to her that she might be too drunk.*

Zach leaned in and whispered, "Do you need a time out?"

She playfully shoved her Handler as she declared, "Probably." Her eyes darted over to Triad's table. *Kevin caught her.* She looked down at her cake and started picking at it with her fork. She heard the chair scraping across the ground beside her and knew who it was, without looking.

"So, you're in a relationship with my brother now? How's that going?" Triad's leader Tiberius enquired as he grabbed a spoon used to stir coffee and dug into her cake.

Kayn stabbed his hand with her fork and hissed, "Get your own damn cake!" Laughing too hard to bother retaliating, Tiberius massaged his fork impaled hand.

Zach's attention snapped away from Triad's table, "Brighton! What in the hell? No stabbing!"

He should consider himself lucky I didn't stab him in the eye.

Lexy aggressively yanked out the chair Tiberius was sitting on, taking him for an unexpected three-foot ride in reverse. She menaced, "You're not bothering my sister, are you?"

Tiberius leaned back in his chair and flirtatiously greeted her, "Hey gorgeous."

"Hey gorgeous yourself," Lexy mumbled as she put her full weight on the back of his seat and tipped him over. With a loud thud, Tiberius was lying on his back on the floor. Lexy distastefully glared down at him.

"Always so deliciously volatile. I've missed this," he commentated from his naughty vantage point, seductively caressing her calf.

"That's odd because I haven't," Lexy countered.

"Liar," Tiberius provoked. He held out his hand like he expected help.

In true Dragon style, Lexy stepped away from the notoriously naughty leader. Scorching flames of animosity flew from her lips as she provoked, "I wouldn't hold your breath."

Tiberius was still lying on the ground laughing as Orin strolled over, politely helped him up and quipped, "You just never learn."

Instead of leaving, Tiberius pushed his seat back to the table and sat down. Without saying a word, Kayn shoved her cake at him and said, "I'll get a new one."

Unfazed, Tiberius dug into her slice. He pointedly looked at Orin as he enquired, "How's Jenna doing with the whole Lexy thing?"

Shit. That was her fault.

Zach nudged her and whispered, "This is getting good."

She was the one that mentioned they were dating.

"I haven't asked," Orin countered. "We don't discuss who we're seeing."

"How's her Handler taking it?" Tiberius probed. "I know Grey can get a bit emotional."

All eyes turned to Grey on the dance floor with Haley and Astrid. *Where did Melody go?* Kayn searched the room. *No Thorne either, interesting.*

Lexy kicked Tiberius under the table. Scowling at him, she declared, "I'm right here. If you have questions about my life… Ask me."

"Are you coming to my room later?" Tiberius boldly enquired.

Lexy rolled her eyes and shook her head, trying to make him look delusional, but Kayn suspected she was entertaining the idea.

"That's not a no," Tiberius taunted as he sipped his wine. "There's an adjoining door between our rooms. It'll be unlocked if the mood strikes you."

"That's my cue," Orin broadcasted. As he got up to leave, he bent and whispered in Lexy's ear, "Don't do anything I wouldn't do."

She really had to catch up with Lexy. She was out of the loop. Were they just a casual thing, because it sounded like he'd just given her permission? Not that Lexy required anyone's approval for anything. Kayn noticed Frost making his way through the flashing lights and smoky air to the table. He was trying to signal her over. *She pretended she didn't see him. She didn't want to miss this conversation.*

Smiling, Frost slid into the seat next to Tiberius and interjected, "Still trying to get blood from a stone?"

"Lexy knows she wants me," Tiberius baited, winking at her.

The volatile hostility in their visual exchange raised the temperature in the room.

Oh, this was so going to happen. Any real romance between Lexy and Tiberius would probably end up being nothing more than a cautionary tale regaled for centuries but until it went down, they were a titillating attraction rivalling every tabloid headline.

Zach caught the waiter's attention on the way by and snagged her two gigantic slices of replacement cake. Kayn was poised to take her first bite when she noticed the conversation had stalled. *Everyone was gawking at her.* So, she did what any comically inclined, somewhat unstable defiant cake eating connoisseur would do. She picked up the mass of chocolate and icing in both hands. It crumbled all over the table as she took a giant uncivilized chomp.

Tiberius was sitting with his mouth agape as Dragon sibling pride shone through in Lexy's thoroughly entertained grin. Zach pressed his lips together to stop himself from laughing. He politely passed Kayn a napkin. Frost watched her savagely devouring her desert in awe. *Open adoration made her uncomfortable.* Kayn grabbed Zach's full glass of wine and chugged it to wash the cake down. She felt Tiberius' penetrating stare and peered up from her cake as he slid a shot glass across the table at her. Giggling, she snatched it mid slide. *He was going to have to do way better than that.* He slid one to Lexy.

Lexy picked up her shot of Tequila and quipped, "I'm going to need a lot of these to forget who you are."

Tiberius was beaming as he shot one across the table at Zach. Her Handler hesitantly picked it up.

Lexy's eyes darted over to Trinity's table. Kayn followed her gaze. *Orin was standing there chatting with Thorne. The Brothers of Prophecy intrigued her. Thorne was the moral one of the three. The other two brothers were quite liberal with their grey areas. Frost was insanely gorgeous. He set her inhibitions free and that's what she needed. Tiberius was a sexy guy with a dark charisma much like Frost's but there was this flawed honesty in the leader of Triad that she found quite compelling. It was obvious that her sister Lexy was finding herself enraptured by the head bad boy of Triad. Her sister, they were sisters. It was difficult to believe but it was sinking in.* Someone's leg brushed against hers. She peered up into Frost's intrigued gaze.

He enquired, "How much longer do you want to stay?"

She didn't want to leave, not yet. "Another hour?" she suggested. Zach sighed. His jaw dropped as Kayn gave his arm a pinch and scolded, "Consider yourself off duty. Just go over there and talk to him." He gave her a look. She corrected herself, "Whoops, I meant her."

"You just stabbed Tiberius," Zach far too calmly stated. He rolled his eyes and downed the rest of his glass of wine.

Frost grinned as he noticed his brother's napkin wrapped hand. Playing footsies with her under the table, he playfully reprimanded, "Sweetheart, you're supposed to play nice."

"That was me playing nice," Kayn mumbled under her breath.

Pivoting on her seat, Lexy said, "Stabbings happen. Tiberius makes me feel all stabby too."

As Grey slid into the chair beside Zach, he declared, "Go. Frost is here, I'm here. Everyone wants to stab Tiberius. He's used to it. We'll keep things PG."

Zach hesitantly got up. He looked at Kayn and asked, "Are you planning to do anything that will get me in trouble?"

"Maybe," Kayn nonchalantly replied as she devoured her massive slice of chocolate cake. Noticing Zach hadn't moved, she peered up at him.

"Are you kidding? It's getting harder to tell," Zach questioned. "Promise me you won't stab him again… Or anyone else."

Feeling Lexy's eyes on her, she glanced at her grinning sister. *She had her back.* Kayn vowed, "I promise I won't stab Tiberius again. Now, get over there already."

"Or anyone else," Zach clarified.

She was planning on doing something to Stephanie at some point this evening. He must have felt it. Party pooper. Her sister winked at her. *Lexy was down for anything. She felt so close to her right now.* "Alright, nobody gets stabbed," Kayn promised. Zach wandered away shaking his head.

Grey gave Lexy a dirty look as he said, "I guess I'm not leaving your side tonight. Come on. Let's dance."

Lexy took Grey's hand, glanced back at Kayn and mouthed the words, "I'll get Stephanie."

Perturbed as Grey towed Lexy away from the table, Tiberius got up and announced, "I'll be right back."

He was probably going to warn Stephanie. Spoilsport.

Frost got up, came to sit beside her and took her hand as he quietly explained, "You know, listening to Zach is the first step in our Clan not having to separate us to secure your Dragon Handler bond."

Tiberius reappeared. He placed a tray with two bottles of whiskey and shot glasses on the table. He declared, "I've invited people back to my room, but first, let's do shots. I'd like to hear about this sister discovery."

Thorne came over to their table with a few Trinity and Melody. They all took a seat. Tiberius filled the glasses and passed a shot to each. "So, you've only known Seth is your father and Lexy is your sister for a couple of days?"

Thorne's eyes widened, he blurted out, "What? Are you joking?"

Tiberius had done this on purpose. That tool. He'd invited Thorne over to drop a bomb. Kevin just warned her about being cocky while explaining things to people. Kayn answered, "Yes, it's only been a few days, and no, he's not joking. It doesn't matter though. It doesn't change anything." *Downplaying it was probably the way to go.*

"I bet the Third-Tier are losing it over this," The leader of Trinity commented. "One more daughter of Seth and the Prophecy has officially started."

Looking at Frost, she asked, "What Prophecy?"

Ignoring her direct question, Frost glared at his brother Thorne as he rebutted, "There's no way they allow another of his offspring to slip through the Correction and Testing process. It's never going to happen." He met Kayn's eyes as he affirmed, "It's nothing important. Forget about it."

How did he think she was going to forget about an ominous declaration like that? She slid her empty glass at Tiberius without a word.

He silently filled it and slid it back, looking like he felt guilty for bringing it up.

She downed the shot of whiskey and looked around for Kevin. *He'd tell her the truth if she could get him alone. She was certain of it. He wasn't at Triad's table anymore. He was gone. That was probably for the best. Maybe, she'd be able to stop her mind from wandering over there. She remembered his old email address. She'd message him when she was alone.*

Thorne changed the subject, "So, you and Lexy are sisters. I can see it." He raised his glass in salute, "To siblings!"

Kayn downed another shot. Frost gave her knee a reassuring squeeze. She turned to look at the man she'd given her heart to. *Most of it.* She felt like a horrible person as she became aware of the token of affection tucked in her bra close to her heart. *The purple clover hidden in her bra was an unnecessary secret. She had to get rid of it. Coveting a token of affection from an ex, was wrong.* She slid her empty shot glass across the table to Tiberius again. *Go big or go home.* Once again, she found herself searching the room for him. *What was wrong with her tonight?* Tiberius sent another shot her way. She downed it and announced, "I'll be back."

Concerned, Frost's hand clasped her arm as she attempted to leave, "Is everything alright? Should I come with you?"

"I'm fine. I just need fresh air," she explained. He released his grasp and she strolled away from the table of enquiring minds. It felt like she was suffocating in the hedonistic blur of flashing lights and rising smoke.

She headed for the balcony. As she stepped out into the warm night air, she knew what she needed to do. Kayn removed the crumpled-up clover from her bra and closed her hand around it protectively. *She was drunk. She wasn't thinking straight. The clover Kevin gave her was confusing their roles. There was no room for sentimentality where he was concerned. She couldn't use that email address. What if Triad was planning to use it to track her?* She tossed the squashed-up clover over the ledge and watched it delicately fall into the courtyard below. When it landed, she had the overwhelming urge to dash down there. From behind her, Kevin's voice assured, "You don't need to keep it. I just knew you'd need proof I remembered us."

Why did he have to use the word, us? She whispered, "There is no us anymore," without looking back at the boy she'd known her whole life.

"Do you really believe that?" Kevin probed as he came over to stand beside her.

As the words slipped from his lips, she knew there was no point in denial. *Their bond was deeper than that.* "I'm glad we finally had a real opportunity to talk about what happened but I still need to find my way back from the Testing. I'm in love with him, Kevin."

"I know," he replied. After a moment of silence, he added, "You still love me too. I know you do. I can feel it."

"In the Testing, I begged you to admit how you felt about me, using those words, and you said it didn't matter," she pointed out. "You were right. It doesn't. Move on. I have. I can't play romantic memory games with you, it's not fair to him."

"Aren't you going to ask me about the Daughters of Seth Prophecy?" her old best friend enquired as he inched closer.

"No. I won't be using that email address either," she affirmed. *It was easier when they were still mad at each other. Carefree memories of mortality before the whirlwind of immortal truths made her want to run away from him as far and fast as she could. Those people didn't exist anymore. He saw the fragile parts of herself, kept hidden from the world.*

"It doesn't matter what you choose to do, I'll always love you," Kevin pledged as his unavoidable eyes bore into her soul.

He was a weakness, a weapon that could be used against her. He may be trying to trick her. She needed to stop this, right now. The Dragon knew how to protect her soul from useless sentiment. "We'll see about that," Kayn sparred as she launched Kevin over the railing and watched him splat in the courtyard. *Unwanted emotional issues resolved. The protective shield encompassed her heart until it vanished, and she didn't care about anything anymore.* She slipped back into the banquet as Triad's symbols went off. They began rushing around searching for their wounded member. *Whoops, Zach saw that.* Her livid Handler took her arm and briskly led her away from the banquet into the hall.

"You can't be offing random people. There are rules," Zach scolded as he escorted her back to her room.

It was hilarious. Kevin hadn't seen that coming, and he claimed to be a psychic. Giggles turned to disappointment when Frost wasn't already in the room waiting.

"Frost won't be showing up any time soon, I'm sure he'll be doing damage control," Zach stated. Trying to stop himself from smiling, he dug a little deeper, "What made you mad enough to toss him over a balcony?"

"He gave me a flower at the beginning of the evening and there were inconvenient feelings," she explained emotionlessly.

His expression softened as they sat down next to each other on the bed. "I can't leave you here emotionally void like this, you know that, right?"

She flopped back, stared at the ceiling and sighed, "Suit yourself."

Sprawling next to her, her Handler mumbled, "You could have just walked away."

No. Walking away wasn't brutal enough to shut her emotions down but tossing him off a balcony was brilliantly played. She closed her eyes for a few minutes and slipped into a deep self-satisfied slumber.

LEXY WATCHED KAYN LEAVE THE TABLE with her chin perched on Grey's shoulder as they swayed to the music. *She was irritated. This wasn't unusual but tonight her primal urges were impressively amped up. Tiberius' presence at the banquet was expected, he was the leader of Triad. Their titillating encounter during the last Summit had left her with this driving urgency to experience all their dark attraction had to offer. No matter how hard she tried, she couldn't shake the sexually charged visions of him above her as he sliced his blade into her skin, showing her a little something she hadn't known about the pleasure he could show her. Their brief sensually charged encounters since the Summit left her yearning for*

more even though she'd accidentally started something with Orin. Being a thousand years old gave Orin a good grasp on the realities of attractions left unfulfilled. He was all for her taking the night to see Tiberius' chapter through till it's end. Orin made it clear he had no intention of getting into anything more serious than booty calls and flirtation until after she'd closed her book of unknowns.

Grey whispered in her ear, "I'm going to need another drink if you're going to insist on thinking about that dick."

She rolled her eyes and sparred, "Jealous?"

He pulled away, considered it and admitted, "Maybe a little."

Lexy playfully shoved him away. As she strolled back to the table, she jabbed, "You'll get over it. You always do."

"What did you just say?" Grey enquired as he caught up with her.

"Nothing important," she countered, as she snatched a shot from in front of Tiberius and downed it.

Triad's leader glanced over at her as she sat down beside Grey. Tiberius bit his lip and grinned as he began playing footsies with her. Lexy grinned and countered by sliding her foot as far up his leg as she could reach.

Grey was laughing with Frost, it didn't look like he'd noticed their flirtation until he turned to look at her, smiled and said, "You know I'm not letting you out of my sight tonight. There's no point in entertaining those naughty thoughts."

Their roles were ridiculously unfair. Grey could do whatever he wanted and her actions had to be monitored. This was the price of being a Dragon. Her Handler was always present to talk her down from the ledge. His job was to stop her dark impulses. She took a sip of wine as she watched the dancers writhing in the light show in a sea of rising smoke. *Everything about this continent's banquet made her want to let her Dragon soar. The pulsating light show stimulated her need to be free.* She met Tiberius' seductive gaze. Their eyes held with the intensity of their passionate game. *She wanted to do bad things.* Grey countered by possessively placing his hand on her thigh, tugging her heart back to where it belonged without words. *Her body and soul had always belonged to her Handler but in the last couple of months, she'd gone from one prospect to three. She'd never been in this position before. Grey had been everything to her for so long. She adored him but he'd been spelled to forget any intimacy between them as he slept. This didn't make his jealousy any easier to digest. Grey didn't understand. He couldn't. She was cursed to remember every heartbreakingly beautiful detail of the nights they'd spent professing their love. He was only ever reacting to half of the story. After forty years by Grey's side, she was finally ready to find something more. She yearned for a physical connection that would still be there at dawn's first light. This was something she could never have with Grey.* Orin shifted closer to her, trying to make sure she understood her options. *Orin was a good friend and undeniably great in the sack but he'd been in a long-term relationship, and by long term, she meant, with the same girl on and off for a thousand years. Neither of them could promise more than drama free shelter from the storm of their endless duties. It had taken her a long time to get to the point of wanting to experience anything physical with anyone but her Handler. She was ready to enjoy the perks of her afterlife now.*

Grey glared across the table at Tiberius and said, "That's me you're playing footsies with."

Tiberius winked at Grey and provoked, "I didn't want you to feel left out. Of course, you're free to join us."

Her Handler rolled his eyes, turned to face Lexy and cautioned, "I'll be upset for like a year if you do this, just so we're clear."

Without the sentimentality of eye contact, Lexy countered, "Lily, Melody, Arrianna…Do I really need to keep going?"

Defeated by the reality of his own actions, Grey looked away and pretended he was listening to Frost. Out of nowhere, Grey turned to her and asserted, "One word from you and I would have walked away from all of them."

Here they were again. Her Handler's feelings for her were returning. As soon as she gave in, they would be gone and she'd be left heartbroken. Determined to stop kicking herself, Lexy didn't respond. She took a pastry from the tray as it was offered to her. As she took her first bite, her eyes were drawn to Tiberius. His foot grazed hers under the table. She bit her lip pensively. With Grey's hand rested on her thigh, she wasn't sure she could reply by action without being caught. *She wanted to though and that was her truth. She'd despised Tiberius with every inch of her being for forty years and now every argument just felt like foreplay between Dragons. Their duelling libidos had led them into some awkward situations, but she wanted him and admitting it was half the battle. He'd been bold enough to acquire the room next to hers, with an adjoining door. Even though she'd led him to believe she wouldn't come to him during his rather public dare, she'd planned to.* Lexy excused herself, turning back to the table when she was far enough away, met Tiberius' intrigued gaze and winked.

Intending to make her way back to her room and use that door, she needed a quick detour to the bathroom. She manoeuvered her way through the crowded dance floor and down the hall with muted toned tapestries to the washroom. Alone in the stall, the hollow clicking of footsteps alerted her someone else came in. *She caught herself hoping it was him.* Lexy peered through the crack of the door. *It was Stephanie. She'd been quite the bitch to Kayn. Her sister. That was still a crazy thought. She could stay in the stall until the Triad girl left or storm out and kick her ass. She was supposed to behave. She'd do her best.* Lexy abruptly opened the stall, startling the Triad.

The petite dark-featured beauty spun around and laughed nervously, "You startled me. I didn't know anyone else was in here."

Lexy strolled over with plans to wash her hands and leave, but there was no soap in the dispenser. *This irritated her but she was still planning to play nice.*

"Didn't you hear me?" Stephanie prodded.

Lexy moved to the next sink and tried the dispenser. *It didn't work. It spoke to her. It shouldn't speak to her when she was this drunk.*

"Should I grunt like a caveman? You know, speak your language? Is the soap dispenser too difficult for you to figure out? I heard you went years without bathing," the tiny Triad provoked.

Tiberius just lost his booty call. He would have been the one to tell her that story. Lexy sighed before asserting, "I'd just quietly go about whatever business you came in here to do if I were you."

Intrigued by her hostility, Stephanie poked the Dragon, "I was thinking about taking Greydon out for a spin. I figure it's all good if you plan to hook up with Tiberius tonight."

She wanted to say Grey would never go there but she knew better. He so would, without batting an eye. "Do what you want," Lexy coldly responded.

"I intend to," Stephanie sparred as she gave the dispenser a shot and it worked. She smiled at Lexy as she whispered her snarky commentary, "It's not rocket science."

And that was it! Lexy shot forward and snapped her neck. Stephanie slumped to the tile. She gave her body a swift boot. *What a bitch! That was satisfying.* She pranced away with a skip in her step. Reaching for the door, the sound of chaos snapped her back to reality. *Crap. Triad's symbols went off. Adding copious amounts of alcohol to her unfiltered rage issues always backfired. She'd might as well own it.*

Grey was already racing down the hall, scolding, "Seriously, Lex! What in the hell?"

"I'll fix it," Lexy mumbled, opening the door to Stephanie's lifeless corpse. She knelt before her and laid her palms on her mortal enemy's chest. As the warmth of her healing energy travelled down her arms into the Triad's body, Grey yanked her away before she brought her back. Her vision wavered. Exhausted, Lexy passed out by the Triad on the tile.

TIBERIUS APPEARED IN THE DOORWAY. Grey turned to defend her actions, but the leader of Triad interrupted, "They obviously had a tiff. I warned Stephanie about being lippy with certain people. That only explains one of the flashes though."

Grey tried to explain, "I told Zach to go have fun and that I'd watch both tonight. It was my mistake. I'm to blame."

The leader of Triad slowly shook his head, staying, "The rules don't apply. They're part Guardian. They can't be Entombed. Don't take ownership of a problem that's not yours anymore."

Amar, Markus and Frost appeared in the hall. Tiberius summoned them over with a wave. Grey tried to take one for the team. Although Markus did agree he'd made a misstep, he wasn't about to place the blame entirely on him. "You should have known better Greydon, but in all fairness, this is a situation we've never encountered so we're going to have to be creative with how we deal with this. Have you noticed a change in your bond in the last couple of days?"

Grey shrugged as he admitted, "Maybe a little."

Thorne's deep superhero voice boomed down the hall, "We've found the other body! Someone tossed Tiberius' grandson over the balcony!"

Annoyed, Frost sighed, "Let me guess, Kayn and Zach are nowhere to be found."

"I saw him usher Kayn out during the ruckus," Lily's voice added as she peeked into the bathroom. "Who started it?"

Grey speculated, "Probably Stephanie but as always, Lexy finished it."

Smiling, Tiberius stared down at the crimson-haired Dragon sprawled on the tile. "I can't turn anyone in. They're Seth's daughters and although the rules don't apply, Ankh is going to have to find a way to control this situation. They can't just be running around murdering anyone that ticks them off."

Markus met Frost's eyes as he apologized, "I'm sorry, Tiberius is right. We need to find a way to manage these two. Contact Jenna and get her to speak to Ankh's Guardian Azariah. Ask her what she thinks we should do. Grey, take Lexy back to your room and wait for us to get back to you."

Grey scooped Lexy up in his arms and carried her back to their room. As he placed her on the bed, Lexy whispered, "I'm not sorry."

He grinned as he climbed into bed next to her and replied, "I know."

4

WHISKY WAS THE DEVIL

Sprawled across the sheets, Kayn stretched and hit someone. She rolled over. *It wasn't Frost. Zach was still passed out next to her. What time was it?* She squirmed closer and gave her Handler a shake.

Zach opened his eyes, squinting in the not so hangover friendly morning's rays, grumbling, "It's blinding. Close the curtains, Brighton." Struggling to get up, clutching his head, he complained, "Man, this headache is brutal. It's morning, isn't it? Oh, did you ever screw up last night. What am I talking about? It's my fault for trusting you weren't going to follow through with your impulses."

Not now. She didn't have it in her to deal with bitching about something that couldn't be undone. She knew what she did. Her brain felt like it was about to explode. She didn't have Frost around last night to feed her a hangover cure. Kayn swung her legs over the edge of the bed and staggered to the bathroom. *Frost left a note on the bathroom mirror.* Squinting to read it, her brain refused to function. *Whisky was the devil. Or had it been the tequila? She'd had wine too. She'd earned this headache. That much she was certain of.* She read the note again. *This time she got the jyst of it. He was gone to the Summit. That was it. No hearts or X's and O's. He was probably mad at her. Could she blame him? Not really.* She ripped the note off the mirror, and sat on the toilet seat, staring at it. *Her inner Dragon had been naughty.* She recalled the surprised look on Kevin's face as she launched him over the balcony and chuckled.

"Are you decent?" Zach called from the other side of the door.

Rarely. "Come in. I'm just sitting here, stewing," Kayn answered.

He walked in and she passed him the note.

Trying to contain his laughter, a snicker escaped as he gave the note back and confirmed her earlier thoughts, "Oh, I'd say he didn't find your impulse control issues funny last night."

It would be better if she just kept her emotions off. If she didn't, she was going to spend the next week thinking about what he was doing. There was a knock on the door.

Zach offered, "I'll get it." While wandering towards the door, he commentated, "Someone's here to Entomb me for being the worst Handler ever."

He was joking, she knew that, but one day it could happen. She couldn't be punished but he could. Oh, she was an idiot. Her inner commentary was going strong even with her emotions somewhat stifled. *She heard Grey and Lexy's voices. Had they stayed behind? Time to face the firing squad.* She got up and strolled back into the room. Lexy was beaming. Grey appeared to be unimpressed with their shenanigans.

He approached, disclosing, "Zach mentioned your impulse control issues were caused by inconveniently timed feelings."

Kayn glanced at Lexy and winked.

"Stephanie from Triad also met with an accident last night. Apparently, she tripped and broke her neck in the bathroom," Zach explained.

Awe, that's so sweet, her sister got her a present. She'd forgotten about her plot for Stephanie.

"As a result, we'll be staying with you guys while the others go to the Summit," Grey explained. "Melody is going with them. Astrid and Haley will be slipping away with Samid. They'll be meeting up with Jenna and Arrianna because they have Dean. Our job is to try to connect Amar's new trio of Ankh."

Curiosity got the best of her and she asked, "How mad is Frost, on a scale of one to ten?"

"Eleven," Grey sternly retorted.

That sounds about right. Yes. It would be best to keep her feelings shut down. Kayn replied, "A week apart isn't that bad. I'll fix it when I see him again."

"Try, we don't get to meet up with the others until we've completed an enormous list of jobs. It looks like it's going to be a long haul. It goes without saying that Markus isn't all warm and fuzzy about Zach's Handler bond, or mine. I was forced to admit I told him to have fun; I'd make sure you didn't get into trouble. While I was partying, Lexy snuck into a bathroom and murdered Stephanie on a whim as you tossed Kevin off a damn balcony. Now, we're all in trouble, mostly me. It's the four of us with no relationship disruptions for the next couple of months."

Kayn's eyes met with Lexy's. They both smiled. *Sister Dragon bonding time. This might be fun.*

"Oh, there's one more thing," Grey announced as he snatched Zach's cell right out of his hand. "Turn in your phones. I have new burner phones for all of us. We're being punished by having no contact with the rest of Ankh. I have the information for the next month. They'll contact us with any changes."

Kayn grimaced. *This was bullshit.* She handed Grey her phone and wandered outside. From her balcony, she saw the staff still cleaning up the splat Kevin made on the cement path in the courtyard. *He shouldn't have given her that flower.* A twinge of guilt began to grow within her. She spun around, marched back into the room and commented, "Reprimanding us by sending us on a murder spree doesn't seem like punishment to me, but why not? Let's get this party started."

Zach glanced at Grey and laughed, "They're not even fazed by this."

"They will be," Grey replied as he struggled to pry Lexy's cell phone from her fingers. "Come on Lex, just give it to me."

Glaring at Grey, Lexy asserted, "In all fairness, we were told the rules didn't apply to us anymore."

"Come on, Lex. Did you really believe that was the case? They can't have you two running around free to do what-ever crosses your mind," Zach argued, playing with his new phone. "At least they are smartphones."

Fiddling around with his, Grey announced, "Yes! We have data plans!"

After placing her phone on the nightstand, Lexy suggested, "Go change into something from the closet and fix yourself up. If we don't eat breakfast before we leave for training in the In-between, we'll still be hungover when we get back."

Kayn wandered back to the washroom. As she passed the closet, she peeked inside. There were three modest silky dresses that looked like they might be her size. They were all the same cut. She chose the colour she liked best and went into the bathroom for privacy. After she'd changed and washed off her raccoon eyes from smudged mascara, she felt like a new woman. Her stomach grumbled. *Lexy was right. She needed breakfast before they went anywhere.*

There was a knock on the door, Grey opened it and stepped out of the way as a lady pushed a cart with their breakfast into the room.

Amar strolled in after her, declaring, "Excellent, you're all up. Eat up. Take those pills beside the orange juice. They'll help your hangover. We have a lot to accomplish in only a small amount of time!"

Oh, he was far too perky for this time of the morning. Wait... what time was it?

Amar answered her thought, "It's ten in the morning but we're not usually big on schedules around here. Today we are. Our three Ankh are in the In-between having much-needed bonding time. They don't know you're coming so their response will be authentic."

As they devoured their meals, Lexy randomly teased, "So, you don't have a lecture prepared then?"

Giving the perfect response, Amar chuckled, "Why? I'd be wasting my time."

He was a smart guy. He totally would be wasting his time.

When they finished, they placed their empty trays on the cart and followed Amar to the room they'd used for travel to the In-between the day before. As they strolled down the marble-floored hallway, Kayn heard rapid footsteps as two giggling children raced down the hall. *Why were there children here?*

Their immortal host responded to her thoughts, "The Aries group headquarters for this continent is beneath this complex. The employee's families also live here. I love having little ones around. I know you probably have a lot of questions. You can ask them when you return."

The sight of playing children lifted the weight on her heart and breathed life into the ornamental organ. *She missed the joyful sounds children made. The tiny beings would rarely be in her lifepath now unless it was a Correction. The thought of having to snuff out a light like theirs for the greater good still felt like the one thing she could never do... even as a Dragon.* Her thoughts drifted to the reincarnation of her brother. *Matty was with the Aries Group. They'd keep him safe until the age of his Correction, but after that, it was up to him.* She recalled his reincarnation's tiny arms wrapped around her and shook her head. *What was she doing to herself? She couldn't think about these things. They would only make her weak. Did Amar know about the children they'd found in that town that Abaddon was keeping?* As their eyes met, she knew Markus told him. *They wanted the same things. She'd been thinking logically about Samid, but when it came to the love of one's family logic didn't apply. Amar wanted his son to have a chance at survival just as she needed Matty to have the same opportunity. If the reincarnation of her brother grew up to be a self-important asshat, she wouldn't want it any less.*

Amar looped his arm through hers, allowing the others to walk ahead as he whispered, "I know where your brother is being kept. If you help me, I vow to help you."

"I can't guarantee his survival," Kayn replied.

"I know you can't, but at least now, there's a modicum of hope. I need to fix the mess I've made. I have three unprepared Ankh. I fear I've robbed them of their chance at survival," Amar explained.

She wanted to promise Amar the moon as she stared into his intense chocolate-brown eyes. Kayn gave his hand a reassuring squeeze. "We'll do our best," she affirmed as they entered the room. Waiting for their arrival were six of Amar's Ankh. *They must be Healer back up. Sucks to be them.* Kayn smiled as she wandered over to stand by Zach.

Sensing her inner turmoil, her Handler took her hand and whispered, "I guess it's Dragon time. Promise you'll come back."

"Always," she whispered. She winked at Zach while lovingly squeezing his hand. The sight of the ancient ornately engraved Tombs always caused her heart to swell with the knowledge they'd been granted this privilege. A sense of faith washed over her as the four, trouble causing North American Ankh climbed into one open Tomb.

Amar announced, "We have four Healers to operate the Tombs and two Ankh to use as an energy source for when your legendary murderous shenanigans weaken them. Let's bond these three so they have a shot at making it out of the Testing."

They gave each other a look and smiled as the lid ground shut sealing them inside.

A female voice from outside of the Tomb said, "Please don't puke in there."

Oh no. They were all hungover.

"Please tell me everyone remembered to take that pill with breakfast," Lexy proclaimed.

"I forgot to take it," Zach admitted.

Manoeuvring past Grey, Lexy gave Zach a good punch. "Ouch. Come on. I didn't know we'd be doing this,"

Zach complained.

Grey mumbled, "If you upchuck on me, I'll kick your ass."

They were jostled around as the Tomb shifted to lock with the one beside it. *Please don't puke on me Zach. Please.* She closed her eyes as the humming strobing luminescent light grew in brightness until it was overwhelming to her senses. Even though Kayn was fully prepared for it, her stomach lurched as they were catapulted into oblivion. Grey released his usual excited hoot as they began spinning with the stomach-churning velocity of a carnival ride for a little longer than usual. She heard Zach's muffled dry heaving beside her as the Tomb abruptly paused. *Oh crap. Don't puke on me Zach.* They all held their breath except for her Handler, who was valiantly trying to stop himself from tossing his cookies. Knowing Zach was hanging on by a thin thread, they awaited the vomit-inducing final descent that turned even the strongest of stomachs. With a wave of nausea for everyone, they plummeted into the In-between. In seconds, the Tomb vanished and they were free falling into the utopia between life and death. Wind whipping her hair around made it difficult to see as Kayn fell through the dampness of clouds until she could see the sand of the endless desert rapidly approaching. They slowed themselves landing gracefully, crouching in the warm, inviting sand. They rose to stand beneath the back-drop of a flaming crimson sunset. *It felt different. She'd always had this sense of belonging but now she felt powerfully connected to each grain of sand beneath her feet. Was Lexy experiencing the same thing?* Kayn turned her head, saw Lexy's serene smile and knew she was…

Giving Zach a brotherly pat on the back, Grey teased, "Next time just take the pill."

Zach was about to reply when a flash of blinding light took them all by surprise. Strolling through the endless desert towards them was Frost. *Oh, thank God. She needed to talk to him.* Kayn was about to rush into his arms fully prepared to spit out a thousand apologies when his form shifted to Grey.

Their confused sandy blonde-haired companion Grey, stared down his Doppelganger and said, "Who is this asshole?"

The being's form shifted again and became Lily with shimmering silky raven tresses flowing behind her and her hips unforgettable hypnotizing sway. *It almost made them forget what they were there for.* As not Lily came closer, she started to laugh. The pitch of her giggling lowered until Lily morphed into her shenanigan loving genetic sire Seth. *Out of every immortal in existence, why did her father have to be this idiot?*

Lexy glanced at Grey and whispered, "That's Seth."

In his blonde Adonis form, Seth announced, "Welcome! Welcome!" He reached out to shake his offspring's Handler's hand.

Taken aback by the Guardian's behaviour, Grey scowled as he took it. Lexy opted out and Seth didn't push her. Instead, the trickster marched over to Zach, greeted him and declared, "I can't wait for the show. I was most impressed with the last one."

How was she supposed to feel about having a parental figure with little to no redeeming qualities? Seth extended his hand and Kayn apprehensively took it.

Seth leaned in and whispered, "I apologize for not being available when you came to see me. I observed the training you did with those four Ankh, and my dear, it was brutal. I felt so close to you."

Was she supposed to say something? Why bother. Kayn removed her hand from his as she baited, "Are you just here for the show? Or do you have something you'd like to say to us?"

"Do you have something you need me to say?" Seth questioned as he glanced down at the sand, grinning at the strategically placed seashell.

None of them were about to fall for that old trick.

Glaring at Seth with venomous distaste, Lexy grilled, "Why didn't you save me? I was only eleven-years-old."

He answered emotionlessly, "I put you there. I was making a Dragon."

Stunned by his admission, the crimson-haired immortal seethed, "I was a child!"

"You not only survived your initial Correction but you kicked everyone's asses who came for you. You were a fighting machine. You are something special," Seth countered, intrigued by her fury.

Lexy stepped back, abruptly spun around and marched away from the group as she mumbled under her breath, "You're a piece of shit."

Kayn slowly shook her head at Seth, following Lexy without giving him the opportunity to say anything else. *She didn't really understand what her sister was talking about but she knew it must have been something horrible to have her harbouring a grudge after all this time.* She was forced to jog to catch up with Grey and Zach right behind her. They disappeared in a flash of light and found themselves strolling through an overgrown field.

Kayn grabbed Lexy's arm to slow her down as she asserted, "Stop. Just for a second. Why are we running away?"

"We are not running anywhere," Lexy curtly responded. We are ending a conversation with someone who isn't worth another word."

Looking stricken to his core, Grey urged, "Drop it, Brighton. I've got this. We'll meet up with you guys after we've had a chance to talk it out."

Kayn remained behind with Zach as Grey and Lexy disappeared in a luminescent flash of light. She glanced at Zach and questioned, "What do you think that was all about?"

"Nothing good," he answered.

They exchanged knowing looks while standing there staring at the empty field. Kayn remarked, "It looks like we have some personal time. Where do you want to go?"

Grinning, Zach held out his hand and stated, "I know where we should go. Trust me?"

"Always," Kayn replied as she took his hand. They vanished from the field in a strobe of dazzling light and reappeared on a gorgeous white sand beach. *They'd been here before. She'd been here with Frost. She'd been actively avoiding thoughts of him. This place wasn't going to help that endeavour.* She was about to think herself up a drink when Zach beat her the punch by handing her a Pina Colada with a tiny decorative dragon printed umbrella in it and a pink curly straw. *Funny.* Kayn grinned as she made herself comfortable in the warm, inviting sand on her tummy with the drink in front of her. *It reminded her of being a child at the beach with her family. Well, the laying on her belly in the sand part, not the alcoholic beverage in front of her.* She inched closer to sip from her curly straw. *She loved drinking out of straws. The weirder the better. Matt and Lexy had too.* Her mind hit pause. *Theoretically, Lexy was still here.* The thought didn't upset her anymore or make her feel a sense of loss. *It now made her feel whole. Complete as a person.* A tiny black hopping sand bug bounced past her. It was the real moments like this that always blew her mind in the In-between. Kayn peered over at Zach. *He was also watching the bug skipping its way across the sand.* She apologized, "I'm sorry, I got us in trouble and we had to leave. Haley was into you at the end of the night."

He quietly replied, "Don't worry about it. That was never going to happen."

Intrigued by his answer, she enquired, "Why wouldn't

it?"

Zach dodged her question, "On the bright side, we get to spend a few months together figuring out this Dragon Handler thing with Lexy and Grey. We haven't really had much time to do that. It could be fun?" He took a sip of his drink and turned to lay on his back as he stared up at the now brilliant paint like splashes of blue in the sky.

Grinning, she teased, "Smooth dodge there, my friend," as she did the same.

"I'll tell you everything when and if there's something to tell. I promise," he pledged.

"I'm holding you to that," Kayn rebutted as she stared up at the vibrant splotches of blue above while running her fingertips through the warm silky sand. She found herself wishing there were clouds so they could guess what they looked like. Her memory flashed back to a vision of her and Kevin watching clouds after school. She blinked, willing the thoughts to disappear. As she opened her eyes, Zach was poised above her with sunlight framing his face like a halo. Once again, her memory fed her a vision of Kevin that day at the track a year after he'd been taken by Triad. She sat up and exhaled. As she did, she noticed they were now sitting in a field full of purple clover. *This wasn't helpful.* She plucked a clover out of the earth and stared at it. *She'd made quite the mess of things.*

Zach shimmied up beside her, took the small flower from her hand and questioned, "Kevin gave you one of these at the banquet, didn't he?"

"He did," Kayn replied. "He thought I'd need proof he'd regained his memories."

"That upset you, so you tossed him over a balcony?" her Handler cautiously enquired.

"Basically," she answered, realising how insane it sounded.

With his curiosity peaked, Zach asked, "Why did Lexy kill Stephanie?"

"Why wouldn't she? Stephanie was pushing her buttons, and we were told the rules didn't apply to us anymore," Kayn quickly responded.

"By Seth," Zach clarified with a smirk.

"I see your point there," Kayn laughed as she plucked another flower from the ground. She tugged off one of its thin, tasty-ended petals.

Zach playfully slapped it out of her fingers and reprimanded, "Quit kicking yourself." He got up, offered her his hand and announced, "Let's have some fun."

Taking his hand, she saucily baited, "Why Zachary, whatever do have in mind?"

"Zachariah," he corrected, giving her a light-hearted shove. "I even know your last name."

Laughing, she gave him a retaliatory push and sparred, "Only because it's my nickname."

"Point taken," Zach admitted as he laced his fingers through hers and added, "It's better if we hold hands until we know where we're going. I don't want to spend the rest of the day searching for you." The meadow was alive with buzzing bees and fluttering butterflies as he towed her through the grass searching the ground. Finding what he was looking for, Zach chuckled as he knelt, picked up a seashell and pitched it off into the field. A towering wall of water appeared in the distance.

Beaming, she sweetly said, "Awe, love monkey. You shouldn't have." As the towering tsunami started coming, they fled. Trees, bushes and long, dense grass broke through the soil and rapidly rose to a full forest ahead. *Zach must have thought of an escape.* As they raced for the edge of the woods, she called out, "There's no cliff for the water to flow over!"

"I didn't think that far ahead," he yelled back.

Kayn stopped running and so did Zach. They stood there holding hands, prepared to face their temporary demise with dignity. They squeezed their eyes shut. *Zach was probably dreading the sensation of mind-altering agony as the wave crushed them like ants on the sidewalk but she wanted the pain, it made her feel alive.* Nothing happened. They opened their eyes. *Crazy.* A towering wall of water so enormous it attached to the sky above was paused a few feet away. *This was new.* Curious, Kayn stepped closer and just as she reached to touch the massive wall of water it vanished, revealing Lexy and Grey casually strolling through the field in their direction.

Lexy hollered, "We know where they are! Let's get to work!"

Kayn squeezed her Handler's hand before letting it go. *They were worried about her attachment to Zach, but she wasn't the least bit concerned. Something in his mannerisms reminded her of the mortal version of Kevin, the boy that was her best friend. Perhaps, that was why he'd been chosen as Kevin's replacement.* Zach took off ahead with Grey. The Handler's wandered away together having an animated conversation. Kayn smiled at Lexy as she approached. *If someone told her Lexy was her sister when they'd first met, she would have never believed it. She saw it now though, in her smile. This had been the craziest couple of years. She'd lost her life and then gained these incredible things she'd never thought possible. Coming to the In-between was a gift. It was exquisitely beautiful. It rarely rained. Had she ever seen rain here?* As Kayn looked up at the sky, raindrops started trickling, speckling her face with moisture.

Grey marched back and sighed, "Alright, which one of you thought of rain?"

"It was me, my bad?" Kayn admitted as she wandered through the moist grass alongside Lexy. *The air smelled of summer rain.*

"Come on Brighton," Zach scolded. "This is unnecessary, and yes, you've seen it rain here before. Remember these two chasing us through the forest with bows before our Testing?"

She'd forgotten about that. Whoops.

Touching Grey's shoulder, Lexy teased, "Suck it up princess, you won't melt."

Grey playfully tugged Lexy to him. "Fine, we'll dance in it then," he flirted.

They were kind of adorable.

They swayed as Lexy laughed, "There's no music."

Grey twirled Lexy, pulled her back against him and provoked, "Suck it up buttercup."

Music began, seemingly piped in from the dark clouds above. Grey dipped Lexy with a fluidity of movement that could only be gained by knowing your partner intimately. They were joyful in each other's arms. *It wasn't fair. Grey couldn't see what everyone else could. They belonged together. Her sister had been doing this one-sided romantic dance for too long. She needed to wake up in the morning next to the man she loved with the knowledge that her feelings were returned. She could never have that with Grey if his memories of their intimacy continued to be erased before dawn's first light. It was sad though. Their bond was so beautiful.* Frost leapt to mind, followed by a pang of insecurity. *Even though they had something truly wonderful, their relationship would always come with serious complications. She understood how Frost's ability worked. She'd siphoned it with her Conduit ability, tasted it and kept it. She had a feeling it was the easiest ability for her to summon because it had also been her twins' gift, back when Chloe was Chloe and not a part of her. Her twin hadn't been able to control it and, in her experience, thus far…neither could she. Neither could Frost. She knew this. They'd assured each other they'd be emotionally faithful, but if she really thought about it, he'd never promised her any more than that.* Kayn picked a buttercup and stared at it, recalling a memory of Chloe's. *She'd needed more time with Frost before they separated. More time to wrap her mind around what they meant. What they were. Their abrupt split was entirely her fault. She was concerned about the way they'd left things, but they had literally forever to figure it out.*

Zach answered her thoughts, "You'll always have me."

She gave him the buttercup she'd tugged out of the ground. *She felt the same way. He would always be her Handler. He wasn't allowed to run away.* She grinned.

"Shall we dance?" He suggested, gallantly holding out his hand.

"We shall," Kayn answered as she took it. They began slowly waltzing to the music. She rested her head on Zach's shoulder and whispered, "You don't think I actually blew it with Frost, do you?"

Zach was silent for a second before responding, "You'll be fine. The timing of your relationship isn't the greatest but he's a thousand years old. He knew what he was getting into."

She was in the train wreck stage. Those were the words he'd used to describe her and she didn't disagree. That's how she felt about the last six months of her afterlife. She proclaimed, "Who wouldn't be a train wreck after being brutally murdered thousands of times in Immortal Testing?"

Zach giggled and whispered, "I've done some messed up things myself but I'm not sure I've hit full train wreck. Give me time."

"I'll be there for you when you go off the rails," she vowed, dancing on the soft dewy grass.

"Unless Frost's here," Zach teased.

"Even then," Kayn promised as they swayed in the calming fragrance of rainfall.

"I'm holding you to that," he whispered in her ear. He dipped her as he proposed, "Let's go kill some teenagers."

As Kayn's feet landed met the sweet-scented moist meadow, her Handler released her. *It sounded like a lovely way to spend the afternoon. She glanced over at Lexy and Grey.* Zach wandered over to their side and they began making plans. Kayn paused for a moment, watching her friends giggling as they plotted their diabolical training games. *She knew her sketchy allegiance to her surprise Handler was a large part of the reason they kept separating her from the only person who truly made her happy. She wouldn't have been confused if Kevin ended up being her Handler. How was this going to work when she could never give Zach her whole heart? Lexy had surrendered hers to Grey without question, he'd been her every-thing. Zach was a platonic friend. Well, except for that one ability experimentation that nearly went too far.* Kayn joined the trio, thought of a sword and it appeared in her grasp as she piped in, "Shall we get to work?"

Lexy enthusiastically agreed, "Let's do this!"

Grey grabbed Zach's arm, stopping him dead in his tracks as he added, "Let the Dragons out to play for a while. We'll rein them in when it's time."

Kayn caught Zach's concerned expression.

Lexy whispered, "He'll get used to it. You guys just need some time to grow your bond free of distractions."

She hesitated, sensing Zach's nervousness. *They had to grow their bond free of distractions. That made sense. Frost was one hell of a distraction.* She followed Lexy as they wandered away through the endless feeling meadow. *It had stopped raining but with each footstep in the moist grass, she was reminded that her thoughts had caused the storm.* Lightning crackled above as dark ominous clouds rolled in. Thunder rumbled its war cry as she felt her emotions beginning to dull. She didn't need to speak to Lexy as they reached the tree line, instinct was already guiding her actions. The two Dragons of Ankh sprinted off into the cover of the trees, aware of each other's presence yet not dependent on it. There was no need for words as the rain pummelled the tree's branches, thinning out as it trickled through. She was reminded of her final moments of humanity as she was pursued through the forest behind her childhood home. The rapid pace of her footsteps crunching through the trails gave new life to the trauma she kept buried within her soul. Hollowness swallowed the final breath of her emotions as she felt the presence of the bonding trio of Ankh. Both Dragons altered direction without need for verbal communication. They were now instinct driven monsters on the hunt for what was left of the trio's humanity. Out of the corner of her eye, she saw Lexy. Kayn's heart raced with anticipation as divine predatory instinct led her to soundlessly creep through the woods without even snapping a twig on the recently travelled path. *There they were.* They heard faint conversation through the pitter-pattering of rain. Little more than a whisper in the wind was all it took to lead them to their prey. Getting as close as they could without being seen was part of the thrill. With no warning, they burst from the bushes into the meadow the three were hanging out in. They ran at the trio. The Newbies scrambled to their feet and booked it into the bushes. *She'd played this game with them before. They knew the rules. Run away or die. Instinct chose the weakest link. She didn't recall his name. She preferred it that way.* Pursuing the snapping twigs ahead, Kayn emotionlessly plunged her blade into his back. As he dropped to his knees and gasped, realization hit her. *She was now the man in the dark. She was the footsteps in the trails. She'd become the monster she had always feared as a child.* Kayn yanked the dripping blade from his spine and carried on with her murder spree as her Ankh symbol strobed. *Lexy took down the girl. There was only one left.* She sprinted through the bushes into the next open area where she saw the cougar she'd run into on many occasions. This time, instead of running away, she stood her ground with her blade clutched in her hands as she called, "Here kitty, kitty, kitty."

The massive feline raced at her. Releasing a war cry, she ran directly at the wild animal. *She was a predator too.* She landed a few swift slashes of her blade as its brutally powerful jaws savaged her flesh, taking down the mighty feline. When all was said and done, Kayn squirmed out from under its limp corpse, leapt to her feet and brushed herself off. Surprisingly victorious for someone critically injured, she noticed her profusely bleeding shoulder and touched her mauled flesh. Mildly inconvenienced, Kayn scowled as she jogged away from the corpse. *She needed energy.* She could feel the aching desperation in her soul for the one thing she wasn't certain she could acquire in this heavenly land but set out to find it anyway. Taking the path less travelled, she sprinted through the overgrown brush. Feeling the weight of the urgent need, Kayn spotted the last Ankh cowering against a tree, attempting to catch his breath. She slowed her roll, casually strolling over to the out of breath Ankh. Their eyes met. He didn't run. His surrender was clear as he stepped away from the tree and remained in place, with his eyes trained on her. She cocked her head, curious as to what his next move would be.

"Are you just going to kill me for no reason?" the boy inquired with a Scottish accent.

She coldly responded, "Not the usual way."

He whispered, "What do you mean?"

She swiftly closed the space, clutched his arms and her palms heated as she ingested his energy. As he slumped to the ground, the rush of his lifeforce surged through her. Kayn marched away from his body into the darkened trails. *She was still hungry.* With all thoughts of relationship woes lost to the driving need of her Conduit ability, she scoured the woods for any form of mystical being as she waited for the immortals they'd subdued to rise again. For weeks, she thought up creatures and devoured their energy until she was no more than a soulless beast void of all humanity. She pursued and killed the new Ankh each time they rose with her sister at her side. Grey and Zach gave the Newbies happy moments to secure their bond as the two Dragons taught strength and perseverance to their souls. Euphoric from energy she'd been ingesting, Kayn curled up in the fetal position on the moss at the base of a tree. She closed her eyes knowing Lexy was sprawled close by.

5

DRAGON DADDY ISSUES

Sunbeams filtered through the branches warming her skin as trillions of tiny dust particles danced in the light. A twig cracked and she was instantly alert.

Seth stepped out of the shadows, revealing himself commenting, "Dragons are such glorious creatures." Their Guardian sire inched closer to Kayn as he baited, "Are you still hungry my child?"

Yes... Yes, she was always hungry. Crouched at the foot of the massive tree, Kayn cocked her head inquisitively as he dared to come closer. Slowly, she rose until she was staring into her father's eyes. With his wrists poised to the sky, Seth offered his hands as a symbolic gesture. He was willing to submit to give her what she needed. Logic didn't play into it as Kayn ingested her father's being until he grew unsteady on his feet. She kept going until his knees buckled.

Seth yanked his hands away and scolded, "You should always be aware of what abilities you're ingesting. Do you understand what you've consumed?"

Feeling the bounty of energy coursing through her, Kayn snapped back to reality long enough to creepily respond, "I want more."

Seth grinned as he offered his energy to Lexy.

The crimson-haired Dragon turned him down cold as she rose to stand with her eyes full of rage. Meeting the Guardian's curious gaze, she accused, "You left me on that farm."

"This again," Seth complained. "For heaven's sake child, it's because of that depraved place that you've survived the unthinkable. Is there no pride in that for you?"

Kayn observed their exchange, quite removed from the emotional content. *She was hungry, nothing more. She felt no need for explanations. His energy was intoxicating. She wanted more and, in a few seconds, she planned to take it.*

"You carnivorous little beast. You're dying for more, aren't you?" Her absentee father provoked, "Come and get it. I dare you."

She loved a challenge. Kayn lunged at Seth as she swung her blade.

He stepped out of her way. She narrowly missed him as he teased, "I see you actually have skills." A sword appeared in his hands with an emerald hilt. He blocked her next swing with a clink of metal. "I wouldn't start a battle you can't win." With a wave of his hand, she soared through the air and landed with a thud in the dirt.

Oh, now he was in trouble. She may not know how to use them but she'd sampled his abilities. Kayn casually brushed the dirt from her short sarong as she stood up, met his eyes and imitated his movement. With a wave of her hand, her genetic sire went flying through the sky. He collided with the tree behind him with a loud thump.

Chuckling as he got up, Seth countered, "A quick learner, I like it." He swung his arm again, attempting to repeat the move.

Kayn countered and neither budged an inch. They held each other in place with the sheer force of energy. Seth wielded his sword. As she looked at her knife, it elongated into a sword with a Rose Quartz hilt. The battle of the beasts began. With each manoeuvre he made, instinct told her how to react until it became clear she was his equal.

A white flag appeared on the end of his sword. He waved it and dropped it into the dirt, to show he'd surrendered. He offered, "You've earned it. Take whatever you need from me."

Kayn released her weapon, and as it hit the dirt, a cloud rose. She took her genetic sire's hands and drank from his being, absorbing his energy until he sank to his knees.

He looked up at her and whispered, "Aren't you the least bit curious about what you've taken?"

She peered down at him as she coolly enquired, "What have I taken?"

"Control," Seth countered from his subservient position. "Use it with caution."

Just as she was about to finish him, he evaporated into the air.

Grey's voice broke through the silence after the Guardian's hasty departure, "We should get back."

Both Dragon's looked up with blank expressions on their faces.

"After we get you back, of course," Grey added with a smile.

She didn't want to come back. Kayn marched away, determined to spend more time getting to know her dark side. *She had abilities to master and immortals to kill. She knew where Seth lived and perhaps, he'd have some Triad lying around his castle.* Without looking back, Kayn felt Zach coming. He didn't try to restrain her or attempt to slow her down. He just followed her as she searched for what she needed. They strolled through the woods until they came to an open grassy pasture full of cattle. *This was new.* Zach's face lit up. *She found herself curious as to why?*

He responded to her thoughts, "On the bus ride home from school we always passed herds of cattle. My family rented the house next to a working farm with cornfields, scarecrows but no large livestock."

She was listening. He'd broken through her urgent hunger.

He was her Handler. It made sense.

Meeting her gaze, he enquired, "Are you still hungry? Are you having a problem? Do you need some of my energy?"

Yes, she did. Planning to feed from him, Kayn moved closer, her heart clenched in her chest. *She didn't want to hurt him. It was inconvenient. Logic tried reasoning with her. She couldn't hurt him. Nothing that happened here was permanent.*

Offering his hand, Zach confirmed, "It's alright, you have my permission."

She tried to take it and was brought to submission by a piercing headache. There was an explosion of light as Ankh's Guardian Azariah appeared. They both dropped to their knees.

"Children, please rise. There's no need to cower before me," the luminescent lady in white assured. As they rose, Azariah addressed Kayn, "We were hoping we'd have the time to grow your attachment with your Handler before your paternity was revealed but my brother jumped the gun on that one, didn't he?"

When Kayn didn't respond, Zach agreed, "A little more time would have been nice. I have no idea what I'm doing, and her attention is focused elsewhere."

"We've taken care of that now, haven't we?" Azariah answered, observing Kayn's demeanour. The all-knowing Guardian said, "Lexy and Grey's bond is not the norm, it took time to build."

"Lexy and Grey have a romantic attachment, this isn't the same dynamics," Zach replied.

Azariah's golden locks flowed behind her in the light as she disclosed, "There was nothing romantic between those two for many years. For more than a decade, they were no more than close friends."

Looking directly at Kayn, he questioned, "I've heard I wasn't the original choice for this duty. It was supposed to be Kevin."

"The afterlife happened, and now, it's you," the angelic woman in white assured. "I have it on good authority, you're fully capable of this job. All you have to do is believe you can do it and you will."

Slowly shaking his head in disbelief, Zach took in Kayn's emotionally void expression and asserted, "She just fed on Seth and tried to kick his ass, knowing he's a Guardian."

"Did she feed on you when you offered yourself to her?" Azariah enquired.

Zach replied, "No, it looked like she was in pain when she tried."

"She was in agony. She can't do anything to harm you, and right now, she's unsure of her own strength. This is about so much more than you know," the lady in the light explained. "We need you to have faith. You never need to fear her. She won't allow herself to harm you."

Kayn cocked her head, listening to what registered as her Handler's complaints. *He feared her.* Her heart tingled. *She didn't want him to be afraid of her.* Emotion washed over her and the light came back into her eyes. She whispered his name, "Zach."

He met her teary eyes as she walked into his embrace and whispered, "I wasn't sure you were still in there."

She quietly confessed, "I wasn't either. Promise me again, you'll always bring me back."

Zach kissed her forehead as he vowed, "I won't second guess this again, I promise."

He'd promised these things to her many times but as her abilities grew volatile, his faith in his own had faltered.

The lady in the light smiled peacefully as she held out her hand. Kayn slowly shook her head as she warned, "I can't take it while I'm still craving energy like this, I'll feed on you."

Ankh's Guardian assured, "The same rules apply. You won't be able to feed on me."

Azariah had never steered her wrong. As Kayn accepted her hand, the urge to feed vanished.

The woman in white squeezed her hand as she said, "You are so important to our future. Both of you." Azariah nodded at Zach as she exclaimed, "Let each other in completely. No secrets. No lies. Live in only the truth of your bond and young Zachariah will always be able to bring you back. This is the most important duty of a Handler."

"I have been truthful," Zach replied.

"Child, you haven't even been truthful with yourself," Azariah answered with heavenly light glimmering around her.

"What do you mean by that?" Zach asked as the woman in white disappeared, they were left with a sense of loss. He looked at Kayn and questioned, "What did she mean by that?"

Kayn knew but suspected he wasn't ready to embrace it so why confuse him. Smiling at her Handler, she assured, "It's not important." Feeling herself again, she laced her fingers through his, as they strolled through the meadow. There was an explosion of light and they were wandering the desert. *She was mentally exhausted. Darkness takes a toll.*

Zach grinned and chuckled, "You tried to kick Seth's ass."

"I vaguely recall that," Kayn admitted, giving his hand a reassuring squeeze. "I know I haven't had my mind in the right place."

He paused, causing her to abruptly stop walking as he explained, "If this scenario happened a week ago, I would have been in a far different mindset. It feels like we haven't spent any time together lately. I guess what I'm trying to say is, I don't know where I fit into your relationship with Frost or your unresolved feelings for Kevin. I can't help you with any of that."

She nodded her silent agreement. *She saw his point.* Kayn smiled as she answered, "That's where you're wrong, you could have helped me. We just haven't been in this situation long enough to read between the lines."

"Why did you do it?" Zach asked.

"I'm afraid you're going to have to be more specific," Kayn countered.

"Why did you act like everything was fine and then toss your ex off a balcony during a ceasefire between the Clans?" Zach enquired.

"Total honesty?" Kayn said. She met his gaze as she revealed, "It's difficult to explain."

"Try me," he urged.

She decided to take this Handler bond out for a spin as she gave him the unfiltered truth, "I'm two people and one of those people loved Kevin with all that she was. We'd been friends since we were five. He was taken by Triad but I never believed they could erase his feelings for me. You were there before the Testing. I know you saw what was happening between us. That magic between two people who care about each other was still there even though his memories had been erased."

"It wasn't just you. I saw it, so did Mel," Zach replied. Smiling at her Handler, she continued, "In the Testing, Kevin killed me. I didn't think he'd be able to do it. Some-thing broke inside of me. I knew I couldn't fix myself. I couldn't change anything, and at first, I blamed my feelings for Frost on Chloe's memories but after a while, I was able to admit I wanted him…Me. Frost kept chipping away at my armour until I just didn't see the point in resisting my feelings for him. I fed from his energy and the attraction I felt became an undeniable force. He makes me happy. Really happy."

"I know, I can see it and it's not that I want you to stop what you're doing or change how you're feeling. I want you to be happy. I just don't understand what my role is yet. It's hard to step back and follow someone else's boundaries when I'm supposed to be surrendering my afterlife in service of you. We're staying in different rooms doing our own things and there's distance between us when he's around."

"You know, I have no idea what I'm supposed to be doing either," Kayn admitted.

"Back to the reason why you tossed Kevin over the balcony," Zach urged.

"He gave me a purple clover so I would know he had his memories back and then warned me to watch my ego. I was flooded with these unresolved feelings. I have this instinct to believe him that supersedes logic. I tucked the flower in my bra and went back inside. Knowing it was there felt like I was being unfaithful to Frost. I know that's silly. It was only a flower but it was symbolic of so much more. Instead of wallowing in self-pity or guilt, I became furious. How dare he show me he still loves me when I've finally moved on."

"I get it. You tossed your ex over a balcony to get out of admitting you still care," Zach concluded as he sat down in the sand.

"Basically," Kayn confessed as she sat next to him. "Okay, that's all I needed to know," Zach said as he started drawing pictures in the sand. "Listen, you can't feel bad about still caring. I don't have relationship experience, but from what I've heard, it takes time and distance to get over someone. It doesn't just happen."

It felt like they were finally on the same page again. They sat there in the warm silky sand drawing pictures with their fingertips, chatting about their afterlife until they sensed a presence. Already knowing who it was, Kayn peered up. She was preparing to tell Seth off when instead of baiting her, he used a different approach as he took a seat in the sand and began drawing pictures of his own. *He was a creepy dude.*

The Guardian of Triad glanced over at the two and asked, "What are you guys drawing?"

Zach nonchalantly sparred, "Isn't it obvious?"

Seth grinned as he continued his masterpiece, ultimately choosing to sculpt a sandcastle rather than draw. *This was how toddlers made friends through parallel play. Was this immortal douchebag seriously trying to be her friend?*

Seth peered up and admitted, "I'd like to try if you'll let me."

A confusing wave of emotion washed over her. This time Zach took her hand before she could shut herself down. He whispered, "Don't go. Face your problems."

She wasn't sure what she should say. He was waiting for a response. She peered up at Seth and declared, "Win over Lexy and I'll come along."

Seth stood up, stomped on his sandcastle and huffed, "Well, then we'll never be able to be friends! She hates me!" He kicked what was left of his sandcastle like an unruly child and stormed away.

"Well, that was awkward," Zach commentated as he continued drawing.

It was awkward. Those were the genes she came from. Sadly, it made sense. Kayn smoothed out her sand to start a new drawing. She used her finger to write K + F in the sand and then glanced over to see what Zach was doing. *Was he drawing a seagull?* She took a shot in the dark, "Is that a seagull?"

"As a matter of fact, it is," he admitted.

"A seagull pooped on me when I was a kid. They say it's good luck," Kayn remarked, regretting her words instantly as she heard multiple calls from ocean gulls soaring through the sky. *Come on! One of them had made them real with their thoughts.* Kayn leapt up, grabbed Zach's hand, towed him to his feet and sighed, "Why?" They laughed as the flock of gulls' dive-bombed, narrowly missing the pair as they dove out of the way and landed on their stomachs in a shimmering cloud of dust. A white and black mound of gull poop splattered on the desert floor. They scrambled to their feet and fled. *They were trying to hit them.*

Laughing, they sprinted through the desert until they reached the edge of the cliff, they'd been looking for earlier. They dove off with the skilled precision of Olympic divers and rapidly descended through damp clouds into their next reality. Kayn's hair whipped around as the air whooshed against her skin. As they came out of the clouds, the forest floor was rapidly approaching. They both used their energy to slow themselves and manoeuvre their descent through the tree line, landing crouched in a thicket. They got up and checked for seagulls. *They were gone.*

"That was a first," Zach exclaimed, brushing himself off.

It wasn't for her. She'd been dive bombed by many a gull on the beach. Kayn questioned, "You didn't see a lot of seagulls growing up?"

"None, until I was with Triad," Zach answered, looking around to see where they were.

Sometimes, she forgot Zach was with Triad for a year before Ankh.
They started walking through the woods with no
destination in mind until they came across a blackberry
bush. They began picking the fruit staining their
fingertips with juice as they snacked on tart berries.
Kayn asked, "Did you have a lot of blackberry bushes
around as a kid?"

"We spent years moving from place to place trying to
get away from my abusive father," Zach explained. "No
blackberry bushes. There were usually strawberries and
raspberries in our garden. We planted them as one of
our family rituals each time, we found a new home. We
lived in the southern States most of my childhood.
When we moved further North there was farmland
and cornfields. How about you?"

"I lived in the same house my whole life with my
parents, my brother and twin sister. I don't know if
you remember much about my house but there were
bushes in the back with trails and lots of blackberries,"
she explained. "Living on Vancouver Island there were
lots of seagulls and wildlife. It was a beautiful place to
grow up."

Zach grinned as he remarked, "You have blackberry
juice in the corner of your mouth."

She tried to get it with her tongue. He just kept
shaking his head and telling her she missed it until he
used his thumb to clean it off. Chuckling, she returned
the favour. He was also purple around the corners of
his mouth. Kayn picked a handful of berries to bring
with her.

"Well, what do you want to do with the time we
have left?" Zach asked as they wandered away from the
bush. She popped a berry in her mouth, swallowed it

and randomly asked, "Have you ever had blackberry wine?"

Zach stopped walking as he admitted, "Never."

"There's something new for our unbucket list," Kayn answered. He was grinning at her. "What?" she laughed.

"You have blackberry juice all over your face. You were a messy kid, weren't you?" he teased.

She grinned. He started laughing. *Her teeth were probably purple.* Kayn stepped closer as she sparred, "You think I'm pretty funny."

"Actually, you're adorable," he complimented.

Kayn gave Zach her best Cheshire cat purple grin as she smashed a handful of blackberries in his face.

He batted her away laughing, "Come on Brighton. That was unnecessary." He dashed back to the bush for ammo.

Kayn raced over to another bush and filled her hands as he began whipping blackberries at her. Each direct hit left purple stains on her thigh length white sarong. She pitched some back at him and soon they were ducking behind bushes having a full out blackberry war. The battle ceased as they sensed the others descending from the sky. Lexy and Grey landed in the dirt before them with catlike agility.

Looking at the mess they'd made of each other, Grey sighed, "You guys have the most fun." He glanced at Lexy and asked, "How come we never have blackberry battles?"

Lexy gave her Handler a playful shove as she answered, "We're supposed to be working right now but next time I see a blackberry bush, it's on." The crimson-haired Dragon of Ankh gave Kayn a curious look as she commented, "I really wish you guys could see yourselves." She strolled over to Kayn and asked, "Did you really tell Seth you'd try being his friend if I did?"

Kayn shrugged as she answered honestly, "I did."

"You know she's not one to forgive and forget," Grey pointed out.

"Oh, she knows," Zach said as he wandered over to the group.

"Okay," Lexy clarified. "Just as long as you know it'll be a cold day in hell before I forgive him for leaving me on that farm."

Grey put his arm around Lexy and whispered in her ear, "We need to get back. Maybe, we should just change the subject?"

There was no point in carrying on this conversation. Kayn decided to make her opinion on the matter crystal clear, "For the record, I really don't care what Seth does or if I ever forgive him."

"Good," Lexy replied.

"We have to go," Grey urged as he led Lexy away.

Kayn and Zach followed as an explosion of light brought them back to the white sand of the clean slated desert. *This magical place always blew her mind.*

Taking Lexy's hand, Grey turned to Kayn and announced, "Let the epic Dragon Handler road trip begin."

Zach had a hold of her hand as the force of the pull back to the land of the living brutally lurched them into oblivion. In moments, they were encased within the Tomb they'd come in spinning at a wild stomach-churning rate. Knowing they'd once again killed the Healers in charge of their travel, both Kayn and Lexy placed their hands against the strobing Crypt's lid and braced themselves for the sensation of their essence escaping their bodies so they could spiritually pilot the Tomb back to the land of the living. It was difficult to maintain the connection as her energy travelled from her hands into the Tomb. The G-force was making her lightheaded.

Grey shouted, "Brighton! Stop us! Before I hurl!"

"I don't know how! I'm not strong enough!" Kayn hollered back.

Zach mumbled, "I'm going to pass out."

Each strobe of light blinded her as Kayn fought to keep her hands securely connected. *She couldn't keep this up for much longer.* Gravity lurched her from side to side. Kayn was nauseous, sweating profusely and confused. *This usually worked. Their energy was supposed to send the Tombs on a spiritual autopilot back to where they began. Why wasn't it working?* She squinted in the glaring light of the rose quartz Tomb trying to catch a glimpse of Lexy between strobes. The light was growing stronger and more brilliant with each cycle. *It was getting uncomfortably hot. They were in trouble. She could feel it. Something had gone wrong.* Suddenly, it felt impossible, and Kayn knew she was carrying the brunt of the spiritual load. "Lexy!" she called out. "Are you still there?" *No answer.* Kayn couldn't open her eyes anymore without burning her corneas. *She was on her own. She sensed it.* Scattered ideas flitted through her equilibrium shuffled mind. *She'd recently fed from a Guardian. How didn't she have enough energy to do this?* The Tomb was now spinning so rapidly the skin on her face was moulded by force. It began lurching to each side as it descended into lord knows where. *What was she supposed to be doing to regain control?* Instinct urged her to do something unusual. Kayn let go of the lid, grabbed a hold of Grey and siphoned his energy. As soon as she felt the intoxicating power surge, she reached for the lid and screeched, "Stop!" The Tomb abruptly halted its nauseating motion. The strobing light ceased so Kayn opened her eyes. There was a dim light coming from right beside her. She lifted her hand and smiled. Her Ankh symbol was still strobing because the other occupants of the Tomb were deceased. *Zach must have been touching Grey.* Kayn placed her hands against the roof and commanded, "Open!" The lid slid aside with the sound of grinding stone. As Kayn climbed out of the Tomb she'd shared with her fellow Ankh, she saw the bodies of the six Ankh running the Tombs deceased on the marble floor. She stood there for a minute feeling impressed with herself. Someone stirred within one and she knew her sister was awake. *That was fast.*

Stretching, Lexy declared, "So everybody's dead then?" She climbed out and wandered over. Surveying the calamity they'd caused, her sister chuckled. Regaining her composure, she sighed, "I'll show you the most efficient way to awaken a group. Come on, Brighton. Let's get everyone into the same Tomb."

They towed the Healers to the Tomb that encased their Handlers, closed it and laid their palms against the ancient stone, feeding their energy directly into the Rose Quartz lined Tomb. The two Dragons stood side by side ready to greet their Handlers and fellow Clan as the stone ground open. They helped each person out and headed for the door, more than ready to get the hell out of this compound and back to their immortal duties. Lexy laid her hand against the door. It wouldn't budge. Kayn followed suit. *Nothing! Seriously?*

A dark-featured olive-skinned female Healer piped in, "Only Amar can open this door."

Frustrated, Kayn perched on top of one of the Tombs and sighed, "I don't suppose any of you have a snack?"

Scowling at her, Grey mumbled, "You've had enough snacks."

Kayn blew Grey a kiss and taunted, "You were delicious."

"You're welcome," Grey jousted as he began to laugh.

Zach slid up onto the Tomb beside her and took her hand in a show of solidarity. Kayn leaned over and whispered in his ear, "I didn't mean to take you out too."

Her Handler smiled knowingly as he replied, "I know."

The girl who told them about Amar being the only one able to open the door offered Grey her hand and introduced herself, "My name's Aubrey."

Giving it a polite shake, he smiled as he replied, "My name's Grey."

"I know," Aubrey baited. "To be honest, I'm a bit of a fan."

"Really?" Grey flirted. "Well, I'm certainly honoured to meet you, Aubrey. That's a beautiful name. Where are you from?"

Lexy rolled her eyes so far back all you could see were the whites. Kayn and Zach chuckled as Grey continued to work his game on the curvaceous raven-haired Ankh.

One of the others strolled over to greet them. *Mike was backpacking through Europe with his best friend when his Correction happened.* Kayn couldn't help herself as she enquired, "Is your family still alive?"

His expression grew solemn as he answered, "I wasn't allowed any contact after I became Ankh. I'd disappeared, so they travelled here searching for me, thinking I'd been kidnapped or worse. I thought if I stayed away, they'd have a chance, but they just wouldn't give up. They kept going back to the States, regrouping and flying back here until their flight crashed."

They all had such wildly different stories but, in the end, they were all the same. They were the only ones left alive. Kayn slowly nodded, understanding what he meant. There was another girl present who wasn't much of a sharer. Kayn's stomach growled as she felt the instinctual urge to feed. *The insatiable appetite of her Conduit ability was pointing out the fact that everyone here was edible. There were a lot of Healers in this room. They were all locked inside. She needed to think about something else. Anything else.* Her mind began to scroll through the reasons why she shouldn't. *Ingesting healing energy was a euphoric experience but then she'd be seeing every-one's brightly coloured auras all day and that side effect was mentally exhausting.* She'd retained the ability a while ago but the auras she saw had dulled with time. *It was helpful while searching a crowd for a Newbie Ankh, but she was glad she could control the brightness.*

Zach interrupted her thoughts, "Are the Newbies still in that Tomb?"

Mike answered, "We thought it might be better for their mental well-being to leave them in there until you left. You did kill them enough to take out six of us."

Zach corrected Mike, "That was Kayn and Lexy. Grey and I played good cop. We got a chance to know them rather well."

Aubrey met Zach's eyes as she probed, "And the verdict?"

Zach's expression darkened a touch as he replied, "Separately, they're great people, but they despise each other. I'm afraid it didn't do much to take Samid out of the mix."

Aubrey understood. She nodded without saying anything else.

The door to the room slid open. Amar smiled and apologised, "I hope I haven't kept you waiting long?" He motioned for their group to come with him and directed his Healers to awaken the others.

Good timing. She was feeling jittery. They followed the handsome dark-featured Amar out of the room, down the long marble-floored hall while Grey gave Amar a blow-by-blow account of their attempt to train and attach the Newbies headed for Testing. When all was said and done, Amar dined with them in the dining hall. After a good-sized meal slathered in hot sauce, Kayn felt far less murdery as they headed back through to their continent.

6

LET THE DRAGON GAMES BEGIN

The other half of the group left their clothing, toiletries and personal items within the Tomb on their continent's soil. The sight of her backpack gave Kayn a pang of guilt. *They all searched through their belongings, hoping for communication from their Clan. There was nothing.* Kayn unzipped the front pocket and smiled as she removed the ring with the fake topaz birthstone Frost had given her from a bubble gum machine as a sweet gesture before they were together, slipped it onto her finger and felt the weight of her mistakes slipping away. *He knows who you are. He loves you anyway. She really wished he'd snuck a note into her bag. A message that wasn't written in frustration as the last one had been.* The foursome climbed the stairs out of the Ankh Crypt and stepped out into the sweltering moisture of the rainforest with their bags in tow. The musical song of the jungle birds made it feel like they were being welcomed home.

Zach nudged her asking, "Everything alright?"

Kayn smiled at her Handler. Knowing there was no point in lying, she revealed her feelings, "I was hoping for a note from Frost in my bag."

Zach placed his arm around her and whispered, "I had something weird in mine."

"Oh, really? What?" Kayn quietly enquired as they wandered away from the Crypt.

"Why would someone put Twinkies in my bag?" Zach questioned.

She shrugged and suggested, "They could have been shoving random snacks in our bags? There were Twinkies in the RV." They walked for a while longer as Azariah's words replayed in her mind. *The whole truth. She was supposed to tell her Handler the truth.* She looked at Zach and disclosed, "Those Twinkies were probably from Frost."

Zach knit his brow as he questioned, "Why would Frost give me six Twinkies?"

She opted to go with the truth, "Let's just say, it's part of a game we've been playing."

Chuckling, he answered, "Say no more. I get it. Putting some in your bag would be too obvious."

A colourful bird called out grabbing their attention from a branch of a tree up ahead. She swatted mosquitos off her arm, wiped the sweat from her brow and slowed as they passed a Toucan. She paused and stared at it as memories of being trapped in the jungle with Kevin during the Testing, came back like a gut punch. *She told him Fruit Loops used to be his favourite cereal as a child.*

He'd told her he would try it when they made it out of there. Had he followed through and sampled some? Did it even matter anymore?

Zach joined her. Staring at the Toucan in the tree, he commented, "This is what has you so mesmerized?"

Without context, she admitted, "We used to love Fruit Loops when we were kids."

Zach knew what she meant. He clarified, "You mean, you liked Fruit Loops. Can I give you some unsolicited advice?"

Kayn turned to look at her Handler, knowing what he was about to say.

Zach wiped his hands on his shorts and laced his fingers through hers as he playfully towed her away from the distracting bird, saying, "I know it's difficult to separate your mortal experiences from Kevin's because he was always around but maybe if you altered your wording just a touch, everything you see wouldn't lead you back to thoughts of him."

He had a point but it was easier said than done. "I wish it were that easy," Kayn countered.

"Well, maybe you need to make new Fruit Loop memories," her Handler suggested. "When we get back stateside, we'll get some."

"Sounds like a plan," Kayn replied as she let him guide her away.

They'd been trekking through the sweltering jungle for a while when Lexy swatted a mosquito off her arm as she called Grey back, "We're supposed to take the other trail."

Grey laughed, "Sorry, the lights are on but nobody's home. I'm dizzy from the heat. That could have gone badly."

He was preaching to the choir. Kayn used the back of her hand to wipe away the film of perspiration on her forehead. *It was disgustingly hot.*

"Do you guys even know where we're going?" Zach questioned.

"Sort of," Grey answered honestly.

"I hope we're not, sort of lost," Kayn sparred as some-thing large moved through the bushes close by. *What might that be?* Her cell was in her backpack. She wanted to google, large jungle animals of Mexico but there would be no service. She caught up with Lexy and asked, "Are there Tigers in Mexico?"

"That was a Leopard. Don't lag behind us," Lexy replied.

They picked up their pace as they doubled back to the trail they'd passed. After a few minutes of walking in the right direction, they saw a jeep parked on the path. *Was this vehicle for them?*

Grey crouched by the wheel well and stood up with a tiny black box in hand. "Sweet ride, Markus," Grey proclaimed as he unlocked the passenger side door.

Sweet, wasn't the word she'd use. There was no leg room at all in the back. There was however, a day planner clipped to the netting on the back of the passenger seat. Kayn opened it and flipped through the pages. *Were they serious? There were times and locations all over North America marked on a calendar with detailed instructions in the margins. Sixty days in brackets. Two months was highly optimistic. There was no way they were going to pull off all these jobs in only two months. At the back in the address section, it read, join us when you've finished the starred jobs. Only the starred tasks were theirs. Well, shit. There were only a dozen feats to accomplish. It could be done.* Kayn passed the journal to Lexy without saying a word. As Lexy flipped through the day planner, she chuckled.

Grey reached for the planner as he enquired, "What do you have there?"

Lexy passed the calendar to Grey. "It's our schedule for the next couple of months. We'll all be so burnt out we won't know our own names by the time we're finished," Lexy remarked as she looked back at Kayn and added, "I'm sorry. Maybe if I hadn't killed someone too, they might have gone a little easier on us."

"Maybe, what you should take away from this moment is that murder sprees are bad," Zach teased.

"Oh, you have so much to learn my young hot friend, just follow along until you get it," Lexy countered.

Zach beamed as he clarified, "Did you just call me sexy Lexy? Ha, ha, that totally rhymes."

"I called you hot, not sexy, there's a difference," Lexy sparred as she did up her seatbelt and shook her head.

They made themselves comfortable in the Jeep as Grey turned the key in the ignition. He swore and remarked, "There's no air conditioning. Open the windows."

"The windows are already open Grey. Can't you tell by the mosquitos feasting on your face?" Lexy taunted.

"Crap!" Grey cursed, frantically swatting them away. Did you check the back for water bottles?" he queried.

Kayn and Zach gave each other a strange look. *There was no back. There also appeared to be no water. Awesome.* Kayn grinned as she took in her Handler's pouty face. *He was still on a mission to win over Lexy.* Giving Zach's leg a reassuring squeeze, she asked, "Where's our first stop?"

Lexy declared, "We're off to Kansas."

The Jeep lurched as they pulled out, beginning their Dragon Handler bonding road trip. *Murder Spree.* Kayn giggled.

Under his breath, Grey began cursing up a storm. "I despise standard vehicles. Frost did this on purpose," he complained.

Lexy sighed and volunteered, "I'll drive. I don't care if it's standard."

Grey peered over at Lexy. Her crimson locks were whipping around in the wind as he mouthed the words, "Three hours."

Three hours until their first rest stop. She could read between the lines. She tried to take in the lush, brilliantly coloured vegetation as it whirled past her window. *It was too hot to play tourist and sight see.* Kayn rested her head on Zach's shoulder and closed her eyes, intending to get some sleep. She drifted away to the sound of humming tires.

Zach nudged her as he quietly said, "We found a motel with air-conditioning. We're stopping for the night."

Kayn groggily opened her eyes and yawned, stretching her arms above her in the cramped backseat. *It was already dusk. How long had she been asleep?*

Zach passed her a water bottle before she even attempted to get out. *She felt sweaty and foul. When she was younger and mortal, she'd been naïve enough to romanticize life. It felt magnificent. Sometimes it was the little things that caused optimism to surface. After a shower and perhaps a swim, she imagined she'd be feeling much more herself.* Kayn downed the last of her water as she followed Zach through the air-conditioned lobby. *It felt incredible.* It looked like they were headed upstairs but instead, Zach used a key to unlock the door beside the staircase. She stepped inside the cool room, saw the two double beds, staggered over and flopped herself on the closest one. She felt the pressure of Zach sitting on the mattress. He turned on the T.V as she mumbled, "Tell me there's room service. I don't even want to move."

Zach chuckled, "Hungry Brighton?"

"Famished," she countered with her voice muffled by the mattress. She felt him moving around, some rustling and then he tossed something on the small of her back. Kayn grabbed for it and laughed as she saw what it was… *Twinkies*. She groaned dramatically. *She missed Frost more than she should for only a day apart. What was she going to do with herself for the next couple of months?*

Zach sprawled next to her, flung his arm around her and said, "If you'd prefer something heartier, go have a shower so we can meet up with Lexy and Grey. They're already at the restaurant."

She got up so fast you'd think the bed was on fire and dashed into the washroom. After a luxurious shower, she put on a clean tank top and shorts. Kayn stared at her reflection in the mirror. *She was humorously covered in freckles.* She shrugged as she wandered out into a strangely empty room. *Why would he take off?* "Zach?" she called out quietly.

From the patio, his hushed voice urged, "You have to get out here and see this."

Intrigued, she strolled out onto the deck to see what the fuss was about. In the torch-lit courtyard, just beyond the privacy bushes, there was a group of people doing yoga. She knit her brow. *This wasn't that exciting.*

"Not that. Look up," Zach whispered as he pointed at the first-floor balcony directly across the way.

The lights were on in the room. Kayn squinted so she could see what he was looking at. *Why was her vision so blurry?*

Kayn nudged Zach and confessed, "I can't see that far. Somethings going on with my eyesight."

"You really can't see them?" he questioned. "What are the odds they'd be here?"

She rubbed her eyes and tried looking again. *She really couldn't see who he was talking about.* "I give up, who are we stalking? You're going to have to spell it out for me."

He rolled his eyes, took her hands and offered, "Go for it. You must need a hit of energy."

She hesitated for a minute before allowing her gift to do its thing. The heat of her Conduit ability channelled Zach's energy up her arms into her chest and her vision came into focus. *This glitch was new.* Kayn thanked him as she released her hold without taking any more than she needed. *Now, she could see what he was talking about. It was Lucien, head of the Lampir Coven they'd visited not too long ago with some of the others. It still felt strange to refer to them as Lampir when in her mind, they were Vampires. It looked like they were just chilling on vacation. It was strange that they'd find themselves in a resort in Mexico at the same time. Maybe this wasn't a coincidence at all?* Her heart leapt as Frost strolled into the room across the way. *She didn't expect to see him this soon. She had to get over there.* Just as she was about to rush over, Frost made eye contact with her and slowly shook his head.

Zach whispered, "This must be a job. I thought our first job was in Texas?"

"Kansas," Kayn corrected.

He whispered back, "This definitely isn't Kansas. We'd better get to the restaurant and meet up with Lexy and Grey. Maybe, there's been a change of plans?"

They were about to go as their door opened. *Someone came into their room.* They spun around. Lexy motioned for them to get back inside. They ducked. It was a ridiculous move because they were trying to hide from people a floor above. In her head, she heard Lexy's voice ordering them to stand up and get back inside. Kayn darted into the room with Zach close behind her.

Lexy shook her head as she flicked off the light switch, hiding them in the cover of darkness. She closed the curtains. "We really can't leave you two alone for a second," she remarked as she waved them to the door. "Is everybody feeling focused enough to pay attention?"

Rarely, Kayn thought as her heart pleaded with her to get over there. *She had so many things she wanted to say, the first being to apologize for causing their abrupt split.* Lexy stood in front of the door blocking her path. *Her sister meant business.*

Attempting to reason with her, Lexy warned, "I know what you're thinking. Don't even try it. I will take you down."

Out of respect for their sisterhood of Dragons, Kayn backed down, looked at her immortal sibling and curtly said, "Explain."

Lexy grinned as she responded, "There's been a change of plans. Grey got a text while you were sleeping. The other part of our Clan is meeting with the head of the Lampir to discuss information they've received. Part of Lucien's crew has gone rogue. They're trying to start a war between the Hives. Once they've determined who is involved, the others will leave. We'll be sent in to correct his crew and possibly him. We've had a long-standing Treaty with the Lampir. This promises to be a shit show."

They were still going to keep them apart. It felt like they were teasing her by having Frost in close proximity without allowing any contact. Kayn grabbed for the curtains so she could sneak a peek at him.

"That'd be why gawking up there from our deck might seem suspicious," Grey clarified. "We have time to go to the restaurant for a meal before we figuratively clean house."

Just knowing he was there kick-started her libido. The foursome left the room and casually strolled down the hall to the restaurant.

"What if they catch on to what they're doing there and take them out before they call us in?" Zach enquired.

"If our symbols go off, we're on. We'll heal ours before we leave," Lexy answered.

That sounded simple enough. Kayn found herself secretly hoping they messed-up so she could be with Frost for five seconds. *She might be able to sneak him a note with her new number so he could get a hold of her during their forced separation. She should have grabbed a pen from their room. There was always a pen on the nightstand.* With a skip in her step, she followed the others into the restaurant with red wooden chairs around two-seater round tables. The colourful art and uneven cobblestone flooring gave it a relaxed vacation vibe. *This was not the place to be day drinking, she'd break her damn neck. Not that it mattered because she'd be healed before she hit the floor.* Judging by the size of the tables, they were going to be sitting in different places.

Grey looked at Zach as he suggested, "Come sit with me. Lexy can go over things with Kayn. We have a more observatory role anyway. They're doing the job."

Zach glanced at her and shrugged as he strolled away with Grey. *Frost was over there. He was so close, she could still feel him.*

The two girls sat down. When Kayn peered up Lexy was grinning. "So, that's really all there is to the plan?" Kayn questioned as their server appeared to take their drink orders.

Smiling, Lexy ordered, "We'll each have two shots of tequila."

Was it wise to get drunk before a job?

Lexy responded to Kayn's thoughts, "Come on. It's your first seriously sketchy Correction with less than clear details. It would be unwise not to. Plus, it'll be hilarious to watch Grey's reaction when he sees us drinking."

Kayn grinned, as she looked at the menu. *It kind of wasn't their first. Not long ago, they'd killed an entire town full of Demons.* The waiter reappeared with the drink tray and placed four shots of golden hell fire on the table. Kayn passed one to Lexy and raised her shot as she saluted, "To Dragons."

Lexy repeated, "To Dragons," as they downed their first shot.

Kayn had to fight off the urge to grin. *She could feel their Handler's eyes on their table.* Without barely a second of hesitation, she raised her next shot and announced, "To Handlers." They clinked their shot glasses and downed the second one.

"Should we order a few more?" Kayn casually enquired as salsa and chips were placed on the table.

Lexy smiled and nodded at their waiter. She reached for a chip. As she dipped it into the salsa, she cursed, "Shit. Every damn time." Her fingerless glove covered hand heated up. *One of theirs was wounded. It was time to go to work.*

The waiter placed four more shots on the table before they could say they were leaving.

Lexy signalled to their server before he walked away and instructing, "Charge this to room 15. Thank you."

The girls quickly drank the shots and stood up. As Kayn's eyes darted over to their Handler's table. *They were gone. Where in the hell did they go?*

"They're probably already back at the room," her fellow Dragon explained. "Time to clean house."

Kayn was practically jogging to catch up to Lexy as she power-marched through the cobblestone courtyard to the other half of the motel. Feeling both nervous and excited, Kayn asked, "Are we using special weapons like last time?"

"Kill everything with a grey or black aura. Anything wooden will do the trick," Lexy replied. "Either their head needs to come off or a direct hit to the heart. It's rather simple. I've always found it fun once you take the pesky humanity thing out of the situation. They used to be a touch stronger physically, but I suspect that's changed now."

Yes, they were like vampire hunting superheroes. Kayn felt super cocky for a second before she tripped on uneven cobblestone in her flip flops and fell flat on her face. *Son of a... Some things never change.* Embarrassed, she peered up. Lexy was standing above her with a peculiar look on her face. She heard laughter from the peanut gallery and realised both of their Handlers were on the other side of the bright floral hedge to her left. *That wasn't helpful. Oh, they were in so much trouble when she finished this job.*

Lexy's crimson locks glinted in the light of the flickering torches as she held out her hand, yanked Kayn to her feet and coldly ordered, "Everyone with a dark aura dies. We should be able to sneak up to the first floor, correct the Lampir and get out without alerting anyone."

Kayn nodded as she wiped the blood off her knees.

Being freshly healed would make it easier to tell the dark souls from the light. Methodically, Kayn raised her hand to her nose. She inhaled the metallic scent of her blood and allowed the icy veil of nothingness to take her cares away. The laughter on the other side of the bushes ceased as the uncomfortable humidity became nothing more than an afterthought. They wandered into the empty foyer as tipsy girls making the most of their vacation. There were faint orange hues in the auras around the patrons at the front desk. *These were mortals.* They inconspicuously strolled through the lobby and slipped unnoticed into the stairwell and up the flight of stairs.

As they stepped out into the empty hall, Lexy whispered, "Find a weapon. Wood. Only Lampir with dark auras."

Kayn nodded as the two split up. There was a decorative table with a vase of fresh flowers on it. She carefully picked it up and placed it gently on the floor, without making a sound. She broke a leg off the table and snapped it in two, just as one of the doors opened. There was a trail of smoky dark aura. *That's all she needed.* She coldly impaled the Lampir in the chest with the table's leg. His face registered shock, he staggered back, solidified and disintegrated into a pile of ash. As Kayn stepped into his room. She was surrounded. by at least a dozen Lampir. *Good. She'd skipped dinner.* Some fled out the adjoining door. More than half remained. *They were standing there in their human form like they had a chance. Fools.* She heard a commotion down the hall. *Lexy was taking care of her escapees.* Kayn grinned as she motioned for them to come at her, boldly taunting, "What are you waiting for? Let's do this!" Their panicked eyes darted around looking for a way to escape. *They'd had their chance.* All at once their human disguises slipped away, revealing their true nature. *This was how she'd pictured Vampires in her nightmares.* A ballsy salivating female growled as she came at her, abruptly bringing Kayn back to the situation at hand. She'd falsely assumed she'd be able to easily toss the abomination away but instead, it hit her with the brute force of a linebacker. Buckling at the waist, she was launched through the air, out of the room against the wall on the other side of the hall. It knocked the wind out of her. Gasping for air, she realised, she'd dropped her weapon. *Shit!* They rushed at her with snapping beastly distorted jaws. Struggling to fend them off, she reached for the table's leg as they swarmed her, sinking razor-sharp fangs into her flesh. She flailed, wildly kicking them away. Adrenaline surged through Kayn's being as her Healing ability struggled to counteract the effects of their sedating pleasure-inducing venom. The stake was kicked close enough to reach during their feeding frenzy. Kayn impaled a few more. They solidified and turned to dust, as the Lampir virus subdued her. *Saying their toxin was pleasurable was an understatement.* Kayn shivered as she fought to regain her faculties. She struggled and clawed them away. *There were too many.*

She was pinned as they fed from her en masse like sadistically volatile leeches. *The toxin caused inescapable euphoria. She hadn't seen this one coming. Her options were narrowing by the millisecond.* As her Healing ability caused adrenaline to surge through her once more, Kayn released a primal scream. She grabbed hold of the closest Lampir and drained its energy. Its jaws slackened and it slumped against her. *The power of the addictive Lampir energy enveloped her soul as she plummeted into the void of emotional nothingness.* Kayn fed from another. As its eyes rolled back in its head, she released her hold on her predatory foe and siphoned from the next until only the whites of its eyes were visible. It slumped on her chest. The others who were trying to feed on her backed away understanding Dragons were predators too and she was taking her rightful place in the immortal food chain.

Surging with Lampir lifeforce, Kayn leapt to her feet. They gathered in awe. Their drive to feed nixed any self-preservation as did hers. *Convenient.* Kayn pried an axe from the grip of an awestruck abomination and chopped off its head. A fine mist sprayed around her momentarily before it turned to ash. Even the blood covering her became an ashy grey film. She kicked what was left and it dissipated into the air. Kayn continued this action until she'd methodically disposed of the Lampir that hadn't been with it enough to scatter the second she got hold of the axe. She coldly walked through the piles of Lampir ash on the floor and began methodically kicking open locked doors, executing the Lampir hiding in the rooms, until one remained. *Lucien.*

He slowly backed away bartering for his life, "You're making a mistake. I have nothing to do with this. I'm on your side. I know things. I have information you need."

Why was he wasting his last moments trying to bargain with a Dragon? She didn't care about denials or the level of his involvement. She was still hungry. Kayn cocked her head as he continued to negotiate for a reprieve.

As she coldly backed Lucien against the wall, he implored, "Lily will be upset! We're friends! She cares about me!"

As Kayn swung the axe back, she felt an unusual tug at her soul. *She believed him.* His swirling aura changed from smoky grey to a deep purple with flecks of gold and her orders became foggy. *Kill everything with a grey or black aura. Was he innocent?* Something within her caused emotion to flicker. This prompted her to speak, "Why are you here?"

"I was a part of this, but only so I could trap those involved," Lucien confessed.

If she fed on him, theoretically he'd be dead, but he'd rise again if she didn't finish him off with the axe. She was starving and this was a grey area. His aura kept changing hues, making it unclear. Was he a part of the job? Kayn observed the deep violet and gold in the smoky haze of his aura. *He wasn't part of this job.* She dropped the axe and whispered, "I believe you." Relief spread across Lucien's face.

He exhaled deeply as he introduced himself, "My name's…"

Silencing him with her finger, she asserted, "I don't care. I'm starving." Being a creature that took life, he understood what she needed.

The leader of the Lampir offered her his hands, giving his consent, "Feed on me."

She didn't need him to say it twice. She took his hands. His knees buckled as bliss inducing energy travelled up her arms into her torso. *He was delicious. Too tasty to stop herself.* Kayn shuddered. She sunk to her knees as they became weak from pleasure and gave way. Lucien began to struggle. *She couldn't stop.* He groaned with abandon. *This excited her.* Kayn trembled as a wave of ecstasy triggered her ability, releasing pheromones into the air. He was now caught in her intoxicating web.

Lucien moaned aloud as his inhibitions ceased to exist, "My turn." His eyes darkened as he sunk his teeth into the tantalizing flesh of her forearm.

The exquisite agony of his fangs mixed with the sensual pleasure of their shared feeding made her tremble with desire. She moaned as he adjusted his bite. Their eyes met and the aching sense of wanting to be fulfilled was all she could feel. Seemingly from the end of a long echoing tunnel, she heard Zach's voice, "Kayn stop!" *She couldn't. She didn't want to. She wanted him to bite her throat.*

"Kayn, stop!" Zach shouted.

She felt a startling jolt of reality as she was pried away from the Lampir by Lexy, Grey and Zach. They held her down with the full weight of all three as she struggled against them and if she wasn't hallucinating, Markus and Orin grabbed the Lampir's leader and forced Lucien out of the room. *She was in agony. Starving with desire, overflowing with this intense urgency that made it impossible to think about anything but her next feed.* Kayn thrashed around, refusing to submit to her Clan. Her gaze locked with Grey's. She ceased to fight, knowing he was under the spell of her potent, sexually charged pheromones. *He'd allow her to take whatever she wanted from him.*

Zach yelled, "Kayn! Enough! Stop!"

Lexy snatched Grey from Kayn's perilous grasp. He fought against her as Lexy forced him out of the room.

"Kayn. Come back to me," her Handler begged, desperately trying to lure her from the emotionless void.

She wanted more. Their eyes locked and there was nothing her Handler could do. Her perilous pheromones were impossible to resist.

Zach's resolve ebbed as he slid into the quicksand of her ability. "You smell incredible," he whispered as he inched closer until their lips met. Unable to fight it anymore, he succumbed to the pheromones drugging him of his free will as he deepened their kiss. His hands began travelling over her curves and as they slipped beneath the material of her tank top, she felt a sharp pain as the lights went out.

7

BOYFRIENDS AND LYCANTHROPES

Melody and Frost were watching Kayn's naughty ability-related issues from the balcony. As soon as the Handler and Dragon duo started going at it, Frost opted out. He strolled back into the room just as Markus and Orin rather comically tackled the Lampir's leader onto the bed. *He was the last person Frost wanted to see right now.* He grabbed a Corona from the minibar and made a quick exit.

Melody grabbed a beer and chased after Frost as he power-walked away from the girlfriend-related drama. As Mel caught up, she asserted, "You know she can't help it."

Frost stopped walking away. He faced Mel as he replied, "I knew we were going to have fidelity related issues, but she lasted all of twenty-four hours. My ego just had a bit of a smackdown. I need a minute. I'm going to drink this beer and try to chill myself out."

1

"So, you're fine with it?" Mel enquired.

"Fine, isn't the word I'd use. Concerned, is more where I am in my head," he commented under his breath. Taking a swig of chilled Corona, he wiped the perspiration from his brow.

"Is there anything I can do to help?" Mel probed, placing her hand on his shoulder.

He playfully swatted her hand away and teased, "Not tempting me to retaliate is a start."

"I would never do that... Ever!" Mel clarified giving him the dirtiest look in her repertoire.

Chuckling, Frost started walking. He glanced back and ribbed, "Relax. I was joking." Mel kept pace with his strides through the courtyard as he disclosed, "I need to get a message to Zach through Grey. He needs to know she can't use my ability on mortals until she's gained control. Even then, we don't know what she's capable of. Her Conduit ability is something we haven't dealt with before."

Mel responded, "I thought we weren't allowed any contact."

"We're not allowed contact because our Oracle told Markus, removal from their peer group would be the only way to regain control," Frost explained. "It's a smart move. Jenna's usually right."

They wandered to the pool area in darkness, where they sat dangling their legs in the lukewarm water. Hearing voices, they both looked up and waved at the Aries Group as they strolled past the flickering torches. They'd come to dispose of the evidence, disguised as a cleaning crew.

1

After a pause in the conversation, Mel enquired, "Aren't you even a little jealous?"

Glancing her way, he responded, "Why?"

Curiosity got the best of her as Mel pried, "So, you have an open relationship?"

He took a swig of beer and said, "There's no point in trying to put a label on it. It's too soon after the Testing for any of you to have your heads on straight. Kayn just fed from a dozen Lampir and can't control her Conduit ability. I'd imagine, each one had gifts, they've been added to her collection. She's likely to be an unhinged shit show for a good month. It's probably better for our relationship if we're not in the same place right now."

Mel smiled as Markus' voice came from behind them, "It's time to go."

Frost got up, grabbed his bag and asserted, "I need to get a message to Grey."

"That could be arranged," Markus replied as they strolled out into the dimly lit parking lot.

KAYN AWOKE TO THE SOUND OF spinning tires on the highway. The evening's events filtered through her memory and she winced.

"It was me. I killed you," Lexy confessed from the front seat.

Grey was sleeping beside her. Zach was her sister's co-pilot. A vision of their steamy make-out session replayed in her memory. *She'd been naughty.* Grey's breathing changed. She glanced his way.

Grey mumbled, "Don't pee where you sleep," as he rolled over.

Hilarious.

Zach taunted from the front, "So, does this mean we're getting married now?"

"Alright. I get it," Kayn sighed. "Thanks for taking me out before I broke the Handler Dragon intimacy seal."

"Not a problem," her sister replied.

Grey added his two cents, "You should never sleep with your Handler. I'm grateful we've never crossed that line."

Lexy mouthed the words, "Oh my God," at her reflection in the rear-view mirror.

Zach glanced back and grinned at Kayn as he assured, "I could think of worse things."

He could think of worse things… Nice. It was too dark to see the road and there were no streetlights. So, she stared out into the endless span of pitch-black nothingness as Zach searched for a radio station. Every station was Spanish. *Maybe, she should get Zach to teach her Spanish?* A beautiful song came on the radio, and even though she couldn't understand the lyrics, the passionate vocals made her feel a part of it. She thought of Frost with a surge of guilt. *She hadn't even managed to stay faithful for twenty-four hours.* Kayn reached over and touched Lexy's shoulder as she questioned, "Aren't they supposed to be at the Summit?"

"They've already left," Lexy answered.

Headlights were approaching on the other side of the road. *The first driver they'd passed all night. Well, that she'd* noticed. She felt oddly uncomfortable as the headlights came closer. She only managed to say, "I have a weird…" The vehicle veered into their lane. Kayn was laughing hysterically as they crashed and began flipping down the darkened highway with the sound of crunching metal. She was flung out of the wreckage mid flip. Her body landed with an explosion of excruciating pain and skidded along the unforgiving pavement. Kayn lay there broken and bruised, aware she was seriously wounded, but not incredibly concerned. *That sucked.* The Ankh symbol on her hand heated up, warning her the others were injured. Her vision blurred, making what she could see hazy and unidentifiable. Her chest was burning. Each breath took effort until it became nearly impossible. *Something was watching.* Aware of panting coming from the shadows, she struggled for a final breath as the lights went out.

It felt like moments lapsed when she became aware of muffled noises. Kayn assessed the damage with her eyes closed. *Her entire body felt hot. Her healing ability was working overtime.* Logic urged her to buy herself time to heal before allowing anyone to know she was awake. *She was going to need energy. The steady panting was still there. Warm, moist breath on her skin. Fingers crossed they weren't mortal. Usually, when they were forced off the highway, it was another Clan trying to steal an underage Ankh. She sensed that wasn't what this was. She didn't recognize any of the voices with a deep gravely undertone. Someone or something was panting loudly. She felt the sense of caution she'd experienced seconds before the crash.* Even though her eyes were closed, she knew it was still dark with no glare behind her lids. As heat of her Healing ability dulled, she suspected she was good to go. Cautiously, Kayn opened her eyes and got up to see what they were dealing with. There was something crouched over a body, twitching. *What in the hell was that?* She soundlessly inched closer like a cat hunting prey. *She sensed it was Zach. Was something feeding on her Handler?* She grabbed the creature by the throat and choked it out, receiving a shivering surge of energy as it fell limply into the sand. *She wanted more but she'd taken enough, her vision was no longer blurry. She'd have to suck it up and stay focused on the situation at hand. Zach had been injured in the crash but there appeared to be no wound caused by whatever these things were.* Confused, she stealthily moved through the shadows temporarily subduing creatures until there was only one rolling on its back in the sand. Observing the creature's canine subservient mannerisms, Kayn whispered, "What do we have here?" It was cowering before her. She motioned for it to come closer, and it did, crawling on all four human legs. *This was incredibly strange.* She inquisitively tilted her head. *What are you?* The creature imitated her. *They didn't have time for this. Now, they were going to need another vehicle. They had a lot of places to be and people to kill before they'd be back with the rest of their Clan.* Kayn motioned for it to come closer. *Whatever it was, it appeared to be in awe of her.* She reached out like she was going to pet it. In a rapid movement, she had the curious thing in a headlock. It didn't struggle. It succumbed to her will, allowing her to subdue it. *What was this? It didn't make sense. Maybe it had something to do with the Lampir they'd Corrected?*

Kayn wandered around to check on her incapacitated Ankh. *They only had injuries from the accident.* She needed to find something to restrain these partially mortal creatures. She searched their vehicle. There was a bag of zip ties on the floor in the back. These would do in a snap, but the fact that they had them made her a tad suspicious about their intentions. She dragged each one over, turned them on their stomachs and zip-tied their hands behind their backs. *This might not be good enough.* Kayn triple zip-tied their hands and ankles together. *Healing everyone alone would take a toll.* She approached her sister's body, intending to heal her first but she was already awake.

Lexy brushed herself off, got up and asked, "Well Brighton, what are we dealing with?"

"I'm not sure what they are but they didn't hurt us," Kayn replied. "Lampir maybe?"

Lexy flipped one over and checked the distorted creature's gums by it's canines. "They're not Lampir," she disclosed, inspecting the predator's blackened fingernails. "They're Lycanthrope but not fully changed, I haven't seen this before. Did you say they didn't touch us?"

"One was by Zach's neck, I thought he was being hurt, but when I got a closer look, he didn't have injuries that weren't caused by the accident," Kayn explained. She crouched to get a closer look at the creatures blackened nails.

"Either way, running us off the road violated the Treaty," Lexy stated. One began squirming and growling. The crimson-haired force of nature flipped it over. Gazing into its eyes, she interrogated, "You've inconvenienced us. Explain yourself. You have about five seconds before I tear out your heart and feed it to your corpse."

Fear registered in the creature's eyes as it bluntly responded, "We were minding our own business, driving home, there was a fragrance in the air, and we started to change with no lunar prompting. The next thing we knew, we'd crashed into you guys frenzied by the blonde's scent. You were all bleeding profusely. We sensed you weren't mortal. We also detected Lampir toxin in the blonde one's system and knew she might turn. So, we tried to keep our distance, but those pheromones are so intoxicating. What is she?"

With understanding in her eyes, Lexy replied, "She's one of us. She's Ankh and a Conduit but part Guardian as am I."

Kevin had just given her a warning about keeping her paternity to herself. Her sister didn't know. She hadn't had the opportunity to tell her. It was too late now. What's done is done.

Smiling, the Lycanthrope introduced himself, "My friends call me Emerson. I give you my word. We never intended to hurt you."

"Alright then, I'll untie you," Lexy responded. She snapped the triple-tied zip-ties like they were nothing.

Fully returned to his mortal state, Emerson was an attractive older guy. *A green haze surrounded the Lycanthrope. It meant they weren't an evil entity, just different. Her curiosity piqued. How did it happen? Was it virus-based, like Lampir or genetics?*

Lexy answered her thoughts, "Usually genetics. In rare cases, a scratch or a bite can infect someone with the virus." "Good to know," Kayn said as she held out her hand to help Emerson up. The now mortal man accepted her gesture. *Wordless apologies made the most sense to her.* Emerson caught her attention by not letting go of her hand. He raised it to his nose and sniffed her.

His eyes were flecked with glowing yellow as he awkwardly released her hand and explained, "Your scent is difficult to ignore. It's still there but just faintly now."

Kayn smiled at Emerson, looked at Lexy and suggested, "We should wake the boys up."

Staring at her cell, looking thoroughly disappointed, Lexy peered up from the screen and declared, "No cell service. We might be stuck here until someone comes along."

"Maybe, it's just our provider?" Kayn countered.

Grinning, Emerson tossed her his phone. She caught it without looking. "Impressive," he flirted.

Kayn couldn't help but smile. *She wasn't accustomed to being on the receiving end of random flirtations.* Her vision blurred and found herself squinting to see his screen. *This was obviously going to be a thing.*

"You alright?" Emerson asked.

He was attractive for an older man. Well, a man that looked his age. Emerson had to be at least forty. Frost crossed her mind again. Kayn grinned as she answered, "I'm fine. It's just an ability related glitch." Lexy called her over to Grey. *He wasn't dead. It wouldn't be a taxing healing job.* They placed their hands on his chest and healed him first, then moved on to Zach and it didn't take much. There was a glowing light flickering on the other side of the Lycanthrope's wreckage. *They'd made a fire. It wasn't cold. That fire was only going to draw the attention of wild animals.* Zach and Grey were being introduced to their new accidental friends as Kayn tried to make sense of the hollow reverb after each person spoke. One of the Lycanthrope's voices cracked as he introduced himself. *He sounded young. Her vision was blurry. She couldn't make out anything further than five feet away. It left her feeling like she was at a disadvantage. The desert sky was probably full of stars.* Deciding to say nothing, she joined the group gathered around the flickering flames.

Zach smiled at her as she approached. He enquired, "Hungry?"

She was starving for various reasons. "Always," Kayn replied as she took her place at her Handler's side. "What are we having?"

"Whatever sees this fire and comes to eat us," Zach ribbed. "Or we can choose the easy route."

Intrigued, Kayn responded, "What would that be?"

Grey piped in, "I'm sure you're a bit hesitant to uncork Frost's ability but if we set off those pheromones, our friends can change without a full moon. A few can go for help, while the rest hunt us down something to eat."

Was she hungry enough to eat random desert wildlife? Not likely. Did she want to uncork an ability she'd proven on multiple occasions to have no control over? It felt like a bad idea. She tried to look up at the desert sky once more in search of stars and there was nothing but darkness. *Her vision would be restored if she fed.*

Giving her shoulder a reassuring squeeze, Lexy assured, "I'll break your neck if you get out of hand."

What did she have to lose? Kayn shrugged as she took Zach's hand, taunting, "Give it your best shot, Romeo." *All eyes were on the Dragon Handler duo. This was awkward.* Zach nervously cleared his throat as he inched closer and gave her his sexiest come-hither smile. Kayn started laughing.

"Come on Brighton," Zach complained.

"There are too many people around, this isn't going to work," she countered.

"Positive thinking," Grey urged. When Zach didn't jump right in, Grey took the initiative as he declared, "Allow me to show you how it's done."

Kayn gave her sister a helpless look.

Lexy shrugged and whispered, "I'll break his neck too."

Grey spun around, glared at her and enquired, "What did you just say?"

"Nothing important," Lexy sparred. When Grey turned back to Kayn, she winked at her.

This was so messed-up. Grey shot her a seductive smile. *Why not? Her sister would literally kill him if he became too frisky.* Kayn decided to take the ability she'd siphoned for a spin.

Grey confidently moved in, took her hand and placed it on his chest, holding it firmly in place with both hands. She felt his heart beating beneath her palm. Thud, thud... Thud, thud. *She knew what he was doing. He'd played this game with her once before but they'd been close to that inhibition loosening pool in the In-between.* It felt voyeuristic having all eyes trained on them as Grey tried to work his flirtatious magic. *Thank heavens it was dark out. It made her feel less exposed.*

"What would Frost do in a moment like this?" Grey enquired.

Kayn stared into his eyes, riveted as to where he was going with this conversation. *Was he looking for details? She could play this game but knew she shouldn't.* She divulged, "He'd probably try to kiss me." Grey leaned in. Kayn dodged out of the way. *This felt wrong. Lexy was her sister. There had to be an easier way to set off the ability without being forced to do something she didn't really want to do.*

Grey chuckled and teased, "Chicken."

She thought of something she'd been dared to do back in the Testing. *Maybe it would be better if she kept it out of the Clan?* Kayn sparred, "Humour me." She was going to check one off her unbucket list and kiss a stranger. She summoned Emerson. Without hesitation the Lycanthrope in mortal form came over visibly curious about what she had planned. *What would Chloe do?* She allowed thoughts of Frost to fill her mind with steamy visions of seduction and before she could talk herself out of it, she planted a passionate kiss on the mature Lycanthrope who was all but a stranger. She felt a touch of warmth between their lips. *It was working!* She deepened the kiss. *Emerson had serious skills in the kissing department.* Kayn shivered as the pheromones released from her skin into the desert air. Emerson's eyes were flecked with yellow as they pulled apart. *She'd figured it out!* Staring into the Lycanthrope's eyes, Kayn seductively ran her fingers over his defined chest as she suggested with a raspy voice, "Why don't you harness that inner beast and go catch us something to eat?"

Emerson's eyes hazed over as he obediently whispered, "Yes. Of course."

While feeling crazy powerful, Kayn faced the rest of the Lycanthropes and ordered, "I'm going to need a few of you to go for help because we've had car trouble. Would anyone like to volunteer?"

All their hands raised. *She loved how this ability made her feel. Go inner Chloe!* Kayn smirked as their facial features distorted becoming angular and savage. They galloped away on all fours.

Grey whispered, "Another Lily. Heaven help us all."

Smartasses get experimented with. Kayn turned to Grey and suggested, "I think Lexy could use a shoulder massage, don't you?"

"Sure," Grey answered, dutifully massaging Lexy's shoulders.

With an uncompromising look, Zach whispered, "I'll just agree to play along if you promise to leave me my free will."

She winked at her Handler. "Deal," Kayn quietly agreed as she walked away from the trio. *Sometimes it felt like she'd barely been given a moment to absorb what happened during the Testing. They'd kept them so busy they hadn't had the opportunity to settle their souls.* She looked up at the breathtaking display of the stars blanketed across the heavens as howling Lycanthrope echoed through the desert. Beginning to understand how her twin's ability worked, Kayn knelt on the ground and raked her hand over the surface of the sand, causing the delicate grains to dance beneath her fingertips. She felt an ominous vibration. Kayn placed her palm flat on the silky grains, knowing what it was before her eyes met with the rattlesnake's as it hypnotically slithered through the sand towards her. It stopped roughly five feet away, raised its head and began its telltale rattling. She met its penetrating reptilian gaze with her own and warned, "You will not succeed in harming me. Leave."

It darted at her with no restraint as predators often do. Kayn raised her hand and the reptile froze in place. *Interesting. This was new.* She waved her hand. In the time it took to blink, the rattler was soaring through the air away from the group. It landed in the sand and left peacefully without making another attempt. *What had she just done?* She snatched a pebble from the ground, tossing it into the air and tried to stop its descent. She managed to keep it in place for a second. That was more than long enough to envision what could be done with this new ability. She recalled how the Guardian Seth had frozen her entire Clan when he borrowed her and Lexy. Kayn rose to stand with her palm full of sand as adrenaline surged through her being. She tossed it into the air and held up her palm, attempting to freeze it in place. It rained down around her. *That time it hadn't worked.* She grabbed another handful and chucked it into the air. This time it froze. Every grain was mystically suspended in midair hovering, slowly moving clockwise like a mobile over an infant's bassinet. *This was incredible.* She felt like cheering. Zach cautiously made his way to stand at her side. *She didn't want to take any chances with him. He shouldn't be this close.*

He quietly enquired, "Are you freezing time?"

"I am. I think so… You shouldn't be standing this close," she cautioned.

"It's my job," Zach pointed out as he moved closer. "Do it again. Show me."

Kayn grabbed another handful, beaming as she pitched it up into the air. She stopped it by holding up her hand but only for about ten seconds, before it sprinkled down around her like summer rain. Her attention was drawn to an odour, followed by heavy panting. *They were back, and by the scent in the air, she knew the Lycanthrope hadn't shown up empty-handed. They had dinner.*

Zach touched her arm and said, "They're back. Stop messing around. Experiment when there are no witnesses."

She didn't want to stop. Aware her Handler wasn't physically strong enough to stop her from doing anything, she considered her options. *She was the strongest. She could take everyone here.* Kayn felt Lexy's presence and her cocky went down a notch. *Her sister was strong enough to give her a run for her money. She knew why she was there. She didn't blame her. Her ego was beginning to take her away from the duties at hand so she allowed it to happen.* Kayn closed her eyes as Lexy snapped her neck.

ZACH PICKED UP KAYN'S LIMP body. Cradling her in his arms, he wandered over and placed her by the light of the fire. He took a seat beside her and sweetly brushed her hair out of her eyes.

"Is she your girlfriend?" The young, human looking Lycanthrope asked.

"No, I'm her Handler," Zach responded as he watched her lying there completely still.

"She's one of those Dragons. I've heard about them. They are always telling stories about one with the crimson hair." Clicking into Lexy's presence, he backtracked, "All good things of course, about how strong and powerful she is."

"Good save little buddy," Grey chuckled as he tried to mess Lexy's hair.

Scowling, Lexy swatted his hand away, cautioning, "Do you really want to do this right now?"

Grey flirtatiously baited, "I might."

Their gaze held for longer than it should. Lexy got up and declared, "Not this time Greydon," as she stormed away.

"What did I say?" Grey sighed as he scrambled to his feet, preparing to go after her.

Zach stopped him and suggested, "I'll go. Watch mine for a minute." Grey shrugged as he sat beside Kayn's lifeless body, ruffled up Kayn's hair and grinned before turning his attention back to the others.

ZACH RUSHED TO CATCH UP. Keeping pace with Lexy, he implored, "You can talk to me." She laughed. "What's so funny?" He questioned, uncomfortably snatching a rock from the ground and pitching it into the distance.

"You are," Lexy sparred as she copied Zach's action and hurled a stone as far as she could.

He groaned and sighed, "Must you ladies always stomp on my ego?"

Lexy's expression darkened as she countered, "Must Grey always stomp on mine?"

"I see your point," Zach replied. "You've stretched the boundaries of your relationship. He doesn't remember anything and he keeps putting his foot in his mouth. Is that why you're upset?"

Exhaling, she faced him answering, "Do you know what it's like to love someone you can never be with?"

"I know what it's like to want someone who has no interest in me if that counts?" Zach disclosed as he pitched another stone.

"You mean Melody?" Lexy enquired.

Grinning, Zach responded, "It would have been helpful to know she was in love with the leader of Trinity. It still stings that she knew I had a crazy crush on her and she let it simmer without bothering to fill me in. Then, there's the yearlong booty call with Grey that I knew nothing about. That had to suck for you."

Lexy glanced his way and confessed, "It always sucks for me. It's a cruel karmic joke. You know those two had nothing serious going on. Grey was just her relief pitcher. Perhaps she needs a new one now?"

"Right… It's not like I haven't tried. We kissed and it was amazing. I was starting to feel like maybe it was going to go my way, but we met up with Trinity and whenever Thorne's around, it's like I'm not even in the room. How am I supposed to pretend I don't know I'm expendable?"

"You realise you're preaching to the choir?" She teased, playfully nudging him. Lexy hinted, "What about Haley? I thought something was happening there."

"I keep getting sucked back into my feelings for Mel," Zach explained. "Also, I'm Kayn's Handler, which is just as confusing. I know I'm not even the first choice for this job. I mean, she's my friend, and there's nothing I wouldn't do for her, but she has Frost. It confuses my role. Maybe, if I had someone myself, it wouldn't?"

"Maybe," Lexy repeated as she gave his arm a reassuring squeeze. "I've been trying to move on from Grey for years, but every time I do, his feelings resurface. That's why I walked away. He's openly flirtatious. This is how it starts. Eventually, he'll confess his feelings, and I love him too much to turn him away. We're inevitable but it's torture when he wakes up and doesn't remember. For a long time, the incredible night we spent together was worth it, but now it just feels like I'm stuck on the wrong road."

"You deserve better," Zach assured as their eyes met.

Lexy took off her shoe and dumped out pebbles as she sighed, "That's just it. There is no one better. It isn't his fault. I know girls say that all the time, but in this situation, he has proven he loves me with everything he is a thousand times. He's my Handler. He forgets after his memory has been wiped, but his feelings have been coming back faster. For me, he's everything. If there were ever a way for us to be together, I'd be a hundred percent in, but this has been going on for so long. I'm finally ready to see my options, if that makes sense."

"It does… I don't know a lot about the guy. Orin seems nice enough," Zach remarked.

Lexy grinned as she recalled their last encounter. She added, "Orin is amazing but I'm not Jenna and he's not Grey. I don't know where it could go while we're both still in love with other people. There are other complications. Attractions to be dealt with before I can even think about it."

"Tiberius?" Zach taunted as he pitched another stone.

Lexy snatched herself a pebble as she chuckled, "You don't miss a thing, do you?"

"Not usually," he admitted.

"It's complicated," Lexy confessed as she cast her stone. "The dark and twisty ones are always fun," Zach sparred as he grabbed a grape-sized rock out of the sand and tossed it.

"Stephanie or Patrick?" Lexy casually enquired.

Zach's expression altered. He was immediately on the defensive, "What about Patrick?"

"Nothing, it was just a vibe I got after seeing you together," she countered with a sly smile.

Zach's eyes grew calm as he confessed, "While we're being honest, I'll admit it, there's a strange pull. To make it clear, I enjoy sex with women."

"I'm not disputing that, I'm just making sure you know, it's alright to be who you are. Some people are into both," she revealed as a commotion by the fire made them aware Kayn was awake.

"For now, I plan to stay in one lane," Zach clarified as he brushed the sand off his hands on his shorts.

"The best things come from broken plans," Lexy teased as they jogged back to the others.

WHEN THEY ARRIVED, GREY WAS JUST sitting there watching a cross-legged Kayn, gleefully moulding an energy ball. Grey mouthed the words, "Get her before she blows someone up."

Kayn looked at Grey and disclosed, "I have no ill will with the Lycanthrope. I'm going to use it on Abaddon. They'll be here soon. Can't you feel it?"

"Shit! Everyone up! Get ready to fight!" Grey stammered as he leapt to his feet. "Does anyone have salt?"

Lexy dashed back to their unsalvageable vehicle as the Lycanthrope gathered by the fire clutching knives, prepared to rumble.

"Hey, Grey!" Emerson called out.

Grey turned just as the Lycanthrope tossed him a closed switchblade. He caught it and warned, "You should leave. You'll be killed."

"We've never run from a fight before, why start now," Emerson refuted.

Lexy returned with a box of salt and a backpack full of weapons. She tossed the unopened box to Grey, quickly made a circle of safety and ordered, "There's no time. I can feel it too and my radar isn't the greatest. Get in the circle!"

"Why?" Emerson asked as his people joined the Ankh in the safe area encircled by salt.

Grey glanced at Emerson and repeated, "Why? How do you deal with Abaddon?"

"We don't," Emerson replied. "We've heard of them, but we've been basically left alone out here."

"Aren't you in for a treat," Zach muttered. He noticed Kayn was purposely standing outside of the circle and summoned her, "Get in here, Brighton!"

Kayn brazenly remained outside of the circle's protection, moulding a blue-hued orb, appearing to have not a care in the world. She peered over at her Handler, Acknowledging his command with a sly smile, she replied, "That's not necessary. Lexy's in the circle." Her stomach cramped again. *They were close.* She glanced at Lexy and said, "What better time for an experiment? If my way fails, I'm sure you've got the juice to take them out old school." Lexy shrugged her agreement.

Zach pleaded with her, "Get in here. You've already ingested too much dark energy today."

Kayn met her Handler's concern with logic, "And I plan to use it... Right now." She whirled around as the cloud of smoky demonic darkness descended upon the group. It passed Kayn by without trying to subdue her as she played with her orb of blue energy. *She didn't want to blow this entity up, not when she could use its strength to defeat a more dangerous foe.* She clapped her hands together and the orb of indigo disappeared.

"What was that?" An awestruck Lycan exclaimed as he spun in a circle, trying to keep his eyes on the ominous vapour swirling around the group protected within the confines of the salt.

Lexy quickly schooled the Lycanthrope, "The dark fog subdues you and the monsters consume you."

"Figuratively?" Emerson enquired, making sure to remain in the circle.

"No," Grey responded. "It tears you apart and devours you. That's why we said you should leave. But that ship has sailed. You're in the eye of the shit storm now. It's happening." He nervously observed the distracting black cloud.

Zach took three blades out of the backpack and tossed them into the sand, saying, "Just in case Lexy can't channel our energy with Lycanthrope in the mix."

Cracking her neck like a badass, Kayn declared, "You won't need those." She stepped into the demonic vapours path, held up both hands and visibly shivered while ingesting the evil entity through her pores. The darkness coursing through her burned like poison as her veins protruded and darkened. As she exhaled a slight puff of black smoke escaped her lips. Usually a brilliant green, Kayn's eyes became dark pools as the sweet agony of the power she'd consumed snuffed out mortal sentiment.

Zach loudly instructed, "Stay focused, Kayn! It's coming!"

Her Handler's voice echoed like it came from the end of a tunnel, but she heard it. Kayn slowly turned to face the rustling sand. *There it was.* A slick midnight black tar covered reptilian monstrosity was shuffling through the harsh grainy landscape towards her. Saliva dripped from its jagged jaws as it reared its head, to assert dominance over the lone girl between the beast and its smorgasbord. *It was now that she needed it.* Kayn pressed her palms together and released a spine-chilling primal wail as she used every ounce of will to create a new hypnotising orb of energy between her palms. She began slowly manoeuvring her fingers apart and together. Each time, the iridescent yellow orb grew larger. The beast let out a screech as Kayn pitched the shimmering orb at the depravity. It exploded in a splat of meaty pieces that reddened the pebble-strewn sand.

A Lycanthrope, who was no more than a preteen excitedly exclaimed, "That was insane!" The boy stepped out of the circle assuming danger had passed. Lexy tried to grab him but wasn't fast enough as black vapour descended upon him. Lexy yelled, "Get the kid!"

Somewhat removed from the situation, Kayn serenely observed the young Lycanthrope squirming on the ground fighting for his life as the demonic vapour devoured his energy.

"Do something!" a male voice yelled.

How was this her concern?

Knowing there was little else Kayn cared about, Zach stepped out of the protection of the circle and grabbed for the incapacitated Lycanthrope.

The pitch of her Handler calling for help brought her out of the void. Kayn darted over, yanked Zach out of harm's way and tossed him into the protected area.

Zach shouted, "Grab the boy!"

On autopilot, she also yanked the Lycanthrope out of the clutches of the demonic cloud and rifled him into the circle of salt. The young Lycan staggered into Grey's arms.

Lexy called out, "Behind you! There's another one!"

In a blur of curly blonde mane, Kayn spun and raced at the merciless abomination clawing through the sand towards the group. Mid instinctual attack, it occurred to her she didn't have a plan. She dove out of the way, narrowly avoiding a well-timed swipe of the depravity's claws, skidding through the sand on her stomach. The shiny, scaly abomination shifted direction and came at her as she scrambled away. More incapacitating onyx fog appeared. Kayn released a primal shriek as she ingested the vapour through her pores. She succumbed to the euphoria for the blink of an eye and snapped back to reality with the lizard like atrocity's claws submerged in her abdomen. In glorious, delicious agony as the monstrosity lifted her impaled body into the air, with the sickeningly sweet taste of the blood in her mouth, her Ankh symbol strobed. While dangling precariously from the savage beast's claws, Kayn loudly declared, "I've got this!" Her Healing ability was fighting the good fight, healing her from the inside but it could do little more than keep her alive while impaled like meat on a skewer. Choking and sputtering up blood, she clawed at the beast's slick impermeable scales with what little nails she had. Her vision wavered. She opened her eyes to a clear view of the blood-drenched ground in front of her. *This wasn't good. It was pouring out of her. Fingers crossed she'd die before it ate her.* She stopped fighting as she hung like a kabob, watching her blood saturating the ground. *She was tired. She should go to sleep.*

Zach called her name," Kayn!"

Her eyes popped open. *No. This isn't over. Keep fighting.*

Touching the monster's scales at the base of its dagger-sharp nails, she willed an ability to surface. Unable to control which one, she released a potent wave of inhibition loosening pheromone into the air. The Lycanthrope began to change within the circle. *That can't be good.* Kayn gurgled as blood sputtered from her lips.

Zach couldn't take it anymore. Knife in hand, he dove from the protective circle into the sand. Grains sprayed, momentarily obscuring him from view. Before the dust settled, he was sprinting to Kayn's aid. He courageously leapt onto the monstrosities back and hung on for dear life while being tossed around like he was bareback riding a demonic bronco. Its spiked tail operated like a third arm, swiping him off. He tumbled across the sand.

Gasping as the monstrosity impaled her through the small of her back with its claws, she cried out in agony as the depravity savagely tugged its claws in opposite directions, opening her gut to an unsalvageable point. The fire of her healing ability fought against inevitable demise as she watched her Handler struggle to get up. Their eyes met, knowing it wasn't about saving her. *They were immortal. Sacrificial lamb was their job description. They wanted to keep their bodies, so it was about killing the beast before it ingested anyone.*

Her Handler was rifling stones at the monster, hollering, "Drop her! Come on! Come get me you slimy demonic, worthless piece of shit!" The beast's tail coiled around Zach like a snake, raised him into the air and pounded him into the dirt twice before catapulting him a good fifty feet.

That was going to leave a mark. An unexpected surge of adrenaline raced through her. Seething with rage, Kayn shivered as another burst of pheromone released. The Lycanthrope morphed into gigantic beastly feral wolves. They raced to her aid, attacking the beast, chomping on its limbs with their razor-sharp fangs. The demonic monstrosity raised its spiked tail and swiped them off like bothersome flies. The heroic Lycanthrope whimpered, struggling to get up. As they shook off the shock of their injuries, they continued rushing at the beast. *They were all going to die… For what? She'd had about enough of this!* Kayn fiercely ordered, "Release me!" The manifestation of evil turned her and gazed into her eyes. She calmly commanded, "Release me." It freed her from its skewers, dropping her in the sand. *It worked.* She felt her midriff but couldn't look, knowing her intestines were exposed. A scene from her Testing involving demons devouring her insides flashed through her mind. *Suck it up. Getting up was impossible, but she was a Dragon.* Kayn found the will to stand, with her hands clasped over her stomach. Her healing ability was working at full force to heal her game-ending injury, but it wasn't going to work fast enough. *Lights out time was coming. She was dizzy but prepared to keep fighting even if she tripped over her own intestines right before she died.* The beast inched closer until it was an arm's length away. Something changed in the monster's eyes as it knelt before her. Removing a hand from her stomach, Kayn reached out to touch it. The commotion instantly ceased. An injured Lycanthrope was pulling himself through the sand, still trying to come to her aid. *She needed energy to heal. The obvious choice was the mortally wounded Lycanthrope.* Kayn was about to take what she needed when it kissed her foot. *Even though her comprehensive sentiment skills had been dulled to almost non-existent, she couldn't bring herself to take from something that had given its life to protect her. Ingesting the physical manifestation of a powerful demonic entity also left her feeling hesitant. Feeling, was the operative word. Instinct was practically screaming its warning.* She turned to the other Dragon, who'd dutifully remained within the confines of the circle to heal her Clan.

Lexy shook her head, signalling disapproval of either choice.

Her attention was drawn to her Handler. Zach was lying motionless in the sand. She felt hollow as she sensed his soul's departure to the In-between. Renewed hostility encouraged her to ignore precautionary measures and digest the monster's essence. As she turned to the gigantic lizard-like being, it evaporated into a black mist and disintegrated into nothing. *Her time was up. No choices mattered.* Her stomach wound was healing rapidly, but she'd lost too much blood. Her knees buckled as she crumpled to the ground.

In seconds, Grey was kneeling before her. With his hands against her bare skin, he urged, "Take mine. You two have a lot of people to heal. I'll hang out with Zach in the In-between for a while. It's all good."

She couldn't find the will. She was too far gone. With a shuddering final breath, Kayn slipped away, succumbing to peaceful darkness.

8

IMPERMEABLE HEARTS

Kayn gasped as she awoke in a field of buttercups with Zach by her side, watching the clouds in the sky. She glanced over at him as she commented, "Well, that was a shit show."

Chuckling, he replied, "We had our asses kicked."

"Apparently," Kayn mumbled as she watched the clouds rapid movement. *She really had to figure out how her ability worked. Experimenting while in the middle of a fight had proven to be a ridiculous idea.*

"We need to figure out how to manage your energy cravings so we can keep you on an even keel," Zach proclaimed.

This was true. She had issues.

Her Handler teased, "And maybe a way to reign in your ego, just a bit."

She'd never had ego issues as a mortal. That was Chloe's thing.

Zach responded to her thoughts, "Remember, you're the same person now."

This was also true. Kayn plucked a buttercup from the ground and placed it under Zach's chin. *There was a shadow of yellow.* She said, "You like butter."

He laughed as he picked one and countered, "So do you."

Visions of Chloe and Frost flashed through her memory. A hint of jealousy surfaced, she shoved it down. *She was both Frost's girlfriend and his ex. She had memories of both relationships. It was confusing to say the least. Theoretically, she was jealous of herself, and that was silly. Sometimes it was difficult to fathom what she was. Who she was...*

Eavesdropping on her thoughts, Zach whispered, "Sometimes, I forget about how much bullshit you've had to sift through. It's only been, what? Five or six months?"

Less, but time was strange when you died on repeat. She met her Handler's understanding eyes as she replied, "I know I haven't made things easy on you. I'll do better. I'll try harder."

Chuckling, he tossed a handful of grass at her and sparred, "Sure you will."

"I will," Kayn promised. *She couldn't even keep a straight face long enough to say the sentence.*

Giving her arm a reassuring squeeze, Zach warmly responded, "You can't promise me anything and that's okay. You're a Dragon, being reckless and mentally unhinged is part of your mystery."

Gazing into her Handler's eyes, she was grateful for who he was. She began to disintegrate into the air, for she'd been healed and summoned back to the land of the living.

With a gasp, Kayn awoke. The lights were off, she was shaking, and there was this repetitive rattling sound. *She could smell paint. There was music playing. What in the hell?* It only took her a few seconds to determine she was in the trunk of a vehicle. *Well played afterlife… Well played.* Being jostled around by a large bump, she silently cursed. *What fresh hell was this? She'd woken up in some strange places, but she'd never come back from the In-between separated from the rest of her Clan before. Where were they?* She felt around, found a bag and unzipped it. *A roadside assistance kit! Score!* She discovered a flashlight and cheered on the inside when there was juice in the batteries. *There wasn't much room to manoeuvre. Something had obviously happened after she'd died. She wasn't with her Clan. They'd never chuck her soulless body into a trunk. What happened? Who had her? She still felt that same hollow sensation in her chest that she'd felt when he'd died and gone to the In-between without her. Where was Zach's body? Her Handler wasn't with her!* She dug through the bag using the flashlight and found road flares. *She could use these. Think Kayn! Think! There was a large can of tire sealant, matches and a jack. MacGyver could totally make a weapon with this. She wasn't MacGyver though and this wasn't a T.V show. She was just an immortal girl trapped in the trunk of a car for reasons unknown.* The vehicle went over a series of bumps and she began to suspect they were no longer on the highway. She scrolled through the list of feasible explanations. *More Demons showed up after she was dead. No, that couldn't be it. They'd eat her not take her for a car ride. The Lycanthrope put her dead body in their trunk because they knew she was immortal? No, that wasn't it. Had one of the other Clans kidnapped her? Now, that was a possibility, but why? They didn't have any Newbie Ankh to steal.* The can of paint tipped over and the lid came off as they went over another bump.

Come on! Seriously? She was covered in paint. Between the heat of the trunk and the paint fumes, she was going to be stoned out of her mind by the time someone let her out of this trunk. This was bullshit! She shone the flashlight on it to see the colour. *It was brilliant blue. Awesome, she was going to have to kick asses looking like Smurfette. That just shot her cool factor down about ten notches. Not like she'd ever broached semi-cool.* Something rolled past in her peripheral vision. *What was that?* She reached for it and grinned as she saw what it was. *Coffee whitener! Yes! She had fireplace accelerant and matches. Was paint also an accelerant?* She patted herself down and grinned. *They hadn't taken her phone. Why hadn't they restrained her? If it was Triad they would have, so would Trinity. They weren't stupid.* She could hear their conversation over the music. *She didn't recognize the voices but was able to decipher what happened. They were male and they were talking about the police. They were mortals! They had to be! Why hadn't they put her in the backseat? Oh yes… They'd found a dead body in the desert. What were the rules regarding this? She wasn't allowed to hurt mortals unless it was a Correction.*

One of her trunk chauffeur's asserted, "If we bring her to the police, they might think we did it?"

Another voice exclaimed, "If we left her, she would have been eaten by scavengers before we got back. Who would that serve?"

"Listen. I'm going to college in the fall. I don't want to be involved in this. Maybe we should just burn her and it's done. She's already dead," a male voice urged.

"Marisa is meeting us back at the ranch with the others.

She'll know what to do," a voice answered.

They were all speaking English. That was a bit peculiar. How long had she been out? The vehicle slowed and stopped. *Oh, lovely. Maybe they decided to burn the body.* Kayn remained silent, listening for information.

One male voice said, "Listen brother, get your shit together and stop whining before we get there. If Marisa even suspects you're a weak link, she'll just kill you."

Marisa… She'd never heard that name before, but by the sounds of things, this wasn't an honourable situation she'd found herself in. Whoever they were, a girl named Marisa was the one in charge. She needed to get out of the trunk. She was about to try kicking through to the backseat when it clicked, *these people could have her Clan. Being burned alive would suck but she'd been through worse. She needed to find the others and this was the most obvious route. Zach,* her mind whispered. *She had to find her Handler.* She heard a door slam. Tires were rumbling down what felt like a gravel road. *She needed perspective. She'd use this next slot of travel time to prepare an escape route, just in case.* She used the jack to carefully, quietly pry up a corner of the trunk to see the environment outside. *Maybe she'd get lucky and they'd pass a road sign?* She watched through her spy hole, wishing she was wearing enough clothing to hide stuff. *There was no room to hide anything in a tank top and shorts. How was she going to do this? Were they even still in Mexico? She'd had a hole in her stomach so large she had to hold her guts in. That would have taken a while to heal. It felt like she hadn't had much time with Zach in the In-between.,* Recalling a story about some older models having escape hatches, she started feeling around. *You could push the seat forward and climb into the backseat.* As her hand passed over a sticker, she grabbed the flashlight, turned it back on quickly to read it. *The vehicle was a 1989 model. The trunk may be super easy to get out of.* She shoved handfuls of coffee whitener into her shallow pockets and tucked the package of matches into her bra. She put a handful of whitener into each cup. *They might not frisk her again, assuming it was done properly the first time.* The car slowed and parked. *She wasn't incredibly concerned about anything happening to her. She was more worried about Zach. As much as she was his responsibility, he felt like hers. It was more than that, she could sense him. He was close by. She'd made the right move by keeping her cool. They'd brought her to the same place as the others.* She heard footsteps walking around the vehicle. *Should she play dead?* Kayn closed her eyes and remained still. The trunk opened to the glaring sun.

A female greeted her, "Welcome to Umbarto new Dragon of Ankh. I know you're awake, there's no point in playing dead. You've had plenty of time to heal."

Kayn squinted in the sunshine, unable to make out the features of the woman who'd called her bluff. *Blurry vision again. Awesome. She needed energy.* She went with what she'd overheard, "It's a pleasure to meet you, Marisa." As she tried to climb out, she heard multiple whooshes. *What in the?* Kayn glanced down. *Seriously? Five tranquillizers had been shot into her torso.* Plucking them out, she jumped out into the gravel and remarked, "Now, that wasn't very hospitable Marisa." A group of men stood around her with weapons raised. *She suspected these were bad people but their auras were mixed together. She was lightheaded. Whatever they'd tried to subdue her with was starting to kick in.*

"Again!" Marisa commanded.

More tranquillizers whooshed at her, piercing flesh. Irritated as hell, Kayn tugged them out. Oh shit! She staggered and her knees almost buckled. Hot damn, she was crazy dizzy. She addressed the woman in charge, "It would be in your best interest to take me to my friends before I get upset. You can't win this fight." Her vision focused as her healing ability counteracted the drugs. She could see their black smoky auras with purple, blue and green mixed. *Most were Abaddon but there were also mortals in the mix. She was extremely outnumbered but not concerned.*

"I'll bring you to your friends once you've done something for me," Marisa promised. "I'm going to need you to stay down longer so we can get everyone settled."

Good luck with that.

Marisa answered her thoughts, "I don't need luck with a 9 mm." She brandished her weapon, aimed it at Kayn's head and coldly pulled the trigger.

Kayn raised her hand intending to try to freeze time but wasn't fast enough. The bullet went right through her hand into her head and the lights went out.

Kayn awoke with her hands restrained behind her, inside of an almost see-through rough material. *She was so thirsty.* Drenched in salty perspiration, all she could smell were potatoes. *Peculiar. No matter how hard she tried, she couldn't rip apart her restraints. These must be Angel chains. They felt heavier than last time. Being disembowelled really took the wind out of her magical sails. Lovely.*

"Who's in here with me?" Grey's voice asked.

Oh, thank God. "It's Kayn," she answered. "Where are the others? What is this place?"

"I just came too, but if this is what I think it is, I have to get to Lexy," Grey's rattled voice answered.

She heard him struggling with his restraints, grunting and groaning, fighting to break free. *Lexy would be alright. Dragons were durable creatures.* She could feel Grey's anxiety.

"I have to get out of here! I need to be there when she comes too! Get us out of this! Hurry!" Grey panicked without a speck of concern for who might overhear.

There was obviously more going on than she understood. "Can you move at all? Roll towards me!" Kayn directed, knowing how she'd broken free last time. She heard Grey fighting to move closer.

He quietly revealed, "I'm almost touching you."

She needed water and fresh air more than energy. It felt like she was going to suffocate in this bag. Her throat was so dry. Were Zach and Lexy in a similar situation? Kayn squirmed as close as she could, needing contact with his skin. *She was going to need at least one hand free of these chains. She might have to break her thumb.*

"That might work if the restraints weren't spelled and we weren't in sacks," Grey commented.

"I'm just pitching out random ideas quit brain stalking me!" Kayn countered as she tried to tear the material behind her. She could see through it and it smelled peculiar. *Manure mixed with dirt?*

"There's a hole in mine close to my fingers in the back," he directed.

Kayn concentrated moving her fingers around until she felt the change in temperature from a lack of material. "Okay! I can feel air! Shift so we're back to back, I need contact with your skin." They rolled around and adjusted themselves until their fingers touched.

Grey asserted, "Take what you need. Just heal me before you do anything else! Promise me! Lexy needs me!"

"I promise," Kayn vowed as she locked fingers with Grey and tried to take his energy. *It wasn't working. Why wasn't it working? Maybe, she wasn't strong enough?*

"Try again!" He frantically urged. "Come on, Brighton! I have to get to her!"

Kayn willed her ability to start but no dice. "It's not going to work," she gasped.

"It has too," he implored. "You don't understand. She was kidnapped at eleven and held somewhere like this by Abaddon for five years. She endured unthinkable brutality as a child. The details are the same right down to the potato sacks we're in. If she wakes up in a potato sack and there's hay beneath her, I don't know what she'll do."

Kayn's blood ran cold. *She hadn't known that about her sister. That's why she kept saying, you left me there. You left me on that farm to Seth.*

"Kayn! Are you still with me?" Grey prodded as he clutched her fingers with his.

"I didn't know," Kayn whispered as she fought to gather her bearings. *Lexy was a Healer. She was already awake if they were. Hopefully, she was with Zach. She was so dizzy.*

Grey snapped her out of her thoughts, "Now Kayn!"

She clutched his fingers once more and willed her ability to work with everything she had. *She felt it!* Her hands warmed as the energy travelled up her arms and gathered in her core. She snapped the chains that bound her and tore her way out of the potato sack as though it were tissue paper. *It felt like being reborn as the breeze caressed her skin.* Adrenaline was surging through her body as she crawled over, tore Grey's bag off and broke his Angel chains. *He wasn't dead, just unconscious.* She lifted his shirt and placed her hands on his chest, intending to revive him. *She didn't have the juice. She needed energy again. Had breaking Angel chains and tearing open a potato sack really taken that much out of her?* There was noise outside the door. *Time to recharge her battery.* She leapt up and raced over to conceal herself from those who dared enter. *Please be Abaddon. Please be Abaddon. She was starving. It felt like Conduit meals on wheels as one lone man entered with a trail of black smoky aura. Silly demons. They never appear to have any foresight at all.* He was about to call out and warn the others. In a flash, she had him in a headlock, draining the life from his body. He slumped to the floor. The pull to find sustenance was over-whelming as Grey's words replayed in her mind... *Promise me.* She knelt in the hay, placed her hands on his chest and healed him until his eyes fluttered. She declared, "Let's go get Lexy and Zach!"

"Lexy," he whispered, still out of it.

As Kayn was helping him to his feet, the door swung open. She dove in front of Grey as Abaddon unloaded their tranq guns on her. *She lost count at ten. How was she still standing? Weird?* She tossed Grey into the hay, raced at the shooters in the doorway, snapped the first one's neck, and soccer ball booted the other in the junk. His dart gun emptied into her chest as he went down. Smirking at the Abaddon, rolling around in agony on the ground as she rather nonchalantly tugged the darts out of her torso, she heard the click behind her. *Shit!* A shot rang out.

This time when Kayn came to, she wasn't in a potato sack on the floor of a stall. Her arms were once again bound but to a wooden post, with her ankles chained. *These were all things she knew without even having to open her eyes.*

They opened to the commotion of the Abandon towing a struggling Grey into the room. They tied him to the post behind her. *Thanks for making it super easy to escape.* There was an old TV on a rolling cart in front of them. She was tied to a post, standing on what appeared to be kindling. *Wonderful. She had accelerant and a pack of matches hidden in her bra. This would have gone badly. Luckily, she had a plan.* Before she had the opportunity to put it to action, Marisa strolled into the room. *That bitch shot her in the head… twice. She was going to eat her first.* Grinning, Kayn politely enquired, "Are you planning to shoot me in the head a third time?"

The dark-featured woman countered, "Not a chance. I'm quite looking forward to watching you burn. Well, that's only if we can't come to an agreement."

Way to just put your evil plot out there. She wasn't the sharpest tool in the shed or barn as this case may be. Kayn sighed, "Stop pussyfooting around and spill it."

"Why don't I show you what I have to bargain with first?" Marisa rebutted as she turned on the T.V in front of her. It was Zach. *He'd been bound and gagged. Alright, she was irritated by the mistreatment of her Handler, but Zach could handle being bound and gagged. He was fighting awfully hard to get away? Why was he freaking out?* The camera altered position and changed perspective as he was tossed into a shallow grave. He was hysterically screaming through his gag. *During his Correction, his abusive stepfather buried him alive in a cornfield. She'd heard the story, but he was past that, wasn't he?* Marisa's henchmen began pouring gasoline all over him. The person filming changed position and there was a man poised above Zach holding a pack of matches. Her pulse started racing, as she felt her Handler's fear. *This was a shitty way to die.*

Marisa baited, "Now that I have your attention, I'd like to make a little deal with you."

"What would that be?" Kayn enquired, viewing her Handler's predicament. *She was going to rip off these chains and beat the shit out of this demonic piece of crap.*

"I wouldn't try anything. Do you honestly think we were stupid enough to bring you to the same place?" Marisa interjected.

She'd responded to her thoughts again. Irritated, Kayn quipped, "Touch my Handler again and I'll tear you to pieces. Have I made that clear enough for you?"

"Oh, there's no need for me to mess up a hair on that young hotties head," Marisa clarified. "Word gets around awfully fast in our community. All you have to do is create one of those orbs and send us all back through the Hall of Souls for a fresh start."

She wasn't allowed to do that. Kayn countered, "I'm afraid you've been given faulty information."

Marisa picked up a walkie talkie, pressed the button and said, "She says, she can't do it."

On the screen, Abaddon's thug lit a match and held it over top of her squirming terrified Handler. He spoke aloud, "Shall I drop it?"

Zach's terror concerned her. Yes, they all had sensitive scenarios, but she felt like there was more going on here. Something, she wasn't seeing. "No! No, don't! Give me a second!" Kayn bartered. *She'd healed herself from death twice in the last hour. She was so gapped out. I guess being shot twice in the head came with a few glitches. It felt like crickets were chirping away where thoughts should be. She was touching Grey. She could inconspicuously drain him of energy so she'd have enough strength to break the chains.* Kayn connected with the small of his back. The euphoric wave of lifeforce travelled up her arms, causing the fine hairs to stand on end. It gathered in her chest and her foggy brain focused. She broke free. In a flash, she had one of Marisa's men by the throat.

"Simmer down sweetheart," Abaddon's boss asserted. "I'll tell him to drop the match. You know your friend doesn't want to have to find a new body."

The instinct to protect her Handler at any cost left her confused. She hadn't been immortal long enough to know if she was telling the truth and Grey was out cold. She was going to be eighty before she saw Frost again if she kept breaking the rules. What did she have to lose now? It was going to be months before she saw him. Kayn released Marisa's demonic thug, shoved him to the ground and bargained, "I'll do it but Grey goes first. I'll also need to see the others freed."

"Excellent!" Marisa replied. "I knew you were an intelligent girl." She pressed the button on the radio, clarifying he would be released as soon as the duty was completed.

This felt too easy. A woman marched out, pushing another rolling table with a dagger on it. *She'd seen that symbol before.*

Marisa directed, "Make a ball of energy and place it in the blade."

"I don't know how to do that?" Kayn rebutted.

"Okay, let's put a time limit on this." She pressed the button and ordered, "Start burying the boy!"

They started burying her Handler, a shovel load at a time. Kayn calmly asserted, "I really don't know how to do it but I'll try. I also told you, they must be released first. Don't think I won't kill you."

Marisa replied, "I wouldn't be that foolish. Just like I wouldn't be idiotic enough to detain you in the same place. There's an easy fix to this. Put the energy into the blade and I'll release your friends."

As Kayn stepped closer to the blade, Kevin's voice rang out in her head, *'No! Don't do it! We're here! We have the others! You can't arm that weapon! Take yourself out!'* She paused, confused as to how Kevin's voice was in her head. *She was part Guardian. Maybe, that was why? Perhaps, it was because he was the original choice for her Handler? Could she trust him? She looked at the screen. Zach was still being buried. It didn't look like anyone was there to free him.* She took another step closer, without her eyes leaving the blade on the table for a millisecond.

Kevin's voice whispered in her mind, *'Do you remember when we were thirteen and we were caught sneaking your dad's homemade beer out of your carport? I told your dad it was all me. I said it was my idea and you didn't even know I had it. I promised you I would always have your back. Please, believe in me now.'*

Kayn stopped, looked at her captors and said, "I'll do it but let Grey go first."

Marisa nodded her silent agreement as Kayn turned around, strolled back to Grey and slipped her hands beneath his shirt. She felt the heat of her healing energy as it travelled down her arms into his chest. Grey's eyes opened. He gasped as she ripped off his restraints, kissed his cheek and whispered, "Go with it." With icy resolve, Kayn turned to face their captors. *Everyone was scrambling around. On the screen Zach was being saved by Triad. Kevin was telling the truth. She couldn't let them take her.*

Walking towards Kayn with her gun drawn, Marisa announced, "Well, it appears that we've lost some of our bartering tools but I still have one person you care about."

It was sacrificial lamb time. Kayn removed the pack of matches from her bra, struck one and exclaimed, "I've covered myself in accelerant and you've pissed me off." She lit herself on fire as a glorious, blazing F-U to Abaddon. She became an inferno of agony. Her senses were shrieking as Grey took her hand, sucked the flames into himself with a deep breath and used his ability to spray fire from his free hand, scorching the Abaddon. Some managed to dive out of the way and scamper out of the barn. With Marisa's mortal shell engulfed in flames, she emptied her gun's chamber into Grey. He crumpled to the floor, breaking the connection.

Clutching Kayn's charcoaled sizzling blistered arms, Marisa breathlessly hissed, "Send me through the Hall of Souls!"

Kayn coldly countered, "Never." She sunk to her knees as the pain ceased, raised her eyes to the doorway and locked eyes with Kevin's as she lost consciousness.

9

KEVIN OF TRIAD

Kevin spent the first year of immortality blissfully unaware of who he was or what he'd given up. *He wasn't stupid. He knew his memory had been erased because he couldn't recall a thing before coming to Triad.* With the help of his inner voice, he managed to fit in. It may seem odd to just go with it while listening to a female voice in your head but the girl who called herself Winnie had never steered him wrong. He'd managed to bond with his Grandfather who was the leader of the Clan while following orders without question. In no time, he became his shining prodigy. The others often referred to him as the Prince of Triad. *It made him feel important, but every so often, he felt the emptiness of something missing. He knew he'd suffered a loss, he just wasn't sure who.* Thankfully, he managed to make friends along the way. Patrick and Stephanie became his closest companions. The trio lived life to its hedonistic fullest as any self-loathing immortals would do. They were always there to secretly console each other when life in Triad became too dark. Eventually, his relationship with Stephanie became more. Plagued with unexplainable guilt, instinct urged him to slow the intimate part of their relationship. He was relieved when she seemed content keeping it casual.

The trio stuck together through the utter insanity of that first year. Their training was harrowing to say the least. There was no room for an operational moral compass in Triad. Each day, Kevin embraced his shady duties while being continuously reminded by Winnie that survival was the objective. Each night as Kevin slept, he dreamt of a girl with a smile that defrosted his soul. This intoxicating stranger with curly blonde locks gave his spirit new light and made him resilient enough to withstand the trials of Triad. He awoke each morning, longing for the dreams to continue, and they did, for nearly a year.

Kevin had been coping with the stress rather well until he ran into the girl from his dreams at the track that day. The sight of her snuffed out reason. *She was real. He couldn't believe it.* Captivated by his fantasy, he watched her sprinting around the track. When their eyes met, she wiped out. He raced to her aid. As Kevin took her hand to help her up, he was enamoured. *He wasn't one to be mushy and sentimental, but he was one-hundred percent certain, she meant something to him.* The glorious euphoria was followed by a gut punch as he saw the brand of Ankh on her palm. It was self-preservation that urged him to be a dick as he let her go. As he walked away, he had to fight against the instinct to turn back. *She was real.* In an instant, Kevin's afterlife changed and he couldn't pretend there was nothing before Triad anymore.

Winnie's voice urged him to keep his distance, so he remained by Patrick and Stephanie's side as they joined their Clan by the school. As the girl of his dreams strolled past with a blonde guy, irrational jealousy surged within him. Tiberius began messing with the guy named Grey, calling him his brother from down under. Grey directed part of the conversation to Kevin, making it obvious they knew each other. Tiberius turned his sights to the blonde girl. Her witty interaction with his grandfather left him even more intrigued. As she walked away, visions of her invaded his system like a plague.

Later that day, they ran into each other by the water. She was standing on the dock with her Clan wearing granny panties and a bra. They were all jumping into the freezing cold lake. He was ready to just chuck it all and wave his flag of surrender. *He had to know the truth.* When he questioned his Grandfather about his memory, Tiberius told him he'd erased it so he wouldn't have to carry the pain of losing the love of his life. He gave him a pep talk about wasting his time and hers, because they were in different Clans. By the time he finished his explanation, he felt compelled to do Kayn a service by letting her go.

Kevin wasn't sure why he went to the track that night. Perhaps, it was to make peace within himself, but when Kayn raced into his arms, he instinctually opened them. Her hair smelled of apples and her skin like coconuts. Holding her felt so familiar and right. The emotion in her eyes reached right down into his soul and made him want to do right by her. *She was in pain.*

Losing him had been difficult. His Grandfather's words leapt out of his mouth and the more she tried to bargain with him, the more he fought against what his heart wanted and pushed her away. He spent the rest of the evening confused and guilt-ridden. He dreamt of her and the visions were so intoxicating, he awoke desperate to know more about her even if it was the wrong thing to do.

Kevin only saw her in passing that day because his Clan was busy training, but that night Tri-Clan attended a banquet together. He knew he was going to bump into her. He spent the beginning of the evening struggling to keep himself from even looking at her, but that proved to be impossible because she looked like a naughty librarian. He tried to concentrate on his friends but everything about her was intriguing. Each time she smiled, his eyes were drawn to her. He'd quickly look away so Kayn wouldn't catch him staring. Her presence felt like the warmth of sunshine on his soul. Tiberius involved him in shenanigans that evening by calling him over to her table and introducing him as his Grandson. With music and wine everyone loosened up and had a good time together regardless of their Clan. He wanted to go over to Kayn's table and apologize for the way he'd treated her at the track but decided against it. She'd all but pledged her eternal devotion to him last night but there was obviously something going on between her and Frost. *A guy who was ironically his uncle. Watching her trying to move on felt like a gut punch.* His attention was drawn to Tiberius chatting with a breathtaking girl from Ankh. *He knew who the girl was, they'd all heard the story of the Brothers of Prophecy.* He was sort of paying attention when he was pulled into a diabolical plot to seduce and kill Kayn during Testing. Blindly following an Oracle's word was a normal Tri-Clan request, but he already felt guilty for not remembering the details of their relationship. After seeing Frost giving her a foot massage on the couch, he started drinking heavily. *It stung way more than it made sense to admit.* The rest of the evening was a blur.

The next day Kevin awoke to his cell blinking on the nightstand. There was a text telling him to make sure he didn't get too attached. Everyone had left for the Summit or gone into town and his usual bed mates must have had a good night. He was sitting at the table having a coffee when he had a flash of twin blonde little girls running around someone's yard with bubbles floating in the air. He wasn't sure what it meant, but as he reached for the doorknob, he had another flicker of Kayn pinned against the bathroom counter during a steamy makeout session. He carried her into the bedroom with her legs wrapped around his waist and dropped her as a man opened the door. They were laughing after he closed it. *Were these real memories or was his mind playing tricks on him?* They'd been left at the camp alone with the others heading into Testing. With his uncle gone, there was nobody in their way. He went to find her. *What could it hurt to just take this out for a spin? Maybe it would give her closure? There was no way in hell he was going to be able to force himself to stay away if he kept having these naughty daydreams.*

During that week breadcrumbs of memories returned, and even though he didn't have the full picture in his mind, his heart did. They spent their days living blissfully in the moment, but each night as he slept, dreams showed him how killing Kayn during the Testing would ensure her survival. The closer they became, the more confusion he felt over what he'd been instructed to do. *Kayn was funny and smart. She knew random facts about peculiar things. She was endearingly clumsy and he was desperate to continue being close to her even if it came with a few bruises.* He couldn't bring himself to take her virginity even though he wanted her more than he'd ever wanted anyone. Their love was grown during a mortal life he vaguely recalled. He'd try to talk sense into her and pull away, but selfishly, he couldn't let her go. By the end of their week together, Kevin was head over heels in love with her and what he wanted ceased to be of any importance. She didn't have any abilities and others were going into the Testing well-armed. Kayn was going to die in there, unless he was willing to sacrifice what was left of his humanity to save her. *He knew this…* He ripped off the band-aid the night before the others were scheduled to return and said goodbye. He planned to trade what little of his humanity remained for her survival. She would despise him for a long time. It would tear him apart, but if she survived, it would be worth it.

The next day, when the others returned, they were led away from the campground and brought through their Triad Crypt into another realm. In the blink of an eye, Kevin was standing on the top of a New York City sized floating Crypt. He could see Stephanie, Patrick and the other Triad. They were a good fifty feet apart. This Crypt was intimidating and he couldn't really explain why, but it felt alive.

Tiberius started to speak, "I know you feel like you've created bonds, but trust me, they are no longer your friends. Kill everything that moves in there. The other Clans have been instructed to do the same. Find Triad and stay with them. You can only make it out if you remain together. If you want the girl to survive this, kill her and walk away. Concentrate on getting out with your Clan. They'll be looking to you for leadership. Good luck."

Kevin dropped into the Crypt and landed with a splash. After being eaten by sharks repeatedly and dying countless times, he was flushed out of the bottom of one chamber into another. He managed to climb through an opening in the wall as the water rose into a dry chamber. The wall slid shut leaving him alone in the dark. *He had to find his Clan.* He heard multiple growls as dozens of oval glowing yellow eyes opened. *Well, shit! This can't be good.* Before he could even think of a way to escape, he was being savagely torn apart. He heard high-pitched shrieks like they were coming from someone else and then there was nothing.

He awoke in a different room just as the wall slid open and scrambled to his feet. Trinity charged him, weapons brandished. Evasively dodging each swing of their swords, Kevin held up his hands and explained his predicament. "I know we're supposed to fight, but I just got in here. It's not exactly fair, I don't even have a weapon."

A Trinity boy, he'd gotten to know during the last week coldly replied, "Fair? Really? Thank Stephanie," as he swung his sword, lopping off Kevin's arm at his shoulder.

What? Why? In shock, Kevin stood watching his blood spurt in long pronounced bursts, as a Trinity drove a sword into his heart. Blood sputtered from his lips as he staggered backwards and crumpled to the floor.

He woke up with his nerve endings jangling in what appeared to be the stone cell. *There was blood everywhere. His blood. Don't think about it. Do not even think about that.* Kevin leapt up and whirled around with his heart palpitating like a kick drum. *It hurt. Was he having a stroke? Why was his chest burning? Oh, yes... The blood. He'd been stabbed in the heart. Did those assholes really just chop off his arm?* He felt his shoulder and exhaled, relieved it was still there. Paranoia took over as he spun watching the walls trying to pre-empt a redo of what just happened. *He was dizzy.* He staggered but managed to regain his footing. *How many times had he died? That was his blood. It was everywhere. He had to snap out of this or he wasn't going to make it back to his Clan. He thought of Kayn and saw a foggy image of her running through the maze.* Kevin's knees buckled as an excruciating wave of pain unlike anything he'd ever experienced imploded within his brain. He was on the floor, squirming and writhing in agony as the fire beneath his temples raged. *What was this?* Kayn crossed his mind. His breathing calmed as he thought of her wide loving smile. The way it felt to hold her in his arms and how her lips felt against his. How much he loved everything about her. This time the vision of her was clear and painless. He had to keep an eye on her but first things first, he needed a weapon. Sprinting through stone walls that pre-emptively moved like they had motion sensors he stole a blade from the next Trinity he bumped into and fought to remain on task while having frequent vivid flashes of his mortal life. He was remembering everything, just a little too late for it to matter.

A wall slid away revealing Zach. He attacked him. Kayn was crouched in the corner. *He wasn't ready to do it.* He kept track of her, always maintaining his distance. *They'd already said goodbye. He'd confuse things by approaching her.* Another vision of Triad at a banquet flashed. He snapped back to reality. *It would be helpful if these abilities came with instructions.* Winnie's words replayed, *'She only survives if you kill her.'* Kevin wasn't remotely paying attention as he strolled through a sliding wall into the middle of a Triad, Trinity knife fight. *He'd found his Clan.* Triad battled their way through Testing in a haze of excruciating pain and violence. Stephanie jumped on board with the darkest because torture was her thing. *He knew this… They dated.* Eventually, it was just a blur of monsters and artery spray.

During the carnage Kevin became separated from his Clan. He'd been on his own for a while when he came upon Kayn sitting by a fountain. *What was she doing? Everything gathers around a watering hole.* She was perched on the ledge fishing around in the water. *She found a sword. Good for her.* For a moment time stood still, he forgot everything except how she made him feel. In another life she'd be his wife, he'd spend the rest of his days doing nothing but striving to see her smile. Flashes of mortality brought him back to their last encounter as they were forced to part ways standing in the sand of the In-between, crying while clinging to each other. He recalled memorizing the placement of each freckle so he'd never forget, and he hadn't. *He'd felt her love in his dreams before ever knowing who she was. He'd counted her freckles as he slept and longed to touch her hand. His heart remembered her even with his memories erased. Killing her would destroy him. How was he going to do this?* He heard muffled conversation. *Someone was coming. Kayn was oblivious. Damn it. She had to get down.* He threw a ceramic bowl to warn her. She walked into it. He smoked her square on the noggin. *Shit!* Stunned, Kayn stumbled while wielding the sword. He sprinted to her aid, shoved her down and pinned her to the floor as she struggled. Covering her mouth so she couldn't scream, he hissed, "Damn it, Brighton. Just stay the hell down." He heard the clashing of swords and leapt up, fully prepared to fight. *Plot twist, Trinity was having a tiff. They were fighting each other.* Kayn raced into an open sleep chamber while he was dumbfounded by Inter-Clan battle. A door slid shut. Without a speck of common sense, he sprinted after her. Outnumbered, Kevin placed his hand against the stone. *They noticed him. At least she was safe. This was going to suck.* The wall slid open and he dove inside. It shut a millisecond before they reached it.

They stared at each other, just breathing. "Why in the hell did you let me in? You're not supposed to let me in," Kevin reprimanded while pacing back and forth, avoiding eye contact. He stopped moving, turned to face her and scolded, "We are supposed to be enemies. They could be watching us right now."

Pointing out the stones situated around the room, she declared, "Let there be silence inside of the circle."
Kevin let out an exasperated sigh. *She didn't even know the words.*

She tried again, "Let there be silence outside of this circle?"

She had no sense of self-preservation. Why did she let him in?

"How's Stephanie?" Kayn coldly enquired.

Aggravated, he took a step closer. Under his breath he harshly responded, "Are you joking? This is our Testing. This is serious shit. I've always been your enemy. You have always been mine. We took a vacation from reality. You can't keep dramatically pausing in the middle of the fight to stare at me." She shook her head in disbelief so he callously clarified, "We have nothing left. We're done. Stay away from me. Run away and hide if you see me. I don't want to have to hurt you. I don't want that on my conscience."

With her back up, she retaliated, "You know what! You followed me in here! Where do you get off saying I'm being friggin dramatic? You were looking at me too!"

"Listen, I was told to entertain you," he fibbed. "I was ordered to get to know you. You're a nice person. I like you and I'm not a complete ass, regardless of what you might think. That is the only reason I came in here. I'm here to warn you, just this once. I have to kill you the next time you're standing in my way when my Clan is around."

Stepping closer, Kayn questioned, "Could you kill me? Could you sink that knife into my chest without dying inside yourself?"

He had to make her hate him. Turning his expression to stone, Kevin took out his blade and backed her up against the wall, saying, "Last week was nothing more than a lapse in judgment on your behalf. I knew you would let me in. Maybe, I came in here to kill you?"

With complete trust in her eyes, Kayn grabbed the end of his blade, raised it to her heart, and placed the tip against her skin. She whispered, "Then just kill me and quit acting. That's what you have been doing all week right? If you have no feelings at all for me, it should be easy."

With their gazes locked, he fought the urge to take her into his arms as images flashed from their mortal lives. *He loved her too much. He couldn't do it. He just couldn't.* They stood there, staring into each other's eyes until his teared up.

As she lovingly caressed his cheek, he closed his eyes. *Damn it.* Folding like a cheap deck of cards with a touch, he shifted the thin material on the neckline of her dress, tenderly tracing the thin ridge of a scar with his thumb. A memory flashed of sitting with her while she was in a coma. A surge of emotion overcame him as tears began flowing down his cheeks. *He adored her with everything he was and all he ever would be.* Kevin slid the shoulder of her dress down and seductively kissed her throat with his blade pressed against her chest. *He couldn't control himself. He had to have her.* Nuzzling her neck, he buried his face in her curls, whispering, "Damn it, Kayn." Surrendering to emotion, he dropped the knife and it tinged to the floor. She snuggled into him as they clung to each other. *He would let her kill him. Maybe it would work the same way if she killed him?* He whispered against her hair, "You have to kill me the next time you see me. Make it look real. I want you to. I need you to be the one to do it. We have to look like enemies."

Squeezing him tighter, Kayn whispered through her tears, "I knew you'd come back to me."

No. No. She didn't understand. He would always love her but being together wasn't an option. With agony in his eyes, he asserted, "I'm not back… We can never go back to who we were. Don't you get it? You have to stop loving me." He abruptly turned and walked away from her.

"You love me too," Kayn whispered. "I know you do."

Yes… with his whole heart but he shouldn't. He was going to have to be cruel. If she despised him it would be easier for her to kill him. His heart was aching as he placed the heel of his hand in the grooves on the door to leave. As it slid open, he bluntly barbed, "Loving you would be pointless."

The wall ground shut and the coast was clear. He sprinted away, desperate for distance between them. He raced through each wall as it opened, purposely trying to get lost in the maze so he couldn't find his way back to her. He had to get a handle on his emotions. Memories of Kayn continued to flash through his mind as he died countless times in increasingly traumatizing ways by various creatures. After having the flesh melted from his bones by lava spitting tigers, he'd been pursued by clowns with chainsaws and had fallen into a pit of fire ants. *He was beginning to under-stand what this place really was… It was hell. He'd lost his Clan because his focus wasn't on them. It had to be now.* He found his way through the insanity back to Patrick, Stephanie and the others. They endured the simulation of eternal damnation until they hit a break in the madness.

Out of the blue, Stephanie asked, "Did you have a chance to kill your girlfriend yet?"

Knowing it was important to act like he no longer cared, Kevin kept his expression vacant as he answered, "I don't have a girlfriend, Steph. I had fun and it's over. She means nothing to me."

"Good… I'm tired of playing nice," she replied.

He kept his reaction shoved down as he sparred, "You don't have to play nice anymore. Just be yourself."

"Ouch," Steph sparred as a lone Monarch butterfly fluttered down the long stone corridor.

It felt like a trap. Completely unfazed, Stephanie held out her hand. It landed on her palm, and for a second, Kevin wondered if his instincts were wrong. They gathered around to take in the Monarch's beauty, grateful to see something colourful in the endless stone maze.

Stephanie scowled and said, "Ouch! The little stinker just bit me! Monarch butterflies don't bite?" Instead of yanking her hand away, she allowed it to continue feasting on her flesh as she observed.

"Don't just let it bite you!" Patrick scolded.

Stephanie smiled as she clapped her hands and squished the beautiful thing. Kevin shook his head. He strolled behind his group while they bickered about whether any species of butterflies on Earth bite. They passed through an open wall into a room. It slid shut. The ceiling rumbled. They all looked up. *Shit!* The slab of stone above sped down and squished them all like bugs.

Regaining consciousness, Kevin inhaled stale Crypt air. *His airway felt like it had been scalded with boiling water.* He was the only one sitting in a long stone corridor. The rest of his Clan appeared as flickering holograms scattered down the tunnel. After they'd solidified, they opted to take turns being the first to enter each room. This plan gave them a reprieve from the torture for a while but there was no stay of execution in purgatory. Each death they managed to avoid only became more brutal in the version that followed until they just began running head on into the madness of their next demise. They fought when they could, but most of the time, they just died gruesomely.

It was his turn to be the first one into the room. Kevin stepped inside and the wall slid shut. He looked up as something dropped through the ceiling and knocked him to the ground. In survival mode, he tossed it away and scrambled to his feet with his heart racing, ready to rumble, clutching his silver dagger. It was Kayn with a knife in her grasp. *The others were going to step through that wall any second. She'd be slaughtered.* There was the briefest moment of a standoff. *Fight me, Brighton.* He shoved her against the wall. *Fight back.* They began to struggle. The stone slid open and they fell through into another room. Kayn landed on top of him with her knife poised above his stomach. He nodded his consent. *Come on! Kill me!*

With their gazes locked, she whispered, "I can't."

"It will make me feel a whole lot better if you stab me first," Kevin quietly asserted as grinding of stone on stone let them know their moment alone was over. They scrambled to their feet. He grabbed hold of her arm and towed her through the next few sliding walls. As they paused to catch their breath, Kevin gasped, "If you're not going to kill me, you have to get out of here.

If I get caught helping you it will just make things worse. We can only get out of this place with our Clans. I can't afford to have them all pissed off. Go find your's."

She shoved him and accused, "You were the one that yanked me through the last couple of walls! You could have just left me there!"

The walls began to shift again. They sprinted down the next corridor. A large part of the floor was gone. Without missing a beat, Kayn leapt over it but didn't make it. She was dangling from the ledge. Kevin made the jump. He grabbed hold of her wrists as she slipped. Beneath her was the sound of rushing water. Struggling to hold on, he hollered, "I can't keep doing this! We can't keep doing this!"

Staring into his eyes, Kayn shouted, "Then let me go!" She slid a bit. He grasped a hold of her tighter.

The wall started to open behind them and he said, "Hold your breath," as he released her. She plummeted into the darkness. He heard a splash. Stephanie and Patrick were standing there as he leapt in after her. He sputtered to the surface of the swiftly moving current, vigorously treading water as he searched for her. She was fighting to grab hold of the roots and foliage as the force of the rapids mercilessly took them downstream.

"Kevin!" she called out as she disappeared.

He heard the roaring of the waterfall, held his breath, and dropped a good fifty feet, managing to hit the water at a good angle. He surfaced, swam for Kayn's partially submerged body and towed her to shore. *They saw him jump. Hopefully, they didn't know why. This would cause drama.* He carried her limp body behind the falls and gently placed her on the stone. Being hidden behind a veil of water didn't offer much protection. Intending to lead Triad away if they showed up before Kayn woke, he emerged from behind the watery veil into the breathtaking jungle. Looking around, it was lush greenery in every direction. *They would be here by now.* With no obvious way out, he picked fruit while glancing back at the waterfall until he was confident Triad hadn't followed. When longing for more time with her, defeated reason, he returned with mystery fruit and sat back against the stone with his snack while shaking his head at himself. *Why didn't he just let her go?* She opened her eyes and he teased, "You're not supposed to attempt to do a belly flop from that height. I thought everyone knew that little rule of life."

"Do I hear birds? I swear I can hear birds," Kayn exclaimed as she sat up.

He handed her a piece of mystery fruit. "We're in the jungle," Kevin explained. "I have no idea how that's even possible but we're here. I've looked around. There doesn't appear to be an obvious way out. We could be trapped together for a while."

Kayn took a bite of fruit, laughing as it gushed down her chin.

Why did she have to be so likeable? Her weirdness was undeniably endearing. The fruit juice was still dripping from her chin. He scooted closer and wiped it off with his hand. She smiled, and he returned the gesture. Their eyes met, and with everything inside of him, he wanted to kiss her. She innocently bit her lip. His parted and he had to talk himself out of it. *No. It'll just make it harder.* He quickly retreated to where he'd been sitting before, conflicted. *They really needed to go somewhere with less ambiance. If they didn't,* he was going to do something they'd both regret. He got up and offered her his hand with the mystical soundtrack of the waterfall in the background. He helped her up and she squeezed his hand before letting it go. His heart ached with the knowledge of what he knew he had to do to assure her survival. Kevin's eyes softened. While trying to use ration, he clarified, "We're making this more difficult than it needs to be. We need to find our Clans. We can't get out of the Testing together. What if we lose our chance to get out of this place, while we're wasting time messing with fate?" She grabbed his wrist and urged him closer with a gentle tug. With raw emotion in his eyes, he cautioned, "Don't."

She pushed him a touch further, "Kiss me goodbye?"

He moved in as he gently caressed her cheek. *She had the softest skin.* In awe of her, he confessed, "I'm always fighting the urge to count your freckles... Why is that? I can't even force myself to hurt you. I couldn't let go of your hand without jumping in after you. We're never getting out of here if we don't stay away from each other. It's not that I don't want you. It's that I can't." He took her hand and placed it on the Triad symbol branded on the flesh above his heart. Kayn intimately traced his symbol with her finger as she tenderly kissed his lips. *She was killing him. He wasn't going to be able to stop himself if she kept pushing his buttons like this. He decided to call her bluff.* Emotion caught in Kevin's throat as he whispered, "Is this what you want?" Walking her backwards until her body was pressed against the stone, tension rose to a tumultuous peak. A breath away from their lips touching hers, his conscience gave him a poke.

"I know you want me too," Kayn provoked as she ran her fingers through his hair and drew his lips the rest of the way in.

He did. So badly. His parted lips seductively met hers. He pushed her further by slipping his hands beneath the sparse material assuming she'd stop him, but she didn't. She gasped with breathless abandon as he caressed her, He was trying to push her limits, but she was all in, and heaven help him so was he. *He had to have her.*

She whispered, "I love you."

He abruptly pulled away like she'd launched a bucket of ice water at him. *What was he doing?* He blocked her hand and cautioned, "If you keep trying to seduce me, Kayn. I'm going to give you exactly what you're asking for. I don't have the strength to keep turning you down."

"I know you care about me," Kayn whispered as her eyes searched for the truth in his.

Placing his hand against her chest to keep her from coming closer, he admitted, "Of course I do but the guy you're in love with is gone. That's not who I am. I could never be him and survive in Triad. I had to become colder and stronger to be a leader. The person I need to be to survive is the opposite of what you want."

"I hear what you're saying," she implored. "I know you're right, but can't we pretend for a while longer?"

Fighting against the urge to continue, Kevin groaned, "That's just it. It's time to stop pretending that everything hasn't changed. It's only postponing the inevitable."

"We get to choose our path," Kayn whispered. "We can choose to keep our friendship alive. We can choose to always care about each other."

Kevin wanted to take her in his arms and make her understand that he'd always be hers but that would be the most selfish thing he could do. He gazed into her eyes, knowing he couldn't say the words teetering on his tongue, but his brain was losing the argument with his heart. He could see the longing in her eyes as she aggressively pulled him closer. He couldn't help his reaction as her tongue darted against his, deepening the seduction until every nerve ending in his body was screaming at him to ignore ration and just do it. He began feathering seductive kisses down her throat to her shoulder and on those magical freckles that twisted his insides into knots of desire. Kayn gasped as he cupped her breast and breathlessly whispered against her skin, "Do you want me to take you? I can keep going. It won't make me remember you and it won't make me love you back." She placed her hand firmly against his chest to signal that he'd made his point. Kevin stepped away from her as he explained, "I don't want to hurt you. I have to count on the other Triad to get out of here and they have to feel like they can count on me. I can't be seen helping the enemy. Stephanie's already going to go postal on me for jumping in after you back there. I left my own Clan to make sure you were safe. I jumped off a cliff with you. I followed you into rapids. I left Patrick and Stephanie standing there wondering, what in the hell I was doing? They need to get out of here. They're stuck in hell and I ditched them for one more second with you. We need to stay away from each other. In this new life, we can only bring each other pain."

Kayn said, "You realise that in one breath you say you don't feel the same way and in the next you act like your feelings for me can't be controlled with anything but my complete and total absence from your life?"

He touched her arm. *He didn't want her to think he didn't care because he did… too much.*

Kayn shook her head and whispered, "Don't."

They wandered out from under the falls into the mystical tropical rainforest. The lush, intoxicatingly fragrant jungle was beautiful, but everything paled in comparison to her. *He'd hurt her deeply.* He couldn't make anything better, so he left her there, staring at the mark on her hand and wandered off. The sights and sounds were so realistic. He pushed aside the ferns as he trekked further into the overgrown brush needing space to breathe. He gazed up at the covering of palm leaves above and whispered, "This isn't fair." The palms swayed above, causing the sun's rays to flicker through. *It was like they were waving him away. This place was so realistic.* Kevin ran a hand along a ridged fern. It was difficult to wrap one's mind around this city-sized Crypt. He wanted to understand the science behind it, but this place of magic defied logic. The brightly coloured birds seemed as real as any he'd come across during his travels, and the fertile soil beneath his bare toes felt exactly as it would have back home. *He had to face her. He couldn't hide in the jungle indefinitely.* Kevin made his way back to where he'd left her. She was sitting by the shore in front of a cluster of purple orchids. He watched Kayn curiously touching the sticky stamen of an exquisite Orchid. As he approached, she moved her hand, plucked the flower from the soil and tossed it into the water. She watched it drift away. Kevin sat down beside her and said, "I don't want to keep hurting you."

"I know you don't," Kayn replied. "I should have listened the first dozen times you gave me that speech."

Her blonde hair was glistening in the sunshine like she had a halo. *He cared about her so much. It wasn't fair. He wanted to kiss her so badly it hurt but it was cruel to keep sending her mixed messages.* Kevin needed her to understand their reality, so he picked her a flower to lighten the blow. She hesitated, so he tucked it behind her ear as he questioned, "What would we do in these fantasies of yours? See each other once or twice a year and be forced to fight? Maybe, we'd sneak away from our Clans and steal a kiss or have sex in a closet? It wouldn't be romantic. It would be torture. You would spend every day aching to be with me. I'm a guy. If I slept with you, it would make things easier. Question answered, and territory conquered. It's not going to be about anything more than that for me because I'm not the same person."

Grinning, she teased, "Don't sugarcoat it or anything."

Kevin grinned and retaliated, "I can see how we would have been best friends though. Everything about you is appealing. You are so weird. You have a warped sense of humour. Your hair always looks messy and I swear, I've never seen you without dirt on your face. I don't even know how you do it. We just got out of the water."

Suddenly concerned, she asked, "Is there actually dirt on my face right now?"

He wiped the streak of mud off her cheek with his thumb. She closed her eyes as he touched her. *He wanted to kiss her so badly.* She opened her eyes. He winked at her like an idiot. Kayn removed the flower from her hair and spitefully plucked off every second petal. *He'd deserved that.* She got up and tossed the orchid into the water. It drifted beside the other one for a second before the current pulled them apart.

She spun around and declared, "Let's get out of here."

Kevin agreed, "Sounds like a plan."

"There's an entrance above the falls," she pointed out. "What if the exit is below the falls?"

"You mean underwater?" he clarified.

"It would be the most inconvenient place for one to be," Kevin confirmed. "That seems to be how this place works."

A colourful toucan flew past. Kayn smiled and jeered, "You brought the Fruit Loops Toucan on your rescue attempt, how adorable."

She was incredibly strange. Kevin cracked a smile, probing, "Fruit Loops Toucan? What are you talking about?"

"From the cereal box," Kayn explained as she stepped into the water. "We ate a lot of it when we were kids."

He'd seen boxes of Fruit Loops in the cereal section at the grocery store, but it never looked appealing.

"Never mind, it's not important," she stated.

"When we all get out of this place, I'll try some and think of you," Kevin assured as he ventured deeper into the water.

While chest deep she countered, "I hope both of our Clans make it out of here, so you can."

He found himself at a loss for words watching her wading away from him. *She wasn't going to make it out unless he violated her trust by hurting her.* "I hope your Clan makes it out too," Kevin quietly replied. They waded out to the ledge of the drop off and swam out to the falls. The closer they came to the falls the less they could see because of the mist. She disappeared beneath the surface just as the rest of Triad came flying over the falls. Kevin swam for shore knowing he couldn't change what had to be done but it didn't have to be here and now. Triad swam to shore. *They'd come after him.*

Seeing Stephanie pulling Patrick's body behind her, Kevin waded in and helped her drag him to dry land.

The others wandered around checking out the scenery as he sat beside Stephanie in the grass.

"I've been extremely patient with this situation, but I'm done," she whispered.

Kevin met the disappointment in his friend's eyes, knowing Stephanie deserved the truth. "I've hurt you and I'm sorry. This won't happen again."

"Promise me you'll do what you've been ordered to do the next time you see her and the conversations over," she said as Patrick began to stir. "We won't get out of here if you keep leaving us for her. You must know that."

He nodded as Patrick opened his eyes. *He'd been fixated on Kayn and he couldn't be anymore. These were his people. This was his Clan. His future was with them, not her.* Kevin got up and announced, "I know how to get out of here. Let's go." He led them under the falls. They surfaced in a pool within a cave. They scaled the rock face and stepped into a sandy corridor. He'd managed to give Kayn a head start, but she'd left a clear trail of footprints in the sand. Kevin stepped in front of his group and whispered his intent, "I have to do this." Stephanie handed him her knife and nodded. Triad silently crept through the sandy stone maze lit by torches until they found her. *He had to break her spirit so she could be reborn. There was no other choice.* Kevin grabbed her from behind and pressed his blade against her throat.

Kayn whispered, "What now?"

He whispered in her ear, "I have to," as he slid his blade across her skin. In shock, she staggered forward, clutching her neck as her blood spurted into the sand. As she bled out, he became hollow inside. *He'd slit her throat from behind like a coward. She would never forgive him.*

His betrayal came full circle when Kayn burst into a room where Triad and Trinity were battling it out. She slayed everyone as retribution. Kevin was looking into her eyes as Kayn took her vengeance by slitting his throat. He awoke knowing he'd succeeded in destroying what he loved the most, and in her place, was a monster. They didn't make it far before an Enlightening took him down. Waking with frayed nerves, he persevered through the simulation knowing his Clan would be trapped in this place if he couldn't pull himself together. Triad fought and died until they finally found their way out of the Testing. When Ankh made it out, Kevin was so relieved that nothing mattered. He could live through a thousand years of her hatred, knowing he'd played a part in her survival.

Triad was already seated at the banquet for the survivors when Ankh came in. Kayn was breathtaking in a golden gown with a sexy slit that stopped at the top of her thigh. The reality of what happened in the Testing hit him. *He'd hurt her because he had to. He'd changed her to save her life. She'd brutally murdered him because she wanted to.* As the Third-Tier festivities began he had a vision. *The King planned to take her virginity.* He tried to warn her, but she wouldn't even look at him. He knew he could trust Patrick. Tiberius and Lexy were also brought on board with the plan. An unlikely group saved her that night and for him it felt like a step in the right direction to atone for his sins.

Months later, their paths crossed for the first time during a job. Triad had aerosol cans of Chloroform and Angel chains with instructions to knock Ankh out and chain them up in a storage container in the desert, so Triad could steal a Correction survivor. He snuck in through the bathroom window, tiptoed to her bed, and lost his train of thought because she was sleeping on top of the covers in her tank top and panties. Kevin sprayed the air above her as she slept. He restrained her with the spelt chains, but she woke up before he had the chance to move her. They had a flirtatious exchange before he Chloroformed her again. He moved her in her scantily clad state and put her in the backseat of his vehicle. Stephanie jumped into the car. While they were driving, Kayn bit a chunk out if her own arm to trigger her symbol so Ankh would know she was in trouble. *He should have gagged her. He knew she had to move on, but it killed him that Frost was the object of her affection.* Unable to stop himself, he kissed her goodbye before leaving her chained up in the broiling storage container to mess with Frost.

Months went by with only brief run-ins with Ankh. They were still connected in dreams. He'd been watching the struggle between Kayn and her Handler with intense curiosity because he was the original choice. He'd like to say he would have been focused on the Conduit ability over mastering her deceased twin's Siren, but he also missed Chloe. Having had a front-row seat as she fell for Frost sucked. When they finally slept together, Kevin woke in the middle of the night wishing he could gouge his heart out. *It wasn't what he'd wanted for her.* From his vantage point, it felt cold and emotionless. He'd fantasized about being with her so many times and in every version it was beautiful. He drank himself into a stupor. He found his way to Stephanie's room, and for a night, he forgot about Kayn Brighton. This was the drill every time he woke up with their love affair shoved down his throat.

When Kayn walked into that pub in Alaska, his heart damn near stopped. It was just her and Zach. It was obviously a trap, but for the opportunity to spend five minutes with her, he was willing to pretend it wasn't. He had the chance to apologize for what he'd been forced to do in the Testing, and once he had, he felt so much lighter on the inside. When he got back to his room, he realised she'd stolen his phone, but it had been worth it. In the proceeding days, he spent his time travelling to the next job while working through his feelings. *Kayn was happy with Frost. It may not be who he would have chosen for her, but she loved him, and he had to learn to suck it up. If he could manage to support her endeavours, perhaps one day they could find a way to be friends again.*

It wasn't long before he began having perilous visions regarding her paternity. Her Guardian status came with treacherous complications. Kayn wasn't adapting to the demanding feeding schedule. She'd figured out how to summon up orbs of energy but had no control over which kind she generated. The shit had hit the fan when she accidentally sent a bunch of demons through the Hall of Souls. Mortality was not bestowed upon evil things. Blissful ignorance was a privilege. They'd be cleaning up that mess for years. Dreaming of when it was just them against the world became his happy place. Even if they weren't together, keeping her a step ahead of anything that wished to harm her was his only plan.

They ended up at the other continent's Pre-Summit banquet together. After he'd gone out of his way to warn her, she tossed him over a balcony. A few days later, here he was again having psychic visions of her. She'd been caught by a devious sect of Abaddon, and as he'd foreseen, they were aware that she could send demons back through the Hall of Souls. *They had to silence the gossip. Every demonic entity would be coming after the promise of salvation.* He had another vision, and this time, they were trying to force her to put her ability into a weapon. Kevin was about to try to contact her Clan when Seth appeared in all his devious glory.

Triad's Guardian explained the rest of Clan Ankh were too far away to intervene. The Dragons and their Handlers were being held by Abaddon at a farm less than thirty minutes away. *They must have been weakened, taking Lexy was nearly impossible.* Triad was closest so they were being sent in. *He wanted to believe Kayn would take herself out before she'd give Abaddon what they wanted but she'd been recklessly unhinged since their Testing.* Kevin used their connection to warn her of Abaddon's true motives. *They couldn't force a dead person to do squat. Taking herself out was the intelligent move.* His Grandfather was pacing and cursing up a storm. *He'd been sure Tiberius had no serious intentions with*

Lexy, but the panic in his eyes led him to believe he was missing a part of the story. Why was he this concerned about indestructible girl?

It didn't take them long to get to where they were being held. One of the Triad could find immortal beings at close range using a heat-sensing aura filter. In seconds they figured out, they'd split up the Dragons and Handlers because there were two accumulations of heat signatures on the property. *They were using Zach to control Kayn and Grey to control Lexy. It was the obvious move.* At one point in his life, he could have guessed every move Kayn would make but not anymore. In his visions, Kayn was with Grey, and they were trying to force her to put her light into a sword so they could use it to pass through the hall of souls. They peeled away and sped to the closest group of heat signatures. Triad got out and raced to the barn. Instinct told him Kayn wasn't in there. She was in the barn on the outskirts of the property. Intuition urged him to use their psychic connection to get through to her. Kevin remained in the car with the engine running as he slipped into his mind. *She needed to be taken out of the equation.* He thought of who Kayn was and what she was destined to become. Visions of freckles on her skin and the way sunlight shone through her hair brought him to her. She couldn't see him, but he could see her. As Kayn stepped closer to the blade, he fought to get through to her, "No! Don't do it! We have the others. Take yourself out!" Kayn paused, appearing confused. *She'd heard him.* She took another step, without her eyes leaving the blade on the table. *Why should she trust me? She was going to need more.* He spoke to her subconscious again,

"Do you remember when we were thirteen and we were caught sneaking your Dad's homemade beer out of your carport? I said it was my idea and you didn't even know I had it. I told you I would always have your back. Please, believe in me now!"

Looking at her captors, Kayn said, "I'll do it, but Grey goes first."

Kevin snapped back to the here and now as screams of agony rang out from the barn. *Lexy's up.* The rest of the Triad sprinted out and got into the vehicle.

Jumping into the front seat, Tiberius yelled, "Go! Go! She's got this!"

Kevin stomped on the gas and floored it to the other group. The barn was already smoking. They pulled up as a man staggered out of the barn fully engulfed in flames. *She'd taken the whole place out.* Kevin raced into the inferno. Shots rang out. His eyes met with charbroiled Kayn's as she went down. Someone walked past lugging a corpse. *That must have been Grey.* He stood in the backdrop of the raging flames in awe of her sacrifice. *She'd listened to him even though she had no reason to. Perhaps, the future he'd envisioned wasn't a fantasy?* He knelt before Kayn, picked her up and walked out with her blistered unrecognizable corpse in his arms.

Impressed, Tiberius commented, "Holy hell. She sure toasted herself. We've got to get out of here. I've called the Aries Group. They're on their way. This may seem insensitive, but we don't have enough room in the car, we're going to have to put the bodies in the trunk."

Kevin placed Kayn's body on a blanket. Someone else tossed Grey on top of her. Scowling at his fellow Triad, he moved Grey, so he was beside her. He tucked them in with another blanket and closed the trunk.

Stephanie nudged Tiberius and teased, "Are we just delivering the bodies to the others or do we have to give that red-headed psycho a ride?"

"Jealous?" Tiberius baited.

"Not in the least," Stephanie bickered as she stared out of the window while drinking from her water bottle.

10

ALCOHOL VERSUS FIRE

Kayn awoke in the darkness to rumbling tires. *Oh, come on! You've got to be frigging kidding me! She was in the damn trunk again. This had never happened to her before, not once... And here she was, waking up in a stranger's trunk. Twice in one day. This time she wasn't alone. What was that smell? Oh, yes. It was burnt clothing. There was another body in the trunk with her. Good times.* She felt her arms. Her skin was smooth as a baby's bottom. *She was healed. Awesome! Who was lying next to her?* Knowing the drill, Kayn felt around in the trunk for a roadside assistance kit. She could tell what some things were by touch but couldn't find the flashlight. She tugged off the charred remnants of her fingerless glove that concealed her symbol of Ankh. If she set it off, she'd be able to see. Kayn dug through the bag until she found something sharp and tried to stick it into her hand. What in the hell was going on? She couldn't break the skin. She felt her trunk mate's face. Ninety-nine percent sure it was Grey, Kayn placed her hands against his torso and willed her ability to play along. *Come on! Come on!* Grey gasped and she cheered internally. He groaned, and she was certain it was him. "Welcome back," she quietly said.

He whispered, "What's a nice girl like you doing in a trunk like this?"

She answered, "Plotting the death of the driver."

"Who has us?" Grey asked as the vehicle swerved.

"If I knew that why would I still be in the trunk?" Kayn teased as the car swerved dangerously again. *Maybe they were being pursued?*

"Let me show you something," Grey said fumbling around in the dark.

It became easier to hear the car's occupants. *It was Triad. They'd shown up as their backup. She recalled Kevin's voice guiding her. They were on their side, at least for today.*

Snickering, he suggested, "We could just open the trunk, kick their asses and take the vehicle."

Playfully shoving Grey, she scolded, "That's my line." *There was nothing wrong with letting them know they were awake.* She heard Grey fumbling around again. The trunk flew open. *Go, Grey.* The vehicle pulled over and they scrambled out as the doors opened. *Grey didn't know Triad had come to help them.* Before she had the opportunity to speak, Grey shot flames from his hands, creating a six-foot blazing wall between the Clans, warning them to stay back.

Gawking at his hands because it had been a long time since his ability operated like it was supposed to, Grey asked, "Did you do this?"

She knew she had. Somehow, when she harnessed their energy to use his ability as a weapon, she'd freed him from his punishment. His Pyrokinesis was running at full capacity. The panic in Kevin's eyes through the blazing inferno while recalling his words about concealing what she was capable of rang in her ears. *She didn't undo the Third-Tier's punishment on purpose. How was she going to be able to stop what came naturally?*

Over the crackling inferno his adversary created, Tiberius said, "No need to light us on fire. We were sent in to help you. Ankh was too far away to respond. We're bringing you to Lexy and Zach."

With hands outstretched, Grey inhaled deeply, sucking the flames back in. Animatedly jumping up and down, he joyfully embraced Kayn. "I can't believe it! My ability has been stifled for so long. You fixed it!"

Oh, no. Grey shouldn't have announced what she'd done. By the devastation on Kevin's face, she knew this accidental act of defiance would come with repercussions. Kevin turned and walked away from her without saying a word. *That can't be good.*

Smiling warmly, Patrick tossed her a shirt and shorts, saying, "Sweetie, you should put these on."

Oh, yes, she'd lit herself on fire. She peered down at her chest. *Well, this was awkward. She was practically naked, wearing nothing but scorched rags.* She slipped the new t-shirt on, reached under and tore away the charred material of her old bra. Grey stood in front of her, blocking Triad's view so she could slip on the shorts.

Handing Grey a clean shirt and shorts as he opened the back door, Patrick urged, "It'll be a tight fit but get in. Lexy and Zach are waiting."

Tiberius baited, "Come on, Grey. Get in. I'll sit in the back with you. We can discuss things we should have talked about a while ago."

"I'd rather get in the trunk," Grey mumbled as he got in.

Kayn shimmied into the cramped space. She ended up on Grey's lap as they tried to fit everyone in like an awkward game of backseat people Jenga. Tiberius was squished into the back next to them with Stephanie on his lap. Kevin's booty call was grinning as they pulled away and began speeding down the dusty backroad towards an unknown destination. *She hated her. It was ridiculous to despise someone you barely knew, but in this case, there were some rather diabolical deeds standing between them and any form of forgiveness.* Scrolling through her list of misdemeanours, Kayn settled on the one thing she couldn't see past. *It was the months of watching her hooking up with the person she loved.* Her thoughts abruptly paused. *The person she used to love... Used to love.* Kevin turned to look at her. He'd been tuned into her thoughts as she made that misstep. Meeting his gaze, she knew he'd taken her mistake as a confession. She slowly moved her head from side to side, to make sure he understood.

Kevin countered by nodding. He was smiling as he turned back to watch the road.

Shut it down. She needed to shut her emotions down. She wasn't thinking straight. Staring out the window, Kayn decided it was best to say nothing.

Shifting Stephanie on his lap, Tiberius complained, "Steph, your butt cheeks are like razor blades."

Stephanie saucily provoked, "Women come in all shapes and sizes. We can't all have big hips, boobs and asses."

Kayn glared at her knowing exactly who that dig was meant for. *She was hungry and Kevin's booty call was trying her patience.*

Grey giggled and answered her thought with one of his own, *'Go for it.'*

Scowling, Stephanie took the hint and moved off Tiberius' knee onto Patrick's. Kayn grinned, knowing they'd all heard her inner commentary. In the distance, she saw the glow of lights. *It was a motel. That must be where the others were waiting.*

Nudging her, Grey whispered, "Take some of mine if you need it."

Kayn was tempted but agitated enough to know she might not be able to stop if she broke the seal. As they pulled into the parking lot, Lexy and Zach were waving from a second-floor balcony. The sight of Zach calmed her as she wandered through the parking lot with the rest to the building.

Kevin touched her arm and asked, "Can we talk?"

She stopped walking, assuring, "I'll come find you after I've seen Lexy and Zach."

Smiling, Kevin replied, "We'll be at the restaurant. We're all staying here tonight. Just so you know."

Kayn made her way to the stairs, but as she grabbed hold of the railing, her eyes were drawn back to him.

Grey called down to her, "Are you coming with me or are you planning to stand there gawking at your ex for the rest of the evening?"

Funny. She chased Grey upstairs, teasing, "You'd better run!"

Lexy and Zach rushed to the top of the stairs where they embraced and made a unanimous decision to go down to the restaurant. Kayn held Zach's hand as they descended the stairs. A sense of calm washed over her, and she no longer felt the intense urgency to feed. Her Handler gently squeezed her hand. Their eyes met, and they both smiled. Their peaceful reunion was broken by the sound of Lexy and Grey arguing up ahead. *Their dining mates were sure to create plenty of complications this evening.*

Leaning in closer, Zach whispered, "Bet Lexy and Tiberius do the deed tonight."

It felt wrong to vote against what she knew her sister wanted. She understood the desire to take a walk on the wild side. Thinking of Frost as they entered the minimalistic pub-style restaurant, she scanned the room for Kevin. He was sitting by himself, waiting for her arrival. The moment their eyes met, she slipped back to the here and now. Wishing they could find a way to resurrect their friendship, she sat across the table. Neither spoke as Kevin passed her a menu. *It was probably in Spanish and Zach wasn't sitting beside her to read it.* Prepared to wing it, Kayn opened the colourful menu and understood everything. *Apparently, she could read Spanish now.* Kayn closed the menu and reopened it. *Yes, she could still read it. This was rather odd.*

"Do you know what you want?" Kevin enquired.

Now, that was a loaded question. She didn't want to lead him on. He needed to know where she stood. Kayn peered up from her menu and said, "Frost."

Without looking up, Kevin stifled a grin while casually clarifying, "From the menu, Brighton."

"You know what I'm saying," she mumbled, reaching for the Corona in front of her. *He'd obviously taken the liberty of ordering her a drink. She didn't really like beer, but he didn't know that. He didn't know much about her now.* Kayn held the cold beverage to her lips, then removed it, and questioned, "Did you put anything in this?"

"I just saved you," Kevin sparred as he sighed and traded drinks with her to prove his point. He took a swig from the bottle she'd accused him of tainting.

He hadn't saved her. "I saved myself," Kayn stated.

Kevin chuckled and teased, "You woke up in my trunk."

Cute. "I would have woken up anywhere, I'm immortal," she countered.

Grinning, he baited, "This is true, but it might have been somewhere extremely inconvenient."

"More inconvenient than your trunk?" She provoked, pausing the conversation as a waiter came to take their orders.

After the witness left earshot, Kevin sparred, "Touché. Would you have woken up if you'd been stabbed with a blade full of yellow light?"

He had a point. Smiling, she met Kevin's eyes and politely said, "Thank you."

"You're welcome," he whispered.

They sat in awkward silence until she added, "Sorry I threw you over that balcony."

"Really?" Kevin probed. He took another swig of his Corona.

Grinning, she admitted, "No. Not really."

"Didn't think so," he chuckled. Raising his drink, Kevin saluted, "To keeping it real."

As they clinked bottles, his hand brushed against hers. Five months ago, she would have had a million questions for him, but right now, she only had one, "Do you know where your Mother and Clay are?"

"I do," he answered honestly. "If you want to discuss this topic any further, we need to be alone."

Curiosity prompted her to leave the restaurant with him, but their meals arrived. As the waiter moved on to the next table, Kayn agreed, "Fine, as soon as we're finished, we'll go somewhere to talk."

They never used to have issues with small talk but finding subjects that could be spoken about in public, proved to be a touch more difficult than it had in the past. *Killed any demons lately? Found any new breeds of immortal creatures? Have you ever been beaten up by a possessed evil toddler?*

Without looking up from his meal, he responded to her thoughts, "Yes. Yes and no, but I heard you guys did."

She took a bite of her deliciously zesty dish. *It wasn't spicy enough.* Kayn dumped a gross amount of hot sauce on it, took another bite and grinned. She inhaled her entire meal in roughly a minute, peered up and saw Kevin with his fork poised above his lips gawking at her. Raising her eyebrows, she questioned, "What?"

"I heard about the thing Dragons have with hot sauce. Seeing it is a whole other story," he answered thoroughly entertained.

She chuckled while finishing her Corona. *It was nice spending time with him. Would it have been like this if he'd stayed with Ankh? There was no way to know if their relationship would have lasted. Maybe, it would have been over in the blink of an eye, and they would have gone back to being platonic friends?*

Finishing his last mouthful, he wiped his mouth with a napkin and announced, "I'll go order us each another drink to bring with us. Do you want another Corona?"

"Sure," Kayn answered as she watched him get up and make his way to the bar. With him away from the table, she inconspicuously checked out how everyone else's evening was going. *Lexy and Tiberius were gone. Interesting. Grey didn't appear to be having a nervous breakdown. Maybe, he hadn't noticed yet?* Grey and Zach were sitting with Stephanie, Patrick and a few Triad she recognized but hadn't had the opportunity to get to know while in same campground before Testing. Zach was having an intimate conversation with Patrick. *She really liked him.* Kevin wandered back to the table with a few Coronas in each hand. Kayn got up to meet him halfway and took two. They snuck out of the restaurant and strolled down to the pool where they put their drinks down, sat on the edge and dangled their feet in the water.

When they were alone, Kevin confessed, "I can't do anything about Clay or my mother. I know where they are and that they're safe. I'm psychic so I know how it all plays out. As soon as they're released, they'll have to start training for the Testing. If they come out now, they won't make it. They're better off in a Tomb for the time being. Tiberius is changing. It's happening slowly and let's just say, I have it under good authority that he won't hurt them after he's had the opportunity to get to know me."

"That makes sense," Kayn responded as she splashed her feet in the tepid water. She glanced his way, asking, "What do you see in my future?"

Smiling warmly, Kevin disclosed, "So many incredible things."

"You're not going to tell me anything, are you?" she teased.

"It's never good to know too much, but if you keep yourself open to me, I'll be able to guide your actions like I did during that last run-in with Abaddon," he explained.

"So, how is that going to work when we're usually adversaries?" she asked. "Won't opening myself up to you just give Triad the upper hand?"

Kevin placed his hand on hers as he answered, "Not if our friendship remains a secret. We need to act that way in front of our Clans, but when we're alone, we can be ourselves."

Gazing into his eyes, she confessed, "I do love Frost."

"I know," Kevin replied. "That's not what I meant. Had I stayed with Ankh, I would have been your Handler. We never would have been together like we dreamt of, not for many years."

Somehow, knowing that made it feel like a weight was removed from her chest.

"I couldn't see past what I wanted for a while there. It was wrong of me to make you feel guilty for moving on. I don't blame you for tossing me off that balcony. I kind of deserved it."

She laced her fingers through his and admitted, "I may have some impulse control issues."

Smiling, Kevin clasped his other hand over hers and bantered, "You've always had impulse control issues."

Her heart soared, knowing his memory was back. *There were so many things she wanted to say but nothing on the list mattered anymore.*

He tucked one of her stray curls behind her ear as he said, "All I knew about you before I helped you up that day at that track, was that you were the girl of my dreams… quite literally. When I saw the Ankh on your palm, I panicked, and it caused me to behave ignorantly. As I got to know you, it was so easy to see why I cared about you and before I knew it, I was head over heels in love with you. That was the best week of my life. I should have stayed with you that last night. I was afraid. I had to find the will to do the unthinkable. It was worse than I'd imagined. After Testing was over, so many beautiful memories came flooding back, and it was too late... you despised me. I hated myself for what I was forced to do but knew it was the only the way you survived. I was this numb shadow of myself during that banquet. When that announcement happened, I knew you were going to have to sacrifice even more of yourself. I just couldn't let it happen. I was with the group that helped you get away. I'd managed to convince myself I had to let you go but that first time we ran into Ankh it was harder than I thought. I wanted to get you alone and tell you everything, but I knew I couldn't. You needed to learn to embrace the Dragon within you. The anger and betrayal you felt towards me at that time was what fuelled the ability. So, I behaved like I was over you even though I wasn't. I couldn't help myself. I kissed you, hoping you'd see the real me. After that, each night when I closed my eyes, I dreamt of you, but it wasn't memories we'd created together. I was dreaming of you moving on with Frost. It was excruciating. Granny Winnie talked me through your loss and explained why each thing needed to happen so you could evolve into what you were destined to become. You were doing exactly what you were meant to be doing. I hid my ability for a while, but when I felt secure enough in my relationship with my grandfather, I told him everything. He's not as horrible as everyone thinks he is. Tiberius is misguided on occasion. I've been helping our Clan for a while now, but according to Winnie, my main purpose is to help guide you through all that is to come, if you're open to it?"

"We'll have to fight each time we run into each other," Kayn pointed out, staring at the glass-smooth surface of the pool.

"It's not a big deal, we're immortal," Kevin repeated the words she'd used earlier.

"True," Kayn answered as she squeezed his hand, agreeing, "Friends then."

"Always," Kevin confirmed, gazing longingly into her eyes.

And for a moment, she saw the five-year-old boy with the mass of wild dark curls that she adored smiling back at her. She looked away and disturbed the peaceful surface of the water by splashing her feet as she changed the subject, "Tell me about your afterlife? I'm guessing you're not with Stephanie. I know she was entertaining my father not too long ago."

"What? Not my Stephanie. How could she?" Kevin gasped, pretending to be shocked. He chuckled as she gave him a light-hearted shove. Kevin confessed, "There's a new girl I'm sort of interested in. Her name's Rebekka."

"That's good. I want you to be happy," Kayn whispered. "She must be a new Triad because I've never heard of her."

"She's so new, we've barely spoken, but I've had visions of what we could be. I don't know how or when it starts, but it's there. So, if the situation arises, don't take her," he implored.

Smiling, Kayn promised, "I won't personally take her. I have no control over the others. We're being punished right now so we have no contact with the rest of the Clan."

"No contact with Frost? For murdering me? Now that's ironic," Kevin teased, playfully shoving her again.

"Isn't it though," Kayn sparred while stared into her empty bottle.

He stood up, held out his hand and suggested, "Lets' go for a walk."

Kayn took Kevin's hand. He tugged her up and they sauntered to the shore with the thunderous crashing of waves in the background. They found dry sand and sprawled under the blanket of stars as they would have before things like immortality and opposing Clans created an insurmountable wall between them.

"I've missed this. I never do things like this anymore," Kevin disclosed, smiling at the night sky.

"What's stopping you?" Kayn asked, looking his way.

Grinning, he met her gaze, admitting, "The pressure of trying to assimilate. The fear of anyone seeing the person I'm trying to hide. Avoiding doing the things that remind me of a life that's gone. There are so many reasons."

"Patrick would enjoy this," Kayn remarked as she watched the twinkling stars.

"Maybe... What about Stephanie?" He teased.

"I'm going to need time to murder her at least a dozen more times to get to an understanding place with her," Kayn mumbled.

"Yeah. Frost irritates me too," he confessed staring her way.

Meeting his eyes, she asked, "Did you know that was going to happen?"

"I thought hooking up with your twin's ex would be too creepy to contemplate," he bantered.

Stargazing with her bestie, Kayn sparred, "Let's blame the pheromones like we did when you made out with Lily."

"Touche," he said, grinning. Glad she didn't ask about her future with Frost, Kevin allowed them to remain in the fantasy. He drew her away from the downwards spiral with a question, "Back when we were kids, could you have imagined this life?"

"I don't know, my imagination has always been rather spectacular," she teased, swatting a crab off her leg as she sat up. She snatched the tiny crustacean out of the sand. He also sat up to look at the sea creature cruising around her palm. She met his eyes, and placed the tiny crab in the palm of his hand as she added, "What's the plan then? Are we just going to avoid each other during each squabble between our Clans? Or do you want me to just kick your ass first and ask questions later?"

"I'm crafty enough to beat you," he assured, smiling.

"No, you're not. You're really going to have to give that ego a rest if you expect our friendship to work," she provoked.

"Fine," Kevin leapt up and beckoned her closer with both hands as he declared, "Give it your best shot."

Intrigued by his cocky behaviour, Kayn got up, grinned and threatened, "You asked for it." With a swift, precise movement, she swept his feet out from under him.

He landed with a thud on his back in the sand. Kevin started laughing and put her at ease by saying, "I wasn't ready."

"Come on, you didn't even try," she muttered, towering above him. While she was busy rolling her eyes, he made a scissor motion with his legs, tugged at the backside of her knees and brought her down in the sand beside him. Kayn remained there for a second. *That was good. He'd knocked the wind out of her.* With no intention of admitting weakness, she started laughing as she complained, "You're still a cheater."

"I said, I was crafty enough to beat you, cheating wasn't a factor," he sparred and winked.

She had to give him that. She'd missed him. She'd missed the playful nature of their friendship. She noted the salty scent of the sea and the glorious sense of calm. *They could be friends again. It was possible.* Their beautiful moment ended as they heard approaching voices.

Kevin sat up and declared, "Back to reality."

Kayn continued to stare at the stars as he stood up. *She didn't want him to go but she knew he had to.* She remained where she was as she nonchalantly said, "Till we meet again, Smith."

He replied, "Till we meet again, Brighton."

He remembered her but it didn't even matter. The irony wasn't lost on her as she watched him wander away. Kayn smiled. *He still had the same walk. His eyes still crinkled when he smiled. A small part of who they were, remained.* She felt peaceful in the knowledge that he appeared to be finding his way just as she was. As she closed her eyes, her thoughts were drawn to Frost. *Where was he right now? Even though she didn't know where Frost was or what he was doing, she felt this sense of certainty. He loved her. He'd spoken the words aloud and she knew he didn't say those words easily. They would have had more time together if she hadn't taken Seth's declaration to heart. Of course, they would have to follow the rules.* She heard the rustling of sand as someone approached. *She knew who it was without looking.* Kayn opened her eyes. *It was Zach.*

"The tides coming in. If you want to get some sleep you'd better come back to the room," Zach's voice urged.

The water had almost reached her. She'd been off in her own little world and hadn't noticed. Kayn sighed and held out her hand. He helped her up as she asked, "How was your visit with your Triad friend?"

"Which one?" Zach dodged her question as they wandered back to the hotel

"I'm not stupid," she declared.

Zach chuckled as he changed topics, "You missed the drama at the restaurant."

She got it. He wasn't ready to have this conversation. "Dra-ma?" Kayn questioned. *Grey had obviously noticed Lexy's absence.*

"Grey," Zach explained.

She'd guessed correctly. An ominous thought crept into her mind. She whispered, "He lit something on fire, didn't he?"

Zach replied, "Multiple things and a few people to be accurate."

"Tiberius?" Kayn questioned, using only his name.

"Tiberius, Stephanie, bushes, some napkins and plants," her Handler clarified. "Let's just say he quite effectively deterred their hookup."

Lexy was going to be choked.

Zach started to explain, "Grey was a mess. He drank us all under the table and when he noticed Lexy was missing, he stormed out, ranting like she was cheating. Guru Grey was frigging unhinged. He completely lost it."

Kayn grinned as Zach used their old pet name for Grey.

Zach continued regaling the unfortunate events of the evening, "Patrick called Tiberius and Lexy came back to calm him down. Long story short, we are so not getting our damage deposit back. Joking. I'm just kidding. We've covered it up. Did you really not see or hear any of this?"

The waves crashed with a thunderous roar. "Nothing," Kayn admitted. *This was her fault. What was wrong with her? She'd taken Grey's cork off and released him into the wild.* As they approached the courtyard. Kayn grimaced at the sight of smoking charcoaled bushes. *Oh, no. She was going to get in big trouble for this. Mental note... Pyrokinesis and alcohol do not mix. She was going to have to find a way to put him back to how he was before someone found out.*

"It's not your fault. Grey's an adult... Sort of," Zach consoled as they made their way back to their room.

Referring to Grey as an adult made her smile again. Kayn winced as she asked, "Did Triad have to call the Aries Group?"

"No. We didn't bother but Tiberius could have. We were lucky it went down in the middle of the night. The bartender was the only one. Tiberius took care of him," Zach replied.

Was he dead? Oh, yes. Tiberius could erase portions of some-one's memories. The bartender probably thought he'd gotten into the sauce.

Zach opened the door, graciously stepped aside and ushered her in, "My lady."

They walked in and found a grossly inebriated Grey, sprawled diagonally on one of their double beds.

Grey mumbled, "Lexy doesn't want me anymore," into the pillow.

Awesome. The whole room reeked of tequila. She couldn't go to sleep. There had to be a way to undo this mess. Maybe, all she had to do was feed from him to take him down a notch or two?

Zach whispered, "I think you've done enough tonight, don't you? Let's go sleep in Lexy's room."

"What if she's not alone?" Kayn replied as they closed the door quietly.

Zach whispered, "Triad's long gone. Tiberius didn't want to set off Grey again in the morning."

Kayn felt like pouting. *She always managed to miss out on the good stuff.* They knocked on the door to Lexy's room and heard the pitter-patter of her footsteps.

Lexy opened the door. Knowing what they were there for, she went back to bed, pulled the sheets over her head and instructed, "Turn off the lights when you're ready to go to sleep."

Zach flicked off the lights, and without a word, they got into the other bed and made themselves comfortable beneath the sheets. Her Handler whispered, "Sweet dreams," as he snuggled against her.

Kayn smiled as she relaxed in the protective warmth of the womb-like safety of Zach's embrace. The trauma of the day ceased as she slipped away into beautiful dreams.

11

DIRTY DEEDS

Lexy's voice sang, "Rise and shine! We're leaving in half an hour. Breakfast has been ordered. The shower is free!"

As Kayn squinted in the sunlight streaming in through the windows, she took note of the skip in Lexy's step and the glow in her cheeks. *Maybe, Grey hadn't stopped a thing?* Smiling knowingly, Kayn stretched and yawned while toying, "You look vibrant this morning. Have a good night?"

"It was eventful," Lexy sparred as she continued to dig through a bag Kayn didn't recognize.

"How eventful?" Zach provoked.

Her crimson-haired sibling countered, "How eventful was your night, Zach?"

Why did she have a feeling that way more happened last night than she'd been privy to? Glancing his way, Kayn casually enquired, "I wonder what she meant by that?"

He tossed a pillow at her and jousted, "Wouldn't you like to know?"

She had a feeling about Zach but not enough life experience to know how to broach the subject without coming off sounding crass. Kayn looked in the direction of the bathroom. Zach leapt up, sprinted across the room and slammed the door behind him. She threw herself back down on the bed and laughed. *He was such a child.*

Lexy answered the door as room service arrived. She charged the food to the room, strolled over and sat on the other bed. She passed the tray to Kayn and announced, "I ordered the same thing for everyone."

Kayn frowned as she took an unsatisfying bite of her bland ham and cheese omelette. Lexy grinned as she revealed a bottle of hot sauce and dumped a disgusting amount on hers, before passing it to Kayn. She did the same.

They were nearly finished when Zach appeared and groaned, "You guys should have told me it was here. Mine's going to be cold."

Lexy took the metal top off his and sparred, "It's been here for all of five minutes, quit whining."

Zach scrunched up his nose as he asked, "Is there one for Grey?"

"He can get his own breakfast," Lexy murmured as she placed her empty tray on the dresser and disappeared into the washroom.

"This doesn't promise to be awkward at all," Kayn whispered.

Nudging her, Zach quietly said, "Do you think Grey knows they slept together?"

Lexy abruptly opened the bathroom door. She gave them the dirtiest look as she stormed past and slammed the door as she left the room.

"You know, I'm not feeling all warm and fuzzy about this road trip anymore. It's liable to be a gong show," Zach whispered even though Lexy left.

Kayn started giggling. *She'd always known it was destined to be a gong show. Two Handlers and their recently tiered up Dragons. What could go wrong?* She peered up at Zach.

He smiled as he disclosed, "It is rather cool. Your thoughts are coming in as clear as if you'd spoken that aloud."

Instead of saying it aloud, Kayn thought, *is there something you haven't told me about last night?*

He responded in his mind, *'Whatever do you mean?'*

She grinned and decided to drop the subject. "I'm going to go wash up. Where did that bag come from?" Kayn pointed at the unfamiliar bag Lexy had been rifling through.

Zach emptied it onto the bed to show her what they had. "There's a toothbrush for each of us in the bathroom, some shampoo, conditioner and a change of clothes. In the front pocket is a charge card from the Aries Group and cash. There's also a rental car in the parking lot. We have a private flight to catch."

She'd never been on a plane. "We're not allowed to fly? I thought the Aries Group had us on the no-fly list? How do you know this?" she asked. *They'd lost the instructions for the next jobs when they lost their bags and phones.*

"There's a phone on the dresser with instructions," he explained.

Kayn called his bluff and snatched the phone. *I'll be damned. Tiberius must have given Lexy one of Triad's cells so he could get a hold of her.* She decided to keep her naughty interpretation to herself as she read the message. *Sure enough, they were going by plane. Her first trip aboard a plane was occurring more than two years after her death. She didn't have anything to fear anymore so it wasn't as big a deal as it might have been before her untimely demise.* Kayn placed the phone back on the dresser and shrugged. "I guess we're flying to Alaska." They were travelling from Mexico to Alaska. *It was so cold there.* She groaned as she flopped back down on the bed.

"It is a little strange, isn't it?" Zach pointed out. "It's odd that we're flying. We never fly."

It was peculiar. They startled as someone aggressively banged on the door. "Ten bucks that's Grey," Kayn called out as she slid off the bed and raced for the door. She opened it to reveal the tragically hung-over blonde guy they all knew and loved. Kayn grinned as she purposely reworded an old saying, "Feeling bright tailed and bushy eyed this morning?"

"You might want to give it a rest until I get my head on straight," he sparred, manoeuvring past her. Grey glared at the empty plates and stated the obvious, "She didn't order me breakfast, did she?"

Zach answered, "No... she didn't."

"My memory is a tad foggy. I was an ass last night, wasn't I?" Grey enquired as he took a seat on the bed by Zach.

"You could say that," Zach replied.

"How angry is she on a scale of one to ten?" Grey asked, holding his pounding head with both hands.

"Easy ten," Kayn answered as she took a seat beside Zach.

"I vaguely recall lighting a restaurant on fire. Is that why she's upset?" Grey probed.

"Um… Yeah… Partially that," Zach responded as he dodged the line of questioning. He got up and started gathering up their newly acquired toiletries. He tossed a shirt at Grey and suggested, "Go have a shower. There's a toothbrush for you in the bathroom. We have a flight to catch." Grey wandered away mumbling about how he was going to smell like booze for a week.

They left him alone for a few minutes, and when it sounded like he was out of the shower, Kayn knocked and said, "We'll meet you at the rental car."

"Sounds good," Grey replied from the other side of the door.

They waited until they were a distance from the room before gossiping. Zach whispered, "I don't think he remembers why he was so upset."

"I don't think so," Kayn whispered as Lexy appeared and silenced their chatter.

As Lexy strolled past, she asked, "How upset is he on a scale of say, one to ten?"

Kayn fought to stop a grin as it curved up each side of her mouth by pressing her lips together. *They'd both had the same question.*

Zach came to her aid by quickly replying, "He doesn't remember last night. He's more worried you're angry at him."

Lexy smiled as she walked back to the room. As they watched her leave, they simultaneously realised, they had no idea which vehicle was theirs. Kayn looked at Zach and said, "I think we should leave them alone to sort this out. I say we just go out to the parking lot and try to guess which car it is."

"I'll race you there!" Zach laughed as he took off.

He was going to make her run. She wasn't feeling motivated enough to run. Oh, hell. Kayn sprinted after him. *There was no way he'd be able to beat her in a race. Kevin had never been able to beat her either.* She slowed her roll, choosing to let him win. He began dancing around raucously cheering as he reached the parking lot. For a split second, her mind travelled back in time, and it was Kevin instead of Zach dancing obnoxiously. As she leaned against a car to take in the splendour of the testosterone show, a nerve shattering pitch made her senses shriek. Squeezing her eyes shut, Kayn covered her ears, screaming for Zach.

He was instantly at her side, "What's wrong?"

"Don't you hear that?" She shouted over the agonizing racket. *Her brain felt like it was about to split in two.*

"What noise?" Zach questioned loudly.

"I can't hear you!" Kayn screamed.

He yelled, "What noise?"

The racket abruptly ceased. With every nerve ending in her body frayed, Kayn gasped as her heart wildly palpitated. She panted, "Whatever that was, it wasn't cool." Even though the sound had ceased, she felt uneasy as she spun around and took in the nearly empty dusty parking lot. "I don't like this. Something is coming," Kayn warned.

Lexy and Grey came sprinting towards them as Grey hollered, "Get in the car!"

Kayn heard a double beep as he unlocked the car she was leaning against. They hopped in and sped away from the lot. Grey's foot was flush with the floor. The car lurched as they peeled onto the main road tossing them all to one side. *What was this?*

"Go! Go! Go!" Lexy yelled, frantically smacking Grey's arm.

Hanging on, Zach hollered, "What's happening? I don't understand what we're doing?"

Grey was driving like they were being chased. Kayn felt the urgency of the situation but didn't know why they'd reacted like this.

Lexy shouted, "Go! Go! We have to be out of range!"

Kayn spun around to look out the back window. *There was nothing there?* They appeared to be alone, speeding down an isolated road. There was a rumbling of a plane's engine overhead. Kayn watched it soaring over the hotel. *What was this?* Something dropped from the plane's cargo hold and descended from the sky.

"Go! Go! We're not far enough away!" Lexy hollered frantically.

They were spitting up gravel going as fast as the car could go. Suddenly, there was a deafening thunder.

Grey yelled, "Seatbelts! Now!"

Kayn spun around as a massive explosion rocked the ground. A wall of wind, earth and fire came surging after the vehicle.

"Brace yourselves!" Lexy yelled as the cloud of dust, debris and fire pursued them.

A millisecond before it hit, Zach whispered, "Shit!"

She was thinking the same thing as the heat of the debris surged through the shell of the vehicle scorching their flesh, followed by agonizing cries and the inability to breathe as the wreckage tumbled down the highway.

When the dust settled what was left of the car was still upright. There was a humming pitch in her ears as she reached for Zach. *He wasn't there.* "Crap," Kayn moaned, seeing the bloody interior and smashed windshield.

Lexy cricked her neck, groaning, "That's why Grey yelled, seatbelts."

"Did his body hit either of you?" Kayn asked as she began tugging on the door, trying to get out. The frame was compromised. *Window it is.*

Lexy answered, "Just Grey. I've got him. Look for Zach."

Kayn climbed out the window. When she attempted to stand, her legs wouldn't hold her. She crumpled onto the dusty gravel road. *Shit, her legs hurt.* Her mind was still fighting its way through the inconvenient aftereffects of mortal shock. *It was Dragon time.* She sucked it up from deep within and got up. This time she stood with no problem. *Her legs had already healed. Cool. Where was Zach's body? It wasn't on the road up ahead as she'd assumed it would be.* She spun around, searching the landscape for her Handler. *He didn't appear to be anywhere. Was she still out cold? Had she imagined this?* She saw Lexy healing Grey and knew it was real. *Where was he?* She called out to the others, "I can't find Zach? Did anyone see where his body went?"

Grey strolled over and said, "Those assholes never give us enough warning. He went through the window with the pressure of the explosion. I'm not sure where we were when it hit. I'm still out of it. Lexy's probably going to need a minute to heal." He took her hand and gave it a casual swing as he suggested, "Shall we go look for Zach's body?"

Kayn couldn't help it as she grinned. With death only a semi-permanent state, these moments were far too comical. "We shall," she replied as they skipped down the road in search of corpse.

Lexy shouted, "You guys are weirdos!"

They both laughed and slowed their skip to a walk. *Perhaps, skipping down a deserted highway in search of a body was a bit much?* The building they'd spent the night in was smouldering in the distance. Kayn paused, and yanked on Grey's arm, enquiring, "Won't the army or the police be showing up?"

"Obviously," Grey replied. "We should hustle our butts. Our new ride will be here soon. They'll call. Hopefully Lexy still has the cell. It might have been thrown out during the accident."

"New ride?" Kayn questioned.

Grey clarified, "Sent by the Aries Group. They'll get us to our flight on time. Theoretically, it's our flight. It won't leave until we get there." He grinned and declared, "Oh, you two are in for a treat."

"What do you mean?" Kayn asked.

"We should find Zach before we worry about anything else," Grey stated, pointing to something in the distance. "Found him. There's probably a hill. That's why we couldn't see him."

Kayn saw the circle of buzzards in the air. *She hated those things. Buzzards were creepy birds. To her, they symbolized death. The demise of someone or something.* They sprinted towards the area below the swarming scavengers. *Hill.* That was funny now as they looked over the edge of a cliff with roaring waves below. Zach's body was on a ledge about ten feet down. *This was inconvenient.*

Kayn called out, "Zach! You still alive?" His body twitched in response.

Grey yelled, "Buddy, that had to suck!"

"You Assholes," Zach groaned.

"There look, he's fine. He still has his wits about him," Grey commented. He peered over the ledge and hollered, "Can you climb up here?"

"Bite me," Zach groaned.

They were gazing over the edge trying to figure out how they were going to get him when Lexy appeared and commented, "The integrity of the ledge doesn't look strong enough for one of us to jump down there."

Before they had a chance to figure out a plan, buzzards descended upon her Handler. As he swatted them away, he rolled off and plummeted into the thunderous rolling waves below.

Kayn took a few steps back, sprinted to the edge and leapt off after him. She managed to slow her descent and hit with the same force as diving from the ledge of a pool. She surfaced in the churning white caps and then allowed herself to sink below the surface to avoid being thrown against the rocks. Opening her eyes in the confusion of the swirling water, Kayn swam towards her Handler's body. *She really hadn't thought this out.* She yanked him below the surface, hoping it would be easier to swim away beneath the waves. *Her head was pounding. The tide was too strong. If she didn't go up to the surface, she was going to be down for the count.* They bobbed up long enough for Kayn to inhale oxygen. She tugged her Handler back under. *If they could make it around the rocks, they'd be all good. Twenty more feet out to sea and she might be able to hold her ground long enough to devise a plan.* Bubbles and swirling water were all she could see beneath the surface. She had a searing headache and knew what that meant. *Her brain was oxygen-deprived.* She was forced to come up for air with the worst possible timing as a massive wave pummelled them into the rocks. Pain surged through her as the wave retreated, sucking them away. *That was going to leave a mark.* Persevering through the agony of what she suspected were broken ribs, Kayn fought with everything she had, to tow Zach away from the rocks before the next wave. Over the thundering waves, she heard Grey and Lexy yelling but couldn't make out what they were saying. Inhaling, Kayn knew she was in trouble when she couldn't get much air. *A broken rib must have punctured her lung.* She dove, towing his limp body with her. *He wasn't helping at all. He must be dead.* She felt the cold resolution of the Dragon within as she fought against the current, knowing she couldn't let his body go.

She bobbed to the surface still in the same place. *This wasn't working. The heat of her healing ability was struggling to repair her injury but if she lost consciousness their bodies could be lost. She wasn't going to be able to keep this up.* Kayn sunk into the deep once more, bringing his corpse along for the ride. *There had to be a way out of this. She needed time to figure it out.* Amid the swirling confusion an idea sparked. She forced her oxygen-deprived brain to concentrate as she looked below instead of to either side or above. *There it was… a visible flow of current going into a space between the rocks.* They surfaced and managed to inhale a touch of air before purposely submerging them once more with a destination in mind. Her pounding headache had been replaced with the instinct to sleep. *She didn't have long.* She shoved Zach's body into the current travelling beneath the rock. They were sucked through by the force of the water, and as she'd hoped, they surfaced in an underground cavern.

Kayn opted to float for a minute, taking shallow breaths, conserving energy as she healed. *It was the craziest feeling, floating in the darkness. It reminded her of the room she'd become trapped in during the Testing where the wicked things were held.* The heat in her chest dulled and she took a deep breath. After an unrestricted dose of oxygen, her problem-solving skills sprang to life. *She needed light.* Kayn tugged off her fingerless glove expecting her strobing Ankh symbol to light up the cavern. *Why wasn't it flashing? Zach had been deceased for a while. Maybe it times out?* She was about to bite into her skin to set off her symbol when a thought leapt to mind, *Blood draws sharks. They'd probably both been bleeding since they smoked the rocks. She had to get them out of the water. There better be dry land in here.* While treading water, she ripped material from Zach's shirt and tore it in half. *She didn't want him to slip beneath the surface while she was messing around.* Once he was secured, she bit her hand hard enough to break the skin and set off her symbol. She kept her oozing hand out of the water as she got a two second glimpse of the underground cavern. *There was dry rock ahead.* Her stomach clenched, warning her of danger. She swam with all her mite and yarded Zach up onto the rock with her. Her symbol flashed again giving her a clear view of fins circling the pool. *They were safe on dry land.* Relief washed over her. She chuckled while lying on the stone ledge. *Well, this rescue attempt had backfired rather epically. She would be a horrible superhero.* She was exhausted. Her eyes grew heavy. *Sleep… Sleep.* She closed her eyes for only a second.

12

SHARKS VERSUS CANNIBALS

Kevin's voice was in her mind, *'Wake up! Wake up, Kayn! You have to get up!'*

Was she wet? Kayn groggily opened her eyes in the dark. *For a second, she forgot where she was. Oh, yes. They were trapped inside of a cliff by sharks.* Water splashed her. Suddenly, she was wide awake.

Kevin's voice prompted, *'The water is rising. Get up!'*

Her back was damp. *Oh, no.* There was only a millimetre of water beneath her but that's all she needed to know to understand the water was rising in the cavern. *If there were still sharks in here, this was going to suck.* Kayn felt around in the darkness for her Handler. She nudged Zach's stiff corpse. *Rigour Mortis was setting in. How long had she been asleep? That lucky bastard was probably enjoying a Pina Colada in the In-between on a gorgeous sandy beach, safe as a newborn baby in his mother's arms.* Kayn needed the visual to see what she was dealing with. *How much time did she have?* She bit herself and her symbol only flashed a few times before the wound healed. *Yes, the tide was filling the cavern. It wouldn't be long before the rock they were on would be submerged and three sharks were circling. Awesome! Could this day get any better?*

Kevin's voice suggested. *'You can get to higher ground. Look again.'*

She bit into her freshly healed hand. This time when Kayn looked up, she saw an escape route. *This guiding her thing might work out. She had to wake Zach. They didn't have much time.* She placed her hands against his lifeless chest and willed her healing ability to surface. At first it didn't work. *Her battery was dead.* She concentrated… *Come on! Please! Work, damn it! Please work!* Shivering heat travelled down her arms into the chest of her deceased Handler until she felt faint. Zach started coughing. *Oh, thank God.* With no time for pleasantries, she gave him instructions, "We have to climb up the rocks to the left. I'm too weak to bite myself and heal on repeat for light from my symbol. I only get a few flashes before I heal. You went off a cliff into the ocean. I jumped in after you. The waves were too strong to swim against, so I managed to get us into this underground cavern."

"Why don't we just swim back out?" He questioned. "Sharks," she answered. "Also, the tide is filling up the cavern and the rock we're on is almost submerged."

"Of course it is," Zach replied in darkness.

Tension in her Handler's voice was followed by light flashing from the Ankh brand on his palm. With each strobe, they momentarily saw what they were dealing with. At least a half dozen shark fins were circling the underground pool, waiting for the tide to rise so they could devour their snacks. It flashed again. It was a steep upward climb with an opening to what appeared to be a cave. *Ironically, she'd been in this situation before minus the sharks. It could be done but they might only be buying themselves more time if the water level rose until it flooded the entire cave system.* They were submerged in darkness once again. It flashed. Standing beside Zach, she urged, "Start climbing. It'll be inconvenient if you heal before we reach the top. We'll scale this during each flash, pause and wait for the next. He went first, using each groove in the stone to climb as they'd been taught. Grasping ridges in the stone, she followed, but the light was dimmer from her vantage point. Reaching for indents and jutting rock as his foot moved upwards to the next, they maintained the pace until Zach vanished at the top. The cavern lit up as he reached over the side to help her.

They sat at the mouth of the cave, regaining their bearings. "That sucked," Zach said, getting up.

She joined him. They peered over the ledge at the growing school of sharks below. *She should have tried to swim out when there were only three.*

Her Handler's hand lit up the cave like a flashlight as he announced, "Let's see if there's a way out."

They entered the cave, and during a flash of Zach's hand, they discovered they weren't the first to choose dry land over a battle in the deep. The walls had primitive carvings, and as they ventured further into the darkness with each strobe, the visual grew more disturbing. There were bones everywhere. Kayn picked up a large perfect one. It looked like something you'd see a dog in a comic strip carrying.

Zach cleared his throat. Kayn glanced back at him as he disclosed, "That's a femur."

Intrigued, she asked, "From what kind of animal?"

"A human. These are human remains," Zach clarified as he crouched and shone his light at a semi-crushed skull. "On the bright side, it doesn't look like this cave will fill up with water."

"Oh, what a relief," Kayn emotionlessly responded as she knelt and picked up the skull. "What else can you tell me about it? Is this something you learned in school?"

"The school of life, I guess... It's a woman's skull," he clarified as they sorted through an uncomfortably large assortment of human remains. He picked up a small one and whispered, "This one belonged to an infant. It's possible we've stumbled across someone or something's trophy case. We should keep moving. There must be another way out."

She wanted to ask if he knew how old the bones were. She had lots of questions that would prove pointless as they continued their journey into the layer of the depraved cave-dwelling being. The glow of Zach's Ankh symbol only lit up ten feet ahead. It felt like they'd been walking for hours when they came to a fork in the cavern.

"Which way, Brighton?" Zach questioned.

Hairs had risen on every inch of her flesh. Grinning, Kayn wiped the sweat from her brow and replied, "Do you want to go towards danger or away from it? You already know my choice. Take a whiff." She flippantly chose the path he'd tempted her to take without waiting for his response.

Zach sighed, "Of course," as he followed her into the more perilous route, dimly lit at intervals by his symbol.

They knew what they were about to stumble upon by the distinctive foul scent of decaying flesh. Sure enough, there were more wall etchings and fresher carcasses. *It was about more for her. She sensed a dark entities presence and she was famished. It had been a tumultuous couple of days. She hadn't fed the beast that raged beneath her mortal disguise.* She picked up her pace as the light from his symbol ceased to strobe.

He whispered, "Slow down. Give me a second to get us light."

A rush of icy air chilled her to the bone. *She wasn't afraid. She was stoked. The ante had been upped.* Whatever this was, she would meet it in its layer and kill it in the darkness it embraced. She inhaled the scent of the dead. With each rancid breath, she became increasingly aware without sight as a crutch. She crouched and placed her hands on the ground. It vibrated every couple of seconds. *There was movement. Whatever it was… It was coming.* She closed her eyes and became one with the dark. *In this predatory form, she required no light.* She heard a grunt from Zach and knew he'd broken his skin. *She could smell his blood. If she could… they could.* Her senses lit up like fireworks as his symbol strobed, adding a creepy ambiance to the cavern. There was a rabid partially mortal creature standing about twenty feet away. Zach's symbol flashed again. *Make that ten feet.*

"It's behind me, isn't it?" Her wide-eyed Handler nervously whispered.

As the light flashed off, Kayn shoved him out of the way and raced at the beastly creature with a primal cry. As it slashed her abdomen with serrated blade-like claws, her emotions numbed. During each flash of light, she dodged out of the way, knowing her moment would come. She leapt on its back, managing to get it in a chokehold. Squeezing with all her might, it tumbled backwards and knocked the wind out of her. Relentlessly maintaining her hold with both arms wound tightly as a Python's grip, she persevered until it ceased struggling. *With no weapon, she had to think on her toes. That was a good enough excuse.* She willed her Conduit ability to the surface, and with unbridled rage, she shrieked in an ungodly pitch while siphoning life from the depraved being. It became limp in her arms. Releasing her hold, she closed her eyes and revelled in the hallucinogenic power of the dark entity coursing through her veins.

Inching closer, Zach asked, "Are you alright?"

Her brain was tingling. Opening catlike iridescent eyes, she coldly answered, "This feels amazing."

"Your eyes are glowing," Zach whispered.

It was no longer dark in the cave. *Not for her.* She could see her Handler's vibrant heat signature with swirling hues of yellow and orange. *This abomination hunted victims in the dark by seeing their body heat, and now, she the ability to do the same.* Zach's symbol continued to strobe at steady intervals as she brushed herself off, announcing, "There's no need to wound yourself again. I can see in the dark now. I'll take it from here."

Squatting before their assailant, her Handler studied it, enquiring, "What do you think it is? It's still part mortal facially."

There was so much they didn't know. So many beings, they'd not yet had the opportunity to come across. They still had so much to learn.

"Do you think there are more of these things in here?" He asked, touching the partially human creature's pointed tips of its ears.

Stoked about it, Kayn answered, "Yes." She lifted the side of the top lip to look at its pronounced beast like curved fangs. "There's evidence of a community. The carvings on the walls of the cave where we entered showed dozens of these worshipping something, and there were an excessive amount of bones. The entrance they use can't be the way we came in. There must be another way out in this system of underground caverns."

"Maybe there's only one of them left?" Zach gave optimism a shot as he got up and held out his hand.

She wasn't stupid. He was trying to handle the situation. Contact with her Handler would undoubtedly take her ability induced aggressive nature down a peg. She took his hand anyway and shook her head, revealing, "No. I can sense a large group. I have an idea but there's no way of knowing if it'll work."

"One idea is better than none," Zach replied as they made their way through the intricate tunnel system holding hands. Dependent on her to see, he nervously suggested, "Maybe, we should just go back and kill the sharks? We can just go back out the way we came in."

"That's not an option. The sharks aren't our biggest problem. The current is too strong. I can't swim against it and keep a hold of you. This is the obvious route. Our odds are better if we make our stand on dry land."

"Without weapons... Really?" Zach countered. "This is so how the others were killed and eaten by those things. They dove off the cliff and got caught in this system of tunnels that's beginning to feel more like a web. Lexy and Grey know we're down here, right?"

"Hopefully," Kayn replied. *Kevin knew she was still alive. She'd heard his voice. He wouldn't just leave her here. That much, she was certain of.* "We'll find weapons and kill everything down here. If we can't find our way out or starve before they find us, our shells will be salvageable," she shared.

"You're so horrible at pep talks," Zach teased, as they started walking again. He yanked her arm and said, "We need to double back. I have an idea."

Intrigued, Kayn said, "Well, don't leave me hanging."

He answered, "Bones brittle from age may be jagged enough to use as weapons if we snap them in two."

And the award for best plan goes to Zach. As he set off his symbol, light strobed throughout the cavern. Understanding he wanted to feel less dependent, Kayn allowed him to guide her while fighting the urge to share her thoughts. *It felt like they were back in the Testing, with the caves and inescapable demises. His idea made sense. Using broken bones as weapons gave them a decent shot at not becoming the next course on the cave dwellers menu.*

When they reached engravings surrounded by piles of human bones, Zach continued injuring himself to see. Choosing to leave the skulls alone out of respect for the dead, they snapped the larger ones in half. Sure enough, broken femurs turned out to be the perfect weapons. *It was irony at its best to kill these creatures with their victim's bones.* Gathering their weapons, they creatively stowed them.

Before commencing their journey, Zach commented, "If Grey were here, he'd use Pyrokinesis to make a torch with what's left of my shirt and one of these bones so I wouldn't have to keep hurting myself to see."

Yes, let's drain her battery for a silly reason. "I can try," Kayn played along as Zach removed his torn shirt and wrapped the end of a bone. *He was so stubborn.* Staring at it, she willed the Pyrokinesis to the surface. *Nothing.* She tried again to light the morbid torch created from human bones. Not a spark, but when she touched it, her hands warmed.

Abruptly dropping the unlit torch, her Handler said, "Please don't feed on me, knock me out and leave me defenceless in a cave system full of cannibals."

She sighed, "I don't know what I'm doing yet. This isn't going to work. I used too much energy healing." *He was nervous but that idea wasn't half bad. He didn't have to fight. If she ingested her Handler's energy and stashed his body somewhere safe, she'd be strong enough to kill anything that came at them.* Kayn looked at her Handler.

"Not a chance, Brighton," he replied to her thoughts. "Who would bring you back?"

"It was just a thought," she explained. His glowing Ankh symbol vanished. It was pitch black, excluding his heat signature. Running an experiment, she wandered away and sensed a wall before she got to it. *This was cool.* Wanting to use the instinct-driven sightless guidance system, she took Zach's hand assuring, "I can find the way out. I've got this." Leading her Handler through the intricate network of tunnels while detecting obstructions like having use of a cat's whiskers, she knew if they fled without clearing the cave, they'd be sent back in. Planning to get her Handler out and volunteer, she let instinct lead the way as she sprinted towards another fork in the caves and veered to the left into the unmistakeable stench of recently slaughtered mortals.

Zach tugged on her hand as he stopped cold. Slicing into his flesh, the morbid scene lit up. Taking in the massacre, he came to the same conclusion, "We can't leave until we kill these things. Now, they'll come to us."

With her heart palpitating erratically and throat so parched she could barely swallow, she was losing her grip. *She'd given the ability enough of a hold to react as they would to get out of the cave system. His blood smelled delicious. Oh, this wasn't good.*

The pattering of multiple feet, panting and agonizing cries filled their ears.

"They're coming," Zach whispered.

There were more than anticipated. With each strobe of light, the wailing grew closer. *She had to take him out and hide his body. Instinct was screaming at her.*

"Don't you dare," her Handler asserted, standing his ground with a jagged bone in each of his hands.

Adrenaline began pulsating and in the next stream of light from his symbol, she saw the colour of the veins down her arms. *She could kill them all with an orb, but she had no idea how to choose between the yellow light which sent them back through the Hall of Souls and the blue. Once it was started, she wouldn't be able to stop, and it would be out of her hands.*

"Have faith in me!" Zach shouted over thunderous steps. "I'm not helpless! I made it through the Testing too!"

The light from his symbol went out, and when it strobed again, the herd of deplorable salivating beings were visible. Each time it flashed they were closer, like freeze frames on a camera. They bravely stood their ground. *Fifty feet... twenty feet... ten feet.* They were upon them with snapping teeth and slicing claws. The duo valiantly swung their bone blades as the ravenous creatures sunk their teeth into their flesh and tore out chunks of meat until all that could be felt was the warm spray of blood and agony. She was sinking into the emotionless void as a swarm of heat signatures descended upon her Handler. Zach's screaming snapped her out of it. She tore the depravities off him in the confusing sensory overload of violence. Her entire body was broiling as it fought to heal.

Suddenly, a familiar soul-shattering pitch brought them all to their knees. Persevering through the piercing noise, she grabbed for one of the creatures and ingested its being as the pitch continued incapacitating everything in the caverns. Placing her hands on Zach's stomach, she released a shriek loud enough to curl the devil's toes while expelling enough healing energy to get her Handler back on his feet. She fought to stay on task as the strongest of the monstrosities began chowing down on her leg. Kayn kicked it away as she rose, weakened by the energy she'd expelled.

Zach breathlessly urged, "Come with me!"

Some were fighting against the noise, crawling towards them. Kayn shouted, "I'll hold them off! Get out of here!

Hide!" His dull heat signature staggered away. She grabbed the closest of her carnivorous assailants and ingested the creature's energy. Shivering as its essence granted her healing ability the juice to soldier on through the impossible. Blocking the path to her Handler, she kicked and snapped necks, detouring those persevering against the incapacitating noise. As the unbearable sound raised a couple of octaves, even the most durable ceased to have the will to battle against it. Momentarily taken down by an excruciating migraine, Kayn dropped to her knees *She refused to submit. Quitting wasn't one of her choices. She needed enough energy to counteract it.* Moving from one dark creature to the next, she devoured energy and slashed throats until all sense of reason slipped away. The sound abruptly ceased. Rising with energy coursing through her veins, she stood in silence, coldly observing a creature crawling away from the massacre. The glow was flush with the ground. *It assumed it would be invisible. This, of course, was not the case.* She left it alive to follow it back to the nest. While lost in an emotionally void state it made the most sense to eliminate the threat. *She would look for her Handler after she'd dispersed the evil things that dwelled in the dark. Instinct told her he was deceased so there was no rush. Death would conceal his location. Nothing touches a dead human's meat with a ten-foot pole.* She unsympathetically stepped over bodies, silently stalking the wounded creature. It got up and staggered away. As she trailed the monster through the caves, she took note of the increasingly foul scent of decomposing flesh. *Perhaps, it was the blood they were after and not the meat? They'd assumed they were cannibals by the clean state of the bones they'd found but the passage of time may have been the culprit.* With each predatory step through the darkness the instinct of the creature's energy she'd consumed sunk deeper into her being. *Left foot, right foot, left foot, right foot. If she became lost in the void, there was no one to bring her back. She had to be with it enough to find and heal her Handler after she'd finished off the cave-dwelling depravities that resided in this underground Tomb.* Struggling to keep her emotions from tapping out, she observed the crimson glow ahead as it dulled. *It was almost gone. This was a annoying.* From the darkness, she heard a series of wild, chaotic shrieks, followed by the rapid pattering of feet as the last of the cave-dwelling monstrosities raced to the aid of their fallen. *These suckers were fast. This was going to be fun.* Adrenaline rushed through her as she raced into the madness with bloody bone weapons clutched in each hand. The Dragon within her didn't care how many there were. Numbers had ceased to be of any concern. Kayn swung the jagged weapons at the whirling heat signatures of the beasts as they launched themselves at her, tearing at her flesh with their fangs and claws. *Small ones kept coming at her legs. Children? She couldn't think about it. They'd kill her as easily as the adults would.* They'd swarmed her from all sides. *Shit. There was too many.* Kayn released a primal scream trying to bring an ability to the surface, anything to give her the upper hand. *Nothing happened. Healing was taking all she had.* She cursed her ego, frantically tearing monsters off and launching them away. *She wasn't winning.* A raging fire engulfed her stomach along with a tugging sensation. *Shit! Come on! She'd felt this before. One of these assholes was tugging out her intestines.* Relieved she didn't have the visual of each wound they inflicted, her ability for rational thought slipped further away.

In the end, she was the only one left standing. The coppery scent of her blood was so potent it was burning her nostrils each time she inhaled. *She was bleeding out.* She instinctively touched her sopping warm, partially missing shirt and got a hand full of squishy entrails. *No. She wasn't going to be able to bring herself to shove these back inside.* Critically injured and nearly lost in the emotionless void, a familiar voice in her head prompted, *'Find your Handler.'* Kayn turned around a few times. *Her thought process wasn't working. Her hair was still wet.* She touched her head. *It was mushy. Oh, crap. She was in trouble.* The voice in her mind prompted, *'turn left.'* She paused. *Oh, no. Which way was left? Her stomach felt heavy.* The voice in her head commented, *'You're dragging your intestines around. Shove them back in.'* Kayn pulled up her big girl panties as she tore off what was left of her shirt and shoved her intestines back into her stomach. *Well, that just happened.* She kept them in by stretching the material around her waist and tying it. *The temperature had become intolerable.* Lightheaded and confused, she stumbled over the massive pile of bodies and fell. *She'd reached her destination. This was where they parted ways.* Sweating and bleeding profusely, she needed to close her eyes for a second.

'Get up, Brighton!' Kevin's voice directed.

She opened her eyes. *Where was she? Zach. She was looking for her Handler.* Her thoughts were scattered fragments. She touched the sketchy blood crusted material covering her stomach. *How much time had passed since they parted ways?* Kayn felt her head wound. *Her hair was crusty. She must be healing by order of importance.* She got up and continued making her way through the darkness as nothingness pumped through her veins. All she had left was the instinct to find her Handler. She'd been scouring the intricate underground maze in search of

Zach for what felt like hours when she lost the ability to find her way through the darkness without sight or touch. Inconvenienced, Kayn sliced her palm with her bone blade. The light from her Ankh symbol flashed twice before she healed. *This wasn't going to work.* She'd gotten a look at the cave ahead. She walked for a while before slicing herself again. On the first flash she spun, scanning the tunnel in every direction. *Nothing. Where was he?* On the second, she stroked her Ankh symbol and thought of Zach. Images flickered through her mind like an old black and white movie. *She was onto something.* Kayn felt her way around for a while longer. *She needed to recharge her Conduit battery with another one of those carnivorous cave-dwelling things.* Usually, calling out for someone in the dark was a horrible idea, but in this case, she'd be killing two birds with one stone. *If any of those creatures were still wandering around down here, this was the fastest way to summon them.* Getting it out of the way while coherent enough to kick ass, Kayn loudly called out her Handler's name, "Zach!" She counted to five and sliced into her hand. Her symbol flashed twice as she surveyed her surroundings. *Nothing attacked her. It felt like the caves had been cleared. How long had those creatures been down here hidden from the world feeding on the forgotten and the lost?* Kayn cautiously continued her journey into the unknown with one hand against the stone. *Was the temperature rising? Maybe it was just her? It felt like something was off.* She wiped the excess perspiration from her brow and sliced into her palm, bringing light to the darkness. The cave split into two tunnels up ahead. She made a choice, uncoordinatedly staggered into the cavern and lost consciousness.

Kayn awoke in a pitch-black area, coldly indifferent to how she'd come to be there. As a Dragon, she preferred the solitude of darkness with only sounds, scents and instinct to guide her way. *She was thirsty.* Finding water was her most urgent need. This prompted her to get up and start moving. *Immortal or not, her system would shut down without it. She wasn't sure how long she'd gone without because the memory of where she was and how she'd come to be there had been wiped.* Kayn inhaled the putrid scent in the air. *It was the unforgettable fragrance of death.* Small fragments of her memory began to return. Before she had the opportunity to downshift, she heard the clicking of shoes and humming voices behind her. She slowly turned as her memory began to reboot. *Zach went over a cliff. She'd followed him in. Sharks blocked the obvious escape route, so they'd chosen to search for another way out through the caves. They'd found bones. They were attacked by monsters.* Picking up the weapons made of human bones, Kayn cracked her neck, expecting another round with the cave-dwellers. *She wasn't seeing heat signatures. It was mortal auras approaching her in the darkness.* As she stepped forward, she was blinded by an explosion of light. Kayn squinted in the glare, unable to see.

"Lower your weapons!" a male voice asserted.

Weapons? Oh yes. She still had the bones in her hands. She heard the cocking of guns as her eyes became accustomed to the light from their headgear. *They were all in hazmat gear with guns drawn. What were they hoping to accomplish with guns?*

"Put your weapons down or we will be forced to take you out!" the same masculine voice bellowed.

She wasn't going to be ordered around by a pack of gun-toting mortals in white jumpsuits. "No," Kayn coldly responded.

"You may have been infected! Weapons down!" another man's voice called out.

"They're human bones," Kayn casually corrected.

"Subdue her," a familiar female voice commanded.

Hearing a whoosh as someone shot a tranquillizer into her torso, it was irritating. Kayn casually plucked it out. Intrigued by their inept knowledge of what they were dealing with, she took in the trembling hazmat suits. She cocked her head and declared, "That was rather rude."

The female voice coolly countered, "You may not be in your right mind. Drop your weapons."

When was she ever?

"On the count of three. One... two," a stranger's voice announced.

She was shot by two darts on two. Sneaky. Kayn nonchalantly tugged the darts out, chuckling. *Whatever they'd just dosed her with was fantastic.*

In her mind, Kevin's voice cautioned, *'It's the Aries group. Submit or you'll cause problems for all of us.'*

She dramatically sighed. *Party pooper.* Dropping the jagged ended bones, Kayn suggested, "Next time try leading with, we're from the Aries Group. Lower your weapons. There's no need to shoot me again. I'll come willingly." Somebody grabbed for her. Kayn cautioned, "I wouldn't do that if I were you."

A female voice ordered, "Stand down!"

Now, she remembered where she heard that voice. It was the lady from the Aries Group with the nice smile that ran some tests on her a while ago at the rodeo grounds. She couldn't recall her name. Kayn addressed the woman in charge, "You shot me before properly identifying yourself."

"When you get a look at your reflection in the mirror, you'll understand," the Agent replied, leading her past the macabre display of creature's bodies in the glare of their headlamps. She questioned, "Did you do this?"

Nodding, Kayn answered honestly, "Yes, but in my defence, they were trying to eat us." *Zach. Where was he?* She froze and questioned, "Where's Zach?"

The woman laughed as she replied, "We have your Handler. We'd just arrived when he found the way out of this maze."

Why had she been so certain he was dead?

The lady from the Aries Group explained, "Your Handler has already been decontaminated and tested. Zach was quite concerned about you, but we couldn't allow him to go back in after being cleared of infection. He'll be happy to have you back safe and sound."

Sound... Hell no. Safe... That depends on how they were planning to decontaminate her. She'd seen Grey decontaminate Frost before. Hopefully, that's not what she meant. She'd already lit herself on fire for the greater good once this week. Up ahead she saw the glimmer of natural light. It felt like walking out of hell into Heaven. Kayn stepped outside into a plastic tube and changed her mind. She was directed into one compartment and everyone else went into another.

A loud voice from a speaker ordered, "Remove your clothes and seal them in that large bag in the corner."

She glanced down at her blood-soaked bra. *Yes. She was impressively covered in blood.* Noticing the red strip of T-Shirt around her stomach, Kayn grinned. *Imagine how freaked out they'd be if she told them what that was for.* She tore away the material used to hold in her intestines and shimmied out of her blood stiffened shorts. She felt her hair, knowing why her curls were matted with blood. She was down to her unmentionables.

The voice directed, "Including your underwear."

It would be less embarrassing if they just lit her on fire to decontaminate her. It might be preferable to a stranger watching her undress while ordering her around. When she was naked as the day she was born, Kayn was told to step into the next room. A woman and man in protective gear were holding sponges. On the floor were buckets filled with liquid that smelled uncomfortably like household cleaner. *Seriously?*

"It looks like you've been through quite the ordeal dear. I know this may seem harsh, but we need to thoroughly scrub you down. It may sting if you have any open wounds under that blood," the woman warned.

It was obvious they hadn't all been let in on the backstory of who she was and what she was capable of. At least after this stranger bathing incident, she wasn't going to end up a virgin sacrifice as she had at the Summit. Healed and super chill from the sedatives they'd shot into her, Kayn smiled as red tinted water pooled on the ground beneath her feet. *Yes, she'd been absolutely covered in it. She was disappointed they hadn't given her an opportunity to look in the mirror. It must have been epic.*

While soaping her up, the lady enquired, "Do you feel lightheaded? Can you tell if you have a fever?"

A voice came over the monitor, "She was shot with three rounds of Etorphine, and she's still standing up. I'd hazard a guess that she's fine."

"What's Etorphine?" Kayn enquired quite curious as to what they'd used to try to subdue her.

The women answered, "It's an Opioid 10000 times the strength of Morphine, traditionally used on large zoo animals. That can't be what they used, dear. You'd be dead."

Yes. This lady had absolutely no idea what she was dealing with. Kayn shrugged and said, "For the record, it's lovely. I'm super relaxed right now." *She must have been insanely amped up when they shot her.* She was ushered into the next room.

Zach's voice came over the speaker, "This is going to hurt."

Kayn's heart swelled. *Her Handler sounded like he was all good. How bad could it be?* She was sprayed by scalding steam from all sides. The surface of her skin bubbled with excruciating blisters. She winced, barely reacting. *This Etorphine was magnificent.* The heat of her ability kicked in, and in seconds, the blisters disappeared. Kayn yawned and asked if they had any snacks.

Zach's voice piped in, "She's all good."

They instructed her to go into the next room, put on a gown and a mask and take a seat. She sat in a covered chair while the people who bathed her began fumbling around. *They were going to take her blood. That made sense.*

The woman whose face was obscured from view except for her eyes drew some blood and said, "This is a precautionary measure. After testing your friend's blood, we're quite certain the virus isn't airborne. I have to say, you're healing ability is miraculous. I'm truly honoured to meet you. My name's Karen. As soon as we're finished up here, I'll get you something to eat. You've been in there for a week. I bet you're starving."

A week without water? She must have died of dehydration and come back. That's how they had the time to get here and set this up. Kayn nodded politely and asked for water.

"Silly me, of course you need water," Karen replied. Taking a six pack of bottled water out of a cooler, she passed her one and left the rest within reach on the counter.

Kayn downed one and drank two more.

The man announced, "She's good to go." They both removed their protective gear.

"I'll take you to your friends," Karen announced as they unsealed a door and stepped out into glaring sunshine.

Squinting and cowering in light after a week in darkness, Kayn smiled as her Handler appeared and ran to her. As they embraced, everything else ceased to matter.

Rocking her in his arms, Zach tried to explain why it took so long, "I've been out for four days, but I had to be stored until they set up their mobile quarantine unit. I was decontaminated yesterday. Thankfully, I was out cold when they did it. Lexy was here to heal me and explain. You died of dehydration. We suspected you'd resurrect long before the retrieval team found you. They've dealt with this virus before. They were prepared for unhinged drama but neither of us were infected."

As Lexy and Grey appeared and joined the embrace, Kayn whispered, "I guess we missed our plane."

"The Aries Group is flying us to our next job," Zach answered. "Alaska's Correction has already happened. He died. The girl in British Columbia also didn't make it. We're off to Seattle, Washington next. Grey and Lexy are taking point so we can have a breather."

Seattle sounded way better than Alaska after being in sweltering heat for more than a week. They heard tires peeling away. Most of the tenting was already gone. *These guys were crazy efficient.*

Karen wandered over, gave them a cooler and said, "Sandwiches with deli meat and cheese. Fill up during the drive. It's a short trip to the airport so eat fast. You can have something else once we get to Seattle."

"You don't have meals on the flight?" Zach enquired.

Lexy nudged him and whispered, "We have to be stored in the cargo bay in containers. It's not optional."

Gobbling down her entire sandwich in seconds, Kayn reached for another, slightly disappointed because she'd never been on a plane. *She wanted the experience. Guess it wasn't in the cards.*

A man came over and handed them credit cards and a phone. He explained, "Buy whatever you need once we arrive in Seattle. It doesn't matter which phone you use. They're not personally assigned. Text the first contact with the name of who has each number. You'll need to be sedated for the flight. I understand sedation is no longer effective for Kayn. We'll still have to dose everyone. It's a paperwork thing. It'll be a relaxing trip even if you're awake. You'll be in your compartment for the duration of the flight, but you have WIFI to keep yourself entertained."

They all sort of shrugged as they followed the unnamed man to one of the remaining vehicles. Kayn glanced back at the now exposed entrance to the cave she'd spent a week in. *She wanted to know more. What were they? Why did they treat it like an outbreak? Many of the immortals she'd encountered were infected by something to turn them into something else. Was this a wide-scale thing or just a random occurrence?* She didn't bother saying anything aloud, opting to keep her concerns to herself. *She'd ask Markus when she saw him.* They piled into the back of the black sedan with a film of dust on it and once again it occurred to her that their vehicles couldn't be more of a cliché. *But they were clichés with glorious air conditioning.* They smiled at each other. Zach took her hand as the driver slid a see-through slightly tinted barrier up obscuring their view of him and doors locked as they took off. They rode in peaceful silence. They'd only been driving for fifteen minutes when they parked at a deserted airfield.

The driver got out of the sedan, strolled around to open the back door and instructed, "Walk over to that first building. There should be someone waiting for you."

"Thank you," Kayn said, because she was Canadian and frankly, she was programmed to thank anyone that did anything for her.

The driver gave her a strange look as he replied, "You're welcome."

They wandered over to the building they'd been directed to in the sweltering afternoon sun. She was still holding Zach's hand as they were instructed to get into four suntan booth sized pods by the lady who'd introduced herself as Karen back at the caves. Lexy and Grey didn't hesitate. They'd done this before.

Kayn enquired, "Can I watch for a minute? The sedatives won't work on me. I'm just curious."

"Sure, why not," Karen answered as Zach climbed into the third pod. "I'll be riding in the cargo hold with you guys for the duration of the flight." She knocked on Grey's container and asked, "Gas, needle or dart?"

He replied, "Gas."

She closed his chamber. It lit up, flashed and hummed. She pressed a button on the side and there was a hissing sound. She slid something down, peered in and said, "He's out." She looked at Kayn and questioned, "Do you want a peek?"

Yes, she kind of did. Kayn wandered over and looked through a small plexiglass observation window. *Grey was out cold. It was kind of cool. That only took a few seconds.* She remarked, "That was quick. How long does it last?"

"Only a couple of hours with each dose. I stay in the cargo hold, just in case one of you wakes up. These chambers are a claustrophobia nightmare. I had to take sensitivity training and do a flight locked in one to get this job. I assure you it's all humane. The chambers are made of Sterenimite. A little something, we picked up at a crash site a decade ago. It blocks all forms of energy. It's practically indestructible. I know you're new, so this probably seems strange but it's a safety measure for our crew aboard the flight. Some of you have abilities that mess with the equipment and impair the crew."

Frost came to mind. Kayn smiled as she replied, "I can see how that could happen. It makes sense." Karen moved to each chamber. They all chose gas, and in a minute, all three chambers were humming in tune. "I guess it's my turn," Kayn said, voluntarily getting into the remaining chamber. "I'll take the gas," she answered her next question before being asked. *This was going to be so boring. There was no way there was enough room to play with her new phone.*

"If you get bored in there, I have a headset and mic. I'll be able to hear you. We can talk," Karen offered.

The chamber filled with gas. Kayn inhaled it hoping for a nap. *Nothing happened.* She recalled the spray Kevin used on her that day they'd been kidnapped by Triad and left to cook in a storage container in the desert. She'd been out for a few minutes at least with whatever that was. *Things had changed. She was stronger.*

Karen's voice piped into the chamber, "You still awake?"

"Wide awake," Kayn answered.

"Do you want me to try another dose?" Karen enquired.

"Fill your boots," Kayn replied, already painfully bored. The chamber filled with gas again and she chuckled. "I can feel it a little now, it's lovely stuff." She heard the lady's laughter.

Karen's voice teased, "So, I read everyone's files. Ankh has some good-looking guys. Can I volunteer?"

Grinning, Kayn answered, "Everyone's hot but the training is brutal and the hours are shitty." The likeable Agent was laughing as Kayn sparred, "I really thought this whole sacrificial lamb job would come with more perks."

"What? You mean you don't consider being gassed on a plane a perk?" Karen teased. She opened the visor so they could see each other.

"Thanks," Kayn said as their eyes met. *She hadn't had a conversation with a mortal in a while.*

"I'd let you out if I could without being fired," Karen apologized.

"You'd definitely get fired for letting me out. How did you end up with the Aries Group?" Kayn asked.

"I've only been working with the Aries Group for a couple of months. I was a lab tech in Florida. I tested the blood of a child who'd miraculously healed after falling ten stories. My partner and I discovered some oddities. It was at the end of our shift, so we hadn't even reported it. We'd planned to double-check our results the next morning. We usually carpooled because we were also roommates, but that night my girlfriend picked me up. I guess my lab partner gave a few friends who were also working that night a ride. They were in a car accident. I was called right away. Everybody knew Laurie was my roommate. Everyone else was pronounced dead at the scene but they were still trying to revive my friend when I arrived at the hospital. Laurie was pronounced brain dead. I was distraught but I stuck around to be there for her family. I went to the lab to keep myself occupied and walked in on the Aries Group covering up our results. We'd stumbled across something we shouldn't have. I was sure they were going to kill me, but they drugged me, and I woke up blindfolded in the back of a van. I was offered a choice between a job and death. That's how I became privy to this craziness," Karen explained.

She hadn't given the mortals who covered up for them much thought until now. They'd given up everything too. She met her eyes through the plexiglass as she replied, "Perhaps, we're not so different after all. I was just a normal girl in high school. My twin had an ability. She triggered our Correction. One day I had this amazing family, and the next, they were gone." Kayn knew she'd hit a nerve as tears formed in her caretaker's eyes.

They spent hours chatting about T.V shows and guys. Time moved quickly, and soon it was time to be released from the pod like chamber she was encased in. Karen opened hers first. She allowed her to watch the protocol for reviving and releasing the others. Another button was pushed, followed by a whoosh of clear air.

"It's potent oxygen," Karen explained. "It usually does the trick. If not, I give the heavy sleeper adrenaline."

The chambers were opened. All three of her Clan members climbed out stretching and yawning.

Lexy asked, "Do we need to rent a car or does the Aries Group have one waiting for us?"

Karen smiled as she answered, "I'm sure someone is waiting because you'll also need passports and ID." She shook Kayn's hand as they parted and said, "I'm sure we'll meet again."

While saying her goodbyes, Kayn awkwardly bumped into an extremely tall man in a suit.

"I'm your driver. I'll take you to get everything you need," a tall, lanky man announced as they descended the stairs into a partially enclosed enormous cargo hold. *They must have driven the plane right into it.* Kayn inhaled the scent of the air. *It smelled like it was raining. It was probably pouring outside.*

13

THIS ONE TIME IN SEATTLE

They'd all had naps and were prepared for the duties ahead. *Except for her.* After a quick shopping spree for clothes, toiletries and snacks, followed by a well-deserved soak in their suites luxurious tub, Kayn felt more herself. Zach knocked on the door. Concealed by bubbles, she sang, "Come in."

He stuck his head in and announced, "We've ordered dinner. I think everyone wants to stay in and binge-watch Netflix. Are you in?"

"Hell yes," Kayn agreed from within her cozy nest of bubbles. Zach grinned as he closed the door. *She didn't have any steam left to burn off today. Room service and movies sounded beyond perfect.* Her mind started to flicker through the last couple of weeks. *That steamy afternoon with Frost before the banquet. She was such an idiot. She would have had more memories to reminisce about if she hadn't tossed Kevin off a balcony for no reason. They'd punished her by separating them from the Clan. Killing those shady Lampir had been followed by an epic car accident and a run-in with pheromone loving Lycanthrope. They'd been kidnapped by Abaddon and she'd lit herself on fire on the word of her ex-boyfriend who now spoke in her thoughts. After waking up in Triad's trunk, they'd been driven to a hotel where they all had plans to spend the night. She'd had a heart to heart with Kevin about his new role in her afterlife. That was also where the repercussions of accidentally strengthening Grey's Pyrokinesis became clear. He got drunk and lit the place on fire in a jealous rage. They'd raced away from the hotel during that high-pitched sound but weren't out of range when the Aries Group blew the place up to dispose of the evidence. Zach fell off a cliff into turbulent waters. She dove in after him, they became trapped in a cave with sharks blocking one escape route and cannibals in the way of the other. She fought infectious cannibals in maze-like underground caverns and ended up trapped for a week, only to be shot with large animal tranquillizers and decontaminated by the Aries Group. She'd taken her first plane ride inside of a pod to keep her from tampering with the equipment. Her mind was spinning. It was time to get out of the tub. There was no point in overthinking this gong show. She was going to give herself a headache.* Putting on an enormous mid-thigh-length T-Shirt that she'd bought to use as pyjamas, Kayn wandered out of the washroom with a wild mane of damp curls.

They were sharing a hotel room with two queen-sized beds. Lexy and Grey were sprawled on one as Lexy flicked through the movies. There was a knock on the door. Zach leapt up, grabbed his card and answered it as she snuggled under the covers. *This was what she wanted to do… Absolutely nothing.*

Zach plopped his behind on the bed, announcing, "Dinner has been served." He handed a pizza box to Lexy.

She opened the box, saying, "Brilliant idea, Zach."

Zach opened their box. Kayn grinned as she saw that he'd loaded half of their pizza with banana peppers and jalapeños. *He always had her back.* She playfully shoved him and praised, "Thanks buddy."

He was chuckling as he dug into a separate bag. Zach tossed packages of hot sauce at both her and Lexy as he replied, "I know what you ladies need."

"I'll tickle your back while we're watching the movie," Kayn vowed as she dumped a grotesque amount of hot sauce on one of the slices and devoured it.

Grey scowled at Lexy and teased, "What? No back tickling for me?"

Lexy held up her pizza, shrugged and countered, "No banana peppers. No back tickles."

Grey fake pouted as he ate his slice. *Things were still off between Lexy and Grey. She could feel it.*

Zach leaned closer and whispered, "That's why we're never sleeping together." Grey tossed an empty styrofoam cup at Zach. It landed between the beds. "Good shot," Zach mocked.

Grey grinned as he slowly shook his head and sparred, "Carry on... It's not like I can't light this whole hotel on fire."

"I dare you to pull that bullshit again and see what happens," Lexy mumbled while staring at her slice of pizza.

"Alright friends, we're staying in the same room tonight and I really don't have it in me to continue watching this soap opera. I'll turn this drama into a horror faster than you can say don't smother me with a pillow. Pick a movie," Kayn urged, irritated.

"Would you like something to drink, hun?" Zach sweetly asked.

"I'd love a glass of water," Kayn answered, grateful her Handler wasn't being a tool.

"I guess nobody thought to get any beer?" Grey enquired as he wandered over to the mini-fridge.

"Oh, you're not drinking anywhere around me for a long time," Lexy muttered under her breath as she flicked through the movies.

Grey stopped staring into the mini-fridge. He turned around, looked directly at Lexy and coldly stated, "I have to drink to be around you. Our days of cuddling in bed are done. I'm sure Tiberius can clear his schedule to cater to your every need."

Lexy got up, met Grey's insolent gaze and countered, "At least he'll remember doing it."

Zach jumped up, blocked Grey and suggested, "Let's get out of here before one of you says something that can't be taken back."

"Don't bring him back if he's drunk," Lexy remarked.

Well, there goes movie night.

Glancing back at Lexy, Grey jousted, "Sweetheart, it'll take me five seconds to find someone more worthy of my company!"

This wasn't good. Grey aggressively slammed the door as he left, leaving Zach standing in the room. Her Handler said, "I'll go and make sure he's alright."

"He'll get over it. I always do," Lexy replied quietly as she continued searching for something to watch.

Zach slipped out of the room. Kayn glanced over at her sister and asked, "Were you guys fighting the whole time I was gone?"

"Worrying, fighting, then worrying some more. Our symbols kept going off. We were afraid you'd been swept out to sea. Jenna contacted us with your location and the warning to wait for the Aries Group to arrive before attempting to go after you because the area was shark invested and we'd only end up making a bad situation worse."

"What are you going to do? He's your Handler," Kayn asked.

"I'm going to get over him and move on with somebody else. Like I should have a long time ago. This is probably a good thing. Maybe if being with him isn't an option, I'll be able to find something lasting longer than a night," Lexy replied.

"You love him," Kayn pointed out, sensing her sister's inner turmoil.

While lost in her thoughts, Lexy whispered, "I always will. More than anything in this world or any other, but I can't keep doing this to myself."

Kayn slipped out from under the covers and got into the bed next to her newfound sibling.

Lexy smiled as she enquired, "How about this one? Do you like scary movies?"

"Sounds good," Kayn replied. They began watching an eighties slasher film full of gratuitous violence. As would be expected, both Dragons fell asleep.

They awoke to find the boys hadn't returned from the night before. It was annoying because they needed to go to high school to stalk a teenage girl today. The backpacks full of supplies they'd purchased the day before were by the door. Lexy texted the first number on her cell, alerting the Aries Group of the change of plans. Kayn and Lexy were going without their Handlers. They were washed, dressed and out of the door in a few minutes. Kayn had just a touch of makeup on and her hair pulled into an inconspicuous sporty ponytail, playing the jock. Lexy was dressed as she felt most comfortable with her free-flowing crimson hair, ruby red lips, heels and jeans that accentuated her curves. The two Dragons strutted out of the room.

"Shit!" Lexy exclaimed. "They have the car."

"We'll take a cab," Kayn announced as she observed the busy street ahead while lugging the backpack full of school supplies intended for Grey. *Lexy was going to have no problem waving down a taxi looking like that. She preferred to hide in the background. Lexy's preference was the waving flag approach. This could be an interesting day. No Handlers. A bonding day with her newfound sibling. What could go wrong?*

Lexy laughed as she responded to her thoughts, "Don't even think it."

In minutes they were in the back of a cab on their way to school. Kayn was honestly excited to experience a few days of normalcy. They'd be walking the halls, eating in the cafeteria. It was an opportunity to just be a teenager. They got out at the school. Her sister paid and their taxi drove away.

Checking her phone when it buzzed, Lexy peered up, announcing, "Grey's paperwork has been replaced with yours. We're siblings from Arizona. We just moved here for our Dad's job. We're using the same first names. Our last name is Smith."

Smith was Kevin's real last name. Kayn grinned as they strolled towards the doors, listening to animated chatter while taking in auras of the swarm of teenagers ahead.

She really should have stabbed herself this morning and healed so their auras would be more vibrant. Kayn nudged Lexy. The two girls paused and stepped aside, allowing the crowd to funnel past. She whispered, "I didn't prepare for this. Their auras are faint."

Lexy casually responded, "No biggie, I stabbed myself this morning after I brushed my teeth. I'll find her."

"Of course," Kayn teased as they joined the herd of teens and marched through the double doors into the hormonal jungle. *They hadn't been given much information to run with but knew the drill.* After a rather witty conversation with an awesome secretary, they had their schedules and were on the way to first class.

They parted ways before Kayn clued in. *Lexy's, I've got this speech, wasn't going to work if they were in different classes. She was going to have to carefully wound herself, so she didn't get blood on her clothes.* The warning bell rang. She opted out. Preferring to focus on what she could see versus being the centre of attention by being late, Kayn entered the classroom. Only seeing faint auras around each person, she inconspicuously slipped into an empty seat at the back of the room and opened her binder. *Invisible had always been her preferred state while amongst her peers when she was mortal. She rather enjoyed people watching. It was easy to see where each student fell in the hierarchy. There were three girls in the front of the room whose mannerisms screamed peacock. They were being ogled by obvious jocks, whose auras were as dull as their personalities.* As she scanned the room, she found a girl with hues of yellow who was a possibility. *She was trying to pay attention to the teacher while visibly upset.* Kayn observed her for the entire hour. When the bell rang signalling the end of class, the petite brunette with a cute pixie cut, gathered her belongings and stood up, revealing a protruding belly. *The girl was at least six months pregnant. She hadn't seen that plot twist coming. It couldn't be her.* Kayn followed the girl out into the hall. Lexy called her name and she turned around.

"I found our girl, Carmen," Lexy announced as she rushed to catch up.

Oh, thank God. "Awesome. So, she was in your last class?" Kayn asked as they compared schedules. *They had a class together.* They raced to the next room number on their schedule and were lucky enough to find two empty seats in the back. This time all eyes were on them. It only took a second to realise they were looking at Lexy, not her. *It was going to be difficult to remain invisible with her sister dressing like that.*

Using telepathy, Lexy spoke directly to her mind, *'She's two rows ahead of us. Can you see her?'*

Kayn inconspicuously peered up from behind her book, and sure enough, there was another girl with a faint yellow hue. *Something concerned her, though. Her aura was no brighter than the pregnant girls from the class before.* Without words, she directed her thoughts to Lexy, *can there be two? In my last class, there was another girl with the same aura, but she was pregnant.* Her stomach clenched as someone knocked on the classroom door. The teacher wandered over with clicking heels and excused herself as she stepped out. Glancing over at Lexy, she knew, she'd felt the same internal warning.

The teacher came back into the room and announced, "Is there a Kayn and Lexy Smith in this class?"

What in the hell was this about? They raised their hands as they got up and strolled over to the door. The teacher motioned for them to come with her. They begrudgingly did, knowing they had to play along. As they stepped out into the hall, they saw officers with ominous swirling black auras. *Maybe she was going to have an opportunity to ripen up that healing ability after all?*

"Ladies, we have a few questions. We're going to need you to come with us," an officer that was obviously Abaddon directed.

Without a speck of concern for their wellbeing, the two Dragons wandered down the hall and out a side door. Kayn thought, *So, I take it we have to behave until we're out of sight?*

Lexy replied without speaking, *'Play along. I'll make it clear when it's time.'*

As they stepped outside with a burst of fresh air, Kayn noticed there was a dumpster and no windows. She looked at Lexy, who slowly moved her head from side to side. *They were Dragons. These guys were morons.* One of the fake cops opened the sliding side door of an unmarked black van and ordered them to get in. They stood there contemplating their options. Kayn leaned closer to Lexy and whispered, "I'm not sure they know who they're dealing with?"

Grinning, Lexy responded, "They know exactly who they're dealing with. We're undercover and they have the power to blow it."

Stupefied, Kayn watched her sister climb into the van. *Were they really going to leave with these guys?* Kayn shrugged as she followed suit. *You were never supposed to allow someone to take you to a second location. Her parents had made them watch that episode of Oprah.* Her mind travelled back to family breakfasts and warm loving embraces. *Her heart ached. It felt like another life... It was.*

Her crimson-haired sister telepathically scolded, *'Change your train of thought. Emotional baggage makes you weak. This is not the time for that. It's Dragon time.'*

The idea of dropping polite pretence and kicking ass always made her feel a delightful surge of freedom. The Abaddon were chatting outside as they sat there moderately amused by their capture's lack of foreboding. *These guys had to be new.* The pretend officers got into the front and started the engine. The unmarked vehicle lurched to one side as it pulled out. They toppled over chuckling. *This was an unfamiliar scenario. There were so many things she still didn't know, and on occasions such as this, it felt like she was flying blind.* Kayn questioned, "Are you going to tell me why we've willingly gotten into this van without an offer of candy on the table?"

Lexy removed her heels, commentating, "Always the comedian." She winked and cracked her neck as she added, "We'll stop and get candy on the way home. As you know, after the Correction happens, there's a race for the survivor. I bet these tools are trying to stop us from interfering. They're obviously new and don't know the rules. It happens. This girl must be important." Balancing like she was surfing on a concrete sea with her palm menacingly against the see-through barrier, Lexy shouted, "Toss me one of my shoes!"

Kayn pitched one of her sister's heels at her. She caught it and winked mischievously. *This was going to be good!*

Lexy started smashing her heel against the shatter resistant window, yelling a colourful list of obscenities. A fanned-out crack formed across the divider. She slammed her fist through the window. With her hand covered in blood, she grabbed one of the men by his hair, yanked him through and tossed him at Kayn, declaring, "Snack time!"

The terrified Abaddon attempted to squirm away as Kayn swiftly pinned him down. She stared deep into his eyes as she declared, "You should have given me candy." She immobilized him by putting her full weight on his shoulders, grasped either side of his face and allowed her ability to take hold. The warmth of his lifeforce travelled up both of her arms, into her chest where it continued to gather until the blissful euphoria caused her to shiver. *Dark energy was always one hell of a trip.* Her emotions sunk into the quicksand of her Dragon soul and for a time all was lost but the numb sensation of nothing at all. When she finally looked up, Lexy was chasing the other man across the dusty parking lot. *She must have climbed through the window into the front.* With power surging through her being, Kayn opted for the direct route as she booted the door. It flew off the hinges and soared through the air, landing in the gravel lot creating an explosion of dust and debris. She casually jumped down from the back of the van into the dusty lot. People trailing ominous black and grey mist, came from every direction, wielding weapons. Coldly calculating her next move, her eyes scanned the junkyard. There were shooters perched on the tops of the stacked rubble of demolished vehicles as dozens of unafraid Abaddon strolled towards her. *If they were normal girls, they'd be in over their heads, but they weren't normal. They were anything but…* Unaffected by rational things like numbers of assailants, she visually searched the parking lot for her partner in debauchery, narrowing in on her almost instantly.

Her crimson-haired vengeance filled immortal sibling leapt to her feet beside a body and brushed herself off, announcing, "Who's next?" They came at Lexy as she booted them away, hurling evil strangers through the air and stomping on the heads of those unfortunate enough to remain underfoot.

Mesmerised by the ghoulish blur of arterial spray and carnage, Kayn was grabbed from behind, and repeatedly stabbed. *Annoying.* She kicked back with immortal force, snapping her surprise assailant's leg. Coolly observing her enemy, shrieking in agony while squirming in dust like a pig with a bone protruding from his calf, she emotionlessly yanked his serrated blade from her back, and watched the sheer terror in the Abaddon's eyes as she stomped on his face.

A voice in her head prompted, *'behind you on your right.'*

Kayn stepped to the left as she spun around. Half a dozen arrows whirled through the air, missing her by a hair. Following instructions from a voice in her mind, she dodged everything coming at her from a distance until she confused right and left in the mayhem and heard popping noises. Aware she'd been shot, Kayn icily peered down at the blood pooling on her shirt as heat from her healing ability enveloped her and wounds closed, forcing the bullets out. Healing extraordinarily fast as Abaddon relentlessly attacked in a blur of scarlet spray and adrenaline until all who'd dared to challenge them had fled, leaving only Dragons in the wake. Hearing a tinny clink in the piles of mortal rubbage, their gazes turned in creepy unison.

An omniscient voice commanded, "No survivors."

Hunting those hidden in demolished cars and heaps of trash, they continued feeding on energy until they were crawling through wreckage as wild creatures. Drenched in the blood of enemies and void of humanity, they were aware of little more than the sun's radiance and the metallic scent of the blood stiffening their clothes as they perched like gargoyles.

"Kayn! Kayn! We're here!" a voice called from below her royal perch. "Come down! We've called the Aries Group. We need to get you guys out of here. They'll shoot first and ask questions later!"

She didn't care but something within her urged her to listen. Zach… it was him. Coldly meeting her Handler's gaze, she inquisitively cocked her head. *She wanted to be left alone.*

Climbing up the wreckage, Zach ceased movement close enough to feel like a nuisance. He tried urging her to come with hand motions while whispering, "Please Kayn. We need to leave."

Obligated to follow his directions even if she didn't want to, Kayn climbed down. Zach held out his hand. *He wanted her to take it.* Her hand rose from her side against her will. This irritated her, but as their skin made contact, the urgency to continue the massacre subsided and reality of what she was doing came into focus.

Gazing into her eyes, Zach prompted, "You're almost there… Come back to me."

She felt the tie to his soul as he gave her hand a gentle squeeze and cautiously inched closer until she was in his arms. As she inhaled his scent, she felt a sedating sense of peace within. *Yes. She wanted to go with him. She felt her emotions beginning to rise to the surface.*

Zach pulled away. He lovingly cupped her cheeks with his hands. While utterly beaming, he said, "Welcome back, Brighton. We need to go."

As Kayn became aware of her situation, her eyes searched for the others. Grey was standing next to Lexy with his arms around her. *That's nice. They'd obviously made up.* Multiple loud shots rang out in the silence. Driven by an instinct to protect her Handler, Kayn shoved Zach out of the way, prepared to take one for the team.

Releasing a guttural wail, Lexy stepped in the bullet's path with her hands raised. The bullets froze in midair.

It took a second to register the hovering bullets. "Holy shit," Kayn whispered. *That snapped her the rest of the way out of Dragon mode.* She looked back to find both Grey and Zach were also frozen in place. The shooters were like statues. Awestruck, she watched as Lexy reached out and touched one of the hovering bullets. *This was extremely cool! Lexy is way better at freezing time.* From behind them, someone started a slow clap. The Dragons spun around to find their inept paternal figure thoroughly enjoying the show.

Seth continued to clap as he marched up to motionless Grey and gave him a pat on the head.

Lexy was the first of the Dragon sisters to speak, "Did you do that?"

"No child," Seth proudly admitted. "That was all you."

"But, I can't do that," Lexy countered as she plucked a hovering bullet out of the air and stared at it in the palm of her hand.

"You couldn't do it. Now you can," the mischievous Guardian clarified as he poked another bullet. It dropped into the gravel at his feet.

"Will I be able to do this?" Kayn questioned as she grabbed another bullet from the air.

Burying the bullet at his feet with a kick, Seth answered, "I honestly have no idea. Stopping time is a Guardian thing and you are part Guardian so it's entirely possible. It doesn't last for long though so you might want to start taking those leftover Abaddon thugs out. Come see me next time you're in the In-between and we'll experiment."

Scowling at Seth, Lexy vehemently retorted, "You left me at a demon farm for five years!"

"Are you really still on that? It's been over forty years. Get over it!" Seth announced as he tried to come closer.

She curtly promised, "I was eleven. I may not be able to kill you, but I'll snap your bones like twigs if you take one more step!"

Seth sighed as he opted out, "So, you're saying you'll need time before we cuddle?"

Rolling her eyes, Lexy sparred, "Enough bullshit black spandex man. How do I unfreeze them?"

It was then that Kayn smiled. She'd become so used to ignoring the weird stuff, she hadn't noticed her genetic sire's choice of form. Seth marched over and placed both of his hands on her forehead. *Her brain felt all tingly.*

Seth was grinning like a naughty child as he whispered, "You're welcome." Without explaining, he vanished. He materialized behind one of their assailants and rather joyously snapped his neck, urging, "Come on you two. The jobs not finished. The Aries

Group is coming. Also, you might want to keep the whole freezing time thing on the down-low." Seth disappeared and reappeared behind the next shooter and effortlessly took him out.

They were both so entranced with what he was able to do, they'd stopped paying attention to the duties at hand.

"We only have a few minutes here, maybe less, Lexy's new," Seth prompted and they joined in to finish the job. He motioned them closer as he announced, "Time to leave. The Aries Group is almost here." He pointedly looked at Kayn as he said, "They shouldn't see you looking like that twice in less than a week, they'll get antsy."

He probably had a point there.

Seth placed his hands on their Handler's shoulders and prompted, "We're out of time. If you want to come along, you'd better be touching them in… 3,2,1."

They grabbed their Handlers, and in a flash, they were back inside their hotel room. The boys were both alert and confused as hell as to how they got there.

Seth pressed his fingers against his lips to shush the group. He grinned at the four, looked at Lexy and urged, "Take a chance. Come see me. I'll help you figure that new ability out." He tossed a bag of stones at her.

Lexy looked like she was about to tell Seth off when he disappeared in a flash of light.

Grey glared at Lexy and questioned, "What new ability?"

Pressing a cautionary finger against pursed lips, Lexy dumped the privacy stones into her hand and placed them around the room.

As soon as the stones were set, Kayn piped in, "Lexy froze time. I'm starving. Dibs on the shower." With that, she dashed away, leaving her sister there to explain.

Once they'd all showered and changed into less murdery clothes, they sealed their blood-soaked garments in bags and left them in the tub, planning to dispose of them later. They decided as a group to stay in and mend fences. Nobody asked any questions or fought about trivial things that couldn't be undone as the four watched a couple comedies and dined on the greasiest entrées room service had to offer while snuggled up in bed.

Utterly exhausted, the four Ankh fell asleep early and awoke to a brand-new day. With Lexy and Kayn being the ones enrolled, the boys opted to stake out the exterior of the school, hoping to head off any complications before they arose. The two Dragons set off in search of the girl slated for Correction. They were relieved as they spotted Carmen because they'd rather epically dropped the ball the day before. They were supposed to be staying in the background, so they'd be familiar yet unknown. If Carmen survived her Correction and recalled seeing them in passing, the odds were higher, she'd come willingly. For days they wandered the graveyard for the creative, attending classes while scrutinizing their prospective Clan member from afar. It didn't take long to realise she was a horrible person who snuffed out the weak in the wilds of this cliché of a high school as lions would gazelles. They both wanted to leave this rotten mortal for whatever or whoever came for her next but that wasn't the job. Their duty was to snatch her after she survived her Correction.

Each day they entered the vehicle feeling like they were wasting their time, but it wasn't their job to determine who got to be Ankh. They tailed Carmen to self-defence class and then home that evening. She was walking to the front door as they pulled into the driveway across the street. Her front door was partially open. Carmen paused. Kayn felt it in her soul as the door shifted ever so slightly in the breeze. They all ducked as Carmen looked back at the street just as Kayn had a couple years ago. Kayn's stomach clenched. *It was happening… Right now. The girl was a heinous bitch, but nobody deserved this.* Kayn looked around the vehicle. *They were all aware of what was happening.* Either it was one of the other Clans or Abaddon in that house. She sensed the darkness within Carmen's house and a tidal wave of hunger washed over her. Kayn was white-knuckling the handle of the door as Grey sat up front blowing bubbles and snapping his gum. *If she ate him it would shut him the hell up.* Her pulse began racing as her veins brightened making her skin virtually see-through.

Lexy glanced back at Kayn and whispered, "Calm yourself down. Breathe in and out until you've got it under control. You know the drill. We wait. We can only take her if she survives on her own or if Azariah gives her another chance." She paused for a second before adding, "Zach, she ingested too much dark energy earlier, she might need to be weaned off. I'd feed her before she eats Grey."

"What?" Grey asked, as he looked back.

"Keep snapping your gum Grey," Lexy threatened. "If she doesn't kill you, I will."

Zach was still gapped out staring at Carmen's house.

Grey scolded, "Earth to Zach! Do something before she eats me!"

Zach looked at Kayn and whispered, "Oh, shit. That can't be good. I'm on it." He offered her his hands.

That was offensive. I'm on it? Kayn was about to accept a snack from her Handler when Kevin's voice yelled, *'No!'* His voice echoed within her mind. Rattled, Kayn yanked her hands away from Zach and stammered, "I can't."

"Why not?" Lexy countered. "If you take too much, I'll bring him back. It's not a big deal."

She wasn't supposed to tell anyone she was being spiritually guided by her enemy. It was a conflict of interest. Kayn shook her head slowly as she explained, "My gut's warning me against doing this. It's never steered me wrong."

Grey piped in from the driver seat, "I'm curious, where did you put the dark energy you ingested earlier?"

"I don't know," Kayn answered honestly. "Seth touched my head and told me it would help. Maybe, it was something to do with that?"

"Why was he there?" Zach enquired. "We were incapacitated. We missed a large chunk of conversation."

"Apparently, Seth's an avid stalker. He knows where we sleep, quite literally." Lexy answered. "That's how he brought us back to our hotel room."

"Gross," Zach commented.

Grey laughed and launched his gum at the dash.

Lexy grimaced and remarked, "That's why we can't take you anywhere."

She needed to cut herself and heal. She had to do something before she ceased to have control over her actions. Kayn reached for a blade. She was poised to slice into her palm as Lexy slapped it out of her hand and quietly scolded, "If Abaddon's doing the Correction, they'll smell it."

Their attention was brought back to the house as the lights turned on in the kitchen. "Weird… They usually cut the power or loosen a bulb," Kayn noted. *Nobody ever makes it out of the doorway.* Kayn flashed back to a vision of herself trying to flick on a light in the entrance of her house. The place was quiet, uneasily so. The vertical blinds had been left slightly open, but they couldn't see what was going on from this vantage point.

"I'm going to get a closer look. If I get caught, I'll improvise," Grey declared as he quietly got out, closed the car door behind him and sprinted across the road.

Zach was about to follow him when Lexy said, "No, let him do it. This is his thing."

Grey snuck through the grass to the blind covered window and found the right angle to peek inside. He stepped away, strolled up the front steps and musically knocked on the door. *What in the hell was he doing?* The door opened. He began chatting up the unharmed girl they'd been observing. A moment later a teenager with a sketchy smoky aura appeared. He placed his arm possessively around Carmen and closed the door in Grey's face.

Grey walked back to the car and got in defeated. "Let's go," he bluntly decreed. He started the engine and pulled away.

"Wait. What's going on?" Zach questioned.

Grey explained, "There's a kitchen full of Lampir and our Carmen appears to be entirely unfazed by her family's corpses on the linoleum. This isn't our girl."

The pregnant girl with the yellow aura. Kayn confessed, "I thought I saw another one, but she was pregnant."

"Maybe this is a test? This definitely isn't playing out like a normal Correction," Zach inferred as he grabbed a bag of Doritos from the grocery bag of surveillance snacks on the floor.

Kayn snagged one. She was about to eat it when Kevin's voice directed, 'You need to go back. If you feed from the Lampir. You'll get the information needed to complete the job. Use Chloe's ability. Seduce your way inside. Lampir love those pheromones just as much as Lycanthrope.' She touched Grey's shoulder and asserted, "Go back. If they're Lampir, Carmen's lack of reaction is mind control. They could just be taking their time doing her Correction."

"Lampir don't partake in Corrections," Grey clarified. "Go back. I'll dose them with pheromones and find out

everything they know," Kayn proclaimed. She devoured her Dorito in one mouthful and grinned at Zach as she realised, he'd bought her the insanely spicy ones. *He really was sweet, most of the time. She needed to give him credit. He was trying.*

Grey turned the vehicle around, blindly trusting her gut instinct which made her feel a tad guilty because it wasn't really hers. *If Kevin ever screwed her over while guiding her, she was totally going to kick his ass.*

Zach leaned in and whispered, "Did I hear that right?" "I'll explain when we're alone," she whispered, wiping

Dorito dust on her black pants. *Seducing her way into a house while smelling like Doritos might prove to be rather comical.* Kayn enquired, "Does anybody have a breath mint?"

Lexy passed her a mint as she asked, "Are you sure you're capable of this right now? You haven't had the best luck summoning up abilities."

Meeting her concerned gaze, Kayn confessed, "I can trigger the pheromones with Zach's help." She popped the mint into her mouth.

Lexy winked at Zach as she passed him a mint and teased, "You're on Romeo."

Chuckling nervously, Zach mumbled, "No pressure or anything."

Grey glanced back and offered his services, "I'll do it." Lexy swatted him and he laughed.

Lexy looked back at Kayn and suggested, "Biting your lip releases Serotonin. Cutting yourself works like a charm, but that's off the table. This is supposed to be a sneak attack." Kayn bit her lip, thinking of the last time she was with Frost and what he was capable of with only a touch. *If he were here, this would be simple. No lingering moral dilemmas to obsess over.*

Zach whispered, "I have an idea. You're already wearing yoga pants. Say you were out for a jog and you tripped. Between the scent of blood, and your pheromones, this will be like taking candy from a bunch of long fanged babies." Comfortable in his role as impromptu make-out buddy, Zach caressed her hair as he seductively moved in. His lips parted as they met hers. She urged her Handler on with an erotic dart of her tongue. Forgetting they had witnesses, she straddled Zach as he moved his hands intimately over the sparse coverage of her clothes. She felt his arousal as she moved against him until and the spine-tingling euphoria as her pheromones released in an intoxicating knee-buckling wave.

Grey began panicking, "Get out! Get out of here! Quick, Brighton!"

She got out, slit her hand with a knife and tossed it back into the car. She casually wiped the blood on her spicy Dorito dusted pants and closed the door. They all ducked and peered up as Kayn marched across the street. She aggressively knocked on the front door. She was invited inside by Carmen with a still oozing bite mark on her neck. *They were feeding on her.* Intrigued by the large mysterious gathering of Lampir, Kayn boldly entered the kitchen and instructed Carmen to leave. Kayn addressed the group, "Please remain seated." She stood in front of the table full of salivating mesmerized Lampir, looked directly at the one that accompanied the girl to the door earlier and enquired, "May we speak privately?"

"As enticing as you are that feels like a horrible idea," he replied as his eyes travelled her body.

"You won't be harmed. You have my word," Kayn assured.

The dark-featured, undeniably attractive Lampir got up from his seat. He held out his hand and bargained, "Promise me you'll let me have a taste and I'll go."

"Do I get a taste too?" Kayn sparred as she opted out of taking his hand and followed him to a doorway that led to a steep flight of cement stairs into the basement.

"Ladies first," he politely motioned for her to take the lead.

No stranger at taking leaps into unknown places, she shrugged and went down the stairs. She heard him lock the door. He turned on a light and what she saw was rather unexpected. There were no windows and cement walls. No natural light at all. They were crashing here. The whole lot of them. "Humour me?" she asked. "Why didn't you dispose of the parent's bodies?"

"Oh, they're not dead," the deviously attractive Lampir revealed as he intimately trailed his fingertips in an enticing path down her arm. "They're in transition."

"So, you're unaware you've stumbled into the middle of a Correction?" Kayn clarified, seductively caressing his dark silky hair.

"Carmen's not up for Correction. She's a distraction," he confessed, with the heat of his breath feathering against her throat.

He had information she needed. Kevin was right. But right now, she didn't care about that. She wanted to feel his teeth sinking into the soft, ivory flesh. She was totally going to let him bite her and he knew it. He parted his jaws and sunk his teeth into her throat. It felt like intoxicating bliss-inducing needles. *It was incredible. She didn't want it to stop.* He pressed the length of his body against hers, making breathy noises of pleasure that caused another unexpected burst of resolve numbing pheromone to release from her skin. *Shit, she was going to get herself in trouble. This ability wasn't easy to control.* She whispered, "Stop."

Obediently, his fangs left her neck. He stared at her in awe as her skin healed and whispered, "What are you?"

Kayn slid her hands beneath the naughty stranger's shirt. Every touch was a thousand times the intensity. She met his spellbound gaze, confessing, "Something new." She was playing with fire and getting burned was on the table, but she didn't care, not in the least. *She wanted more. More of everything.* "Don't you dare move a muscle it's my turn." Kayn slid her hands up his muscular chest until her palms were flush against his cool skin. He wasn't attempting to get away. Her suggestion sealed his fate. Her Conduit ability began heating her hands as the Lampir's lifeforce travelled up both arms and gathered in her chest. She eagerly replenished the energy he'd taken from her in blood. Flashes of memories, information from his subconscious fed images into her mind. It was like putting together a puzzle with missing pieces.

He pulled away and breathlessly questioned, "What are you doing?"

"I was hungry too," she clarified. "Surely, you didn't think the feeding was going to be one sided?" Kayn sensed she was losing her control over him, so she stepped closer, parted her lips and aggressively rekindled their make-out session. He stripped off his shirt and tossed it aside. *Whoops. How far was she willing to take this? She'd better decide and quick.*

He walked her back until he had her flush against the wall as he ominously whispered, "My turn."

The door was locked. *She could just do this. Lord help her, she wanted the release with every inch of her being. Nobody would ever have to know.* She shivered as he sunk his fangs into her throat. Feeding off Lampir energy was crazy addictive, overpoweringly so. *She needed this.* He slipped his hand into her pants and just as he was about to touch her where every nerve ending in her body was crying out to be touched, there was a loud pound on the door at the top of the stairs. Startled, they leapt apart. *No! Not now!* There was another loud crash and her focus returned. *She'd seen their plan. It was diabolically brilliant. Bravo.*

With a flirtatious smile, the Lampir stepped away and introduced himself, "Just in case we end up fighting and I don't have a second chance to say this, my name's Paul and you, my dear... are delectable." There was another crash followed by the sound of splitting wood. "I'm just going to go up there and see who it is before I end up having to fix that door," her sexy cohort announced as he dashed up the stairs.

Kayn remained there watching the empty bottom of the staircase. With the top obscured from view, she could only guess what was going on. After a few loud crashes, sexy Paul's lifeless corpse tumbled down the stairs. *His neck was broken. Snapping a Lampir's neck was only temporary.* They had special weapons that worked on a variety of otherworldly creatures. Only a wooden dagger or bullet to the heart sealed a Lampir's demise. She stood before the lifeless body of her make-out buddy and raised her eyes to the sound of slow steps descending the stairs. It was Zach.

"Is there a reason you're down in this creepy basement? You do realise your symbol went off," her Handler taunted, grinning like a cat that just ate a canary.

She stepped over Paul's body, with her pheromones on overdrive and darted past Zach without touching him, mumbling, "I have the information." *She was seriously horrible at her job. She had no idea what she was doing. Not a damn clue.*

"Well?" her Handler questioned as he pursued her up the stairs.

"Well, what?" Kayn countered.

Zach playfully shoved her and teased, "It sounded like you were too busy making out with this devilishly attractive stranger to question anything?"

Why did she keep trying to use this ability when she had no idea how to control it? They stepped out into the living room just as Lexy staked one of the house dwellers in the chest. He lit on fire and turned to ash. *No! What was she doing? She told Paul she wasn't going to hurt him.*

Lexy peered up and questioned, "Did you finish off the one on the stairs?"

Zach sighed, "I'll do it," he doubled back to the kitchen.

Kayn quietly followed. Grasping her Handler's arm when they reached the top of the stairs, she whispered, "Wait. I promised I wouldn't hurt him."

"Now why on Earth would you go and say something like that?" Zach whispered back. He stopped moving out of respect for her wishes as he quietly asserted, "They were in the process of turning three humans. They're not allowed to do that. Our response is crystal clear in this case."

She'd spoken the words so she felt obligated to stand by them even if he should be punished. Kayn stepped in front of Zach and urged, "Can't we just leave this one. Just once. My word is all I have."

Cupping her cheeks with his hands, Zach whispered, "We can't save every guy you makeout with. You understand that, right? How good was his information?"

"Excellent. I promise," she responded truthfully, still standing in his way.

Zach slowly shook his head as he instructed, "Give him a burst of healing energy and tell him to run. I'll try to keep Lexy occupied. A minute or two is all I can give you."

Nodding in silent agreement, she closed the door behind her and raced down the stairs. She knelt before Paul and placed her hands on his chest. He opened his eyes and gasped. *He must have been almost healed.* She whispered, "Run."

In a blur, Paul disappeared. Kayn remained seated on the cool cement stairs with only the humming of the vacuum as back noise. *They were vacuuming up Lampir ashes.* She chuckled. *This unconventional move was going to come back and bite her in the ass.* She got up and scaled the stairs. The back door was open and the kitchen was spotless. She closed it and walked away. *Why had she let him go? Zach was right. They were turning this girl's family.* She wanted to blame Kevin for setting her actions in motion but all he'd done is tell her what she needed to do. *He hadn't told her to practically sleep with the guy while siphoning information. She'd been the one to take this into unchartered territory.* Kayn wandered back into the living room. Grey was dumping a full container of Lampir ashes from the vacuum into a plastic bag. *Yet another check on the list of crazy shit she was just supposed to roll with.*

Grey peered up and disclosed, "You'll have to kill him eventually, and just so you know, there's always messed up consequences for just letting someone go."

She hadn't gotten away with a damn thing. Kayn nodded her acceptance of the inevitable. She met Grey's concerned expression with one of resolve, "I gave Paul my word. I'll pay for it at some point in the future."

"You know, it's not too late to hunt Paul down and kill him," Grey pointed out. "No harm no foul."

Frost hadn't been gone a month and ironically, she was the one with ability related fidelity issues. Shit. She had to kill this guy, didn't she? Kayn held out her hand and requested, "Toss me that knife on the couch,"

Wiping the sweat from his brow, Grey grinned as he reached over and handed her the knife, saying, "Now, that's the spirit, Brighton."

She'd only taken a step towards the door when it abruptly opened. It was Lexy, looking quite satisfied with herself. Zach was a few paces behind her. *She knew what they'd done by the guilty expression on Zach's face.*

Lexy announced, "The situation has been dealt with. No witnesses. The rules have a purpose. Dead Lampir tell no tales." She winked at Kayn. "What did you find out?"

Oh, yes. She was supposed to share the information she'd recovered from the Lampir's mind. Kayn addressed the group, "The girl we've been following is a decoy. I saw a yellow hue around another girl. She was pregnant. I assumed there was no way it could be her. I was partially right. It's the baby she's carrying."

"Why are we even here when they have to wait to do the Correction until the child is over the age of sixteen? Those are the rules," Grey asked, tidying up.

"If the pregnant mother with abilities is scheduled for Correction, it's within their rights to do it. The infant she's carrying is irrelevant under immortal law," Lexy explained. She turned to Kayn and said, "You told me about the pregnant girl, I didn't see a yellow-hued aura. Maybe, it wasn't the right girl?"

"I'll show you who she is when we get to school," Kayn answered while helping the others dispose of the evidence.

Nudging her, Zach whispered, "It's only nine o'clock. We have a whole night of sleep before school."

She wasn't going to be able to sleep. She was a horrible girlfriend. Grey handed her the container full of Lampir ash. Kayn strolled back through the kitchen and mumbled, "Sorry Paul" as she dumped it out the door and watched the ashes as they floated away. *Oh, yes. Sexy Lampir guy was killed outside. He wasn't even in there.*

"You didn't put the bloody towels in the garbage can outside, did you?" Lexy enquired as Zach strolled by.

He answered, "They're in the basement with the girl."

"Was she awake?" Lexy asked as she finished bleaching the linoleum.

"She's up and bitey," Zach confirmed. "Why didn't we gag her?"

"Grey was supposed to do it," Lexy sighed. "He's outside texting the address to the Aries Group. You two go downstairs and kill Carmen. Take the dustpan and the broom with you. Sweep her up and toss her out the back."

Zach shrugged and exclaimed, "I'll go get the dustpan and broom."

Kayn turned the end table on its side, stomped on it and snapped off a leg. *Such a waste. She should eat her.*

Zach reappeared with the cleaning supplies and stated, "You're not eating anyone else today. I'm exhausted."

Spoilsport.

"I heard that," Zach mumbled. He snatched Kayn's weapon, handed her the broom and said, "I've got this."

After they'd dealt with their final duty, they wandered across the street to where Lexy and Grey were waiting. Grey's cell vibrated as they got back into the car. He read the message in his mind first, upset about something.

Lexy touched her Handler's arm as she asked, "What happened?" Grey passed Lexy his cell as he turned the key in the ignition with dewy eyes. Lexy scrolled through the messages. She looked back and said, "The Ankh from the other continent didn't make it out of the Testing."

They'd all known that was going to happen.

Beaming, Lexy added, "The Trinity from your Testing made it out with the other continent."

Kayn blinked away the memories of the Testing as they flooded her mind. *Her friends from Trinity were free. Mel was probably ecstatic. The rest of their Clan were celebrating, and they were hearing about this via text.*

14

AS YOU ARE

They'd had a mini celebration the night before, so the next day the girls were feeling more than a little rough as they entered the high school in search of the pregnant girl. As they took their seats at the back of the room, the short-haired brunette in question strolled in looking like she'd swallowed a watermelon.

Lexy opened her book, whispering, "I don't see it."

This was rather peculiar because, for Kayn the yellow haze around the girl was brighter than it had been the prior week. She quietly disclosed, "I do. It's more intense."

The greying teacher in his mid-fifties placed his palm on Kayn's desk, interrupting their conversation, "Miss Smith with the blonde hair, you've just volunteered. Head up to the board and answer the question."

He didn't even know her actual name. Oh, she so despised being the centre of attention. Kayn got up and sauntered over to the chalkboard. She'd always had concentration issues, but with the steady hum of thoughts in the room, the squeaky hamster wheel between her ears wasn't going to play along. This was where the ability to hear thoughts came in handy. There were a lot of conflicting answers floating through the minds closest to where she was standing. Deciding to go with the pregnant girl's answer, she wrote, 37 on the board.

The teacher smiled and asked, "How did you get to that answer? You didn't show your work."

When in doubt, just say something confusing. Kayn turned around to face the class as she said, "Magic."

"Funny," the good-humoured teacher sparred. "Go sit down, Miss Smith."

Kayn pressed her lips together to stop herself from smiling as she slipped back into her seat.

The teacher placed a quiz on everyone's desk, and as he handed a copy to Kayn, he said, "You're quite advanced. You should have no problem with this."

Shit. A buzzer went off. Kayn opened her quiz. *Yes. She'd always had a strange gift when it came to multiple choice. Now, if she could only block out the buzz of everyone's thoughts.* She whipped through the test, feeding Lexy the answers and finished long before the bell rang. She watched the expectant teen. *She'd completed her test early too. She couldn't imagine having a baby at her age but at least she got to have one. She never would get married or have babies. Those things weren't in her future at all anymore. It made her heart ache.*

Lexy interrupted her thoughts with commentary, 'Don't let yourself think about it.'

Just then, the pregnant girl excused herself to go to the washroom.

The teacher razzed, "You're not going to have that baby in there are you, Emma?"

"I might," the expectant teen saucily bantered.

Fascinated by the girl who was comfortable enough in her own skin to joke about going into early labour with her teacher, Kayn waited a minute or two before asking to use the washroom. *Emma…That was a pretty name. This girl could be Ankh. She barely knew anything about her and already liked her.* Kayn stepped out into the empty hall lined with beige lockers and made her way to the girl's washroom. Her stomach cramped, she spun around, spooked. There was nobody there. She gave the washroom door a good hard shove just as the expectant teen was coming out and she toppled over. With fast reflexes, Kayn stopped her from falling, apologising, "So sorry. I'm a bull in a china shop."

Patting her protruding belly. Emma laughed and sparred, "I know the feeling."

"Sorry," Kayn repeated as she slinked past and quickly picked a stall. *Idiot! She wasn't supposed to interact with her.*

Emma called out, "It's nice to meet you fellow bull in a china shop!"

Kayn heard the door close as she gave her head a dramatic bang on the inside of the bathroom stall. *She was horrible at this job.* She sat down on the toilet with pants still up and her face in her hands. *The girl was pregnant and the Correction was coming for her. Awesome Emma didn't stand a chance.* Kayn made it back to class just as the bell rang. She collected her stuff and they followed Emma out into the hall as a surge of students appeared. *What was happening? There were so many black auras.*

"It's a distraction. You're right. That must be the girl.

Where is she?" Lexy stammered.

They'd lost her in the crowd. *Oh, no.* Kayn's stomach cramped again. They raced through the swarm of students. *Where was she?* Kayn exclaimed, "They can't do a public Correction."

"Not unless it looks like an accident," Lexy answered as they continued to scour the school.

The Dragons separated as students disappeared into classrooms to draw less attention. Kayn briskly marched down halls, trying each unmarked door until she saw a sign for another women's washroom. Foreboding filled her being as she sprinted there and heaved open the door. Emma was on the floor. Kayn was instantly at her side, shaking her. She wasn't breathing. She placed her ear on Emma's chest. *No heartbeat.* She started CPR. She wasn't allowed to heal her, but if she kept Emma's blood flowing, she might have a chance. One, two, three, four, breath. She looked around. There was a fire alarm. One, two, three, four, breath. She couldn't stop to pull it. She startled as Emma opened her eyes and took a deep breath. Kayn gasped, "Oh, thank god. I thought you were dead."

"I was… I think," Emma gasped. "There was a lady in the light and…"

Joy overcame Kayn as she started to laugh. *Azariah sent her back. They could take her.* She whispered, "This is going to sound absolutely insane but I'm with Ankh. Come with me. We'll protect you."

Lexy appeared in the doorway of the bathroom. They managed to get Emma out of the school undetected. They raced back to their hotel and checked out.

In under an hour, they were speeding down the highway away from the city towards the border. Kayn nudged Emma and asked, "You don't have many questions. Everyone has concerns like why did this happen? My parents will be looking for me. Why did someone just try to murder me?"

"I'm an empath with psychic abilities," Emma confessed. "I've known someone was coming to kill me for a while. This wasn't even the first attempt. My parents died last year in a car accident. I'm an only child with no close relatives. I've been couch surfing and living at the school because my foster home sucks. The father of this baby is an insignificant asshole. Any other questions?"

"No," Kayn commented. "This is by far the easiest kidnapping I've ever been a part of. Thanks for your cooperation."

Emma replied, "You're welcome. Thanks for showing up when you did."

They all laughed. Lexy texted the Aries Group. They needed a passport for Emma. As they approached their last chance to pull off before the border, they still hadn't heard back so she contacted the last number Ankh texted from. They were never going to get over the border with an expectant teenager. After making a unanimous decision to head into Idaho, they grabbed dinner on the go and ate their truck stop diner ham and cheese subs as they sped down the highway. Zach offered Emma a donut.

Emma scrunched up her nose as she declined, "No, thank you. I'm already fat enough, those things will kill you."

Everyone laughed, including the girl. They listened to music on the radio until, Here I Go Again by Whitesnake came on and in no time at all, they were all belting out the tune like road tripping warriors. Grey kept looking at Emma in the rear-view mirror as he drove. He seemed concerned and Kayn knew why. *They'd never had such precious cargo in the car. If they ran into Triad, Trinity or Abaddon the shit would hit the fan.*

Grey announced, "Bathroom break," as he pulled over at a rest stop. Kayn accompanied Emma to the washroom just to be cautious. *This was all too easy.*

As they got back into the car, Grey passed the new girl a two-litre of orange juice and awkwardly explained, "For the baby. It has folic acid. It says heart wise on it."

"Thank you. Should I just drink it out of the carton?" Emma enquired with a grin.

"I swear I don't have cooties," Grey flirted.

Their pregnant willing hostage smiled at Grey as she took a big swig from the carton.

Zach nudged Kayn as he raised his brows and thought, *'Grey likes her. Frost would be laughing his ass off.'*

Her heart surged as Zach mentioned his name but quickly sank as she thought about everything she'd done while they were apart. They pulled away from the rest stop and continued driving down the highway as Kayn struggled to shut her inner commentary down. The phone vibrated.

Lexy read the message aloud, "Our punishment must be over. We're meeting up with everyone in Montana. They're at the Edgewood Inn. Emma's new ID and passport will be couriered there. I have the directions…"

Lexy trailed off and everyone knew she had something else to say. *They had to brand her Ankh.*

"You might as well just spit it out," Emma sighed. "I'm not going anywhere."

Kayn showed her the Ankh symbol on the palm of her hand and pulled off the metaphorical bandage. "We have to brand you Ankh. This symbol prohibits us from passing through the Hall of Souls when we die. We remain in the In-between until our bodies have been healed by our Clan."

"Alright. Let's just get it over with," Emma agreed.

Kayn took Emma's hand and whispered, "I'm sorry," as she branded her palm with her ring.

"Son of a bitch!" Emma shrieked and protectively clutched her hand against her chest. "That was not cool!" their newest Ankh complained.

"I know," Kayn affirmed. "It's done. Welcome to Clan Ankh."

In the silence that followed all she could think about was Frost. *Was he angry? She'd made out with a lot of people.* She recalled the speech Frost gave her about forgiveness. *She'd assumed that was him preparing her for his inevitable ability related infidelity. Hopefully, he practiced what he preached.*

Interrupting her thoughts, Emma questioned, "What did you mean by, our punishment is over?"

Grinning in the rear-view, Grey revealed, "During a banquet, Kayn threw her ex off a balcony and Lexy snapped Kayn's ex-boyfriend's new girlfriend's neck."

Kayn rolled her eyes as she countered, "Come on, we're immortal, it wasn't a big deal."

Zach teased, "Don't let Markus hear you say that Brighton."

"Brighton?" Emma asked.

"Kayn's nickname," Lexy explained as she offered her chips to Kayn.

Kayn took a handful and whispered, "There's way more to the story. It'll make sense later."

Emma took chips as she muttered, "I wish someone would toss my ex off a balcony." Kayn and Lexy both looked at the new Ankh. Emma stammered, "Joking. I'm only kidding."

They drove through the night and into the following day until the scenery became flourishing rolling hills of green. They stopped at each rest stop to make sure their knocked-up Newbie Ankh stretched her legs and got a breath of fresh air. By nightfall, they arrived at the hotel in desperate need of a shower.

"So, what are the other Ankh like? Are they as cool as you guys?" Emma questioned as they all strolled into the lobby.

Grey flung his arm around Emma's shoulder and gave her a friendly squeeze as he whispered, "No way. We're definitely the coolest."

Kayn looked at her sister. She could tell Lexy was a little concerned. Grey's fascination with Emma was obvious. *Why wouldn't he be intrigued by a girl carrying a child? It was something he'd never have. They all liked her a lot. She was kind of amazing.*

They were each handed a key card at the front desk. *Everyone had their own rooms. That was unusual.* Kayn hauled her bag to the stairs. Everyone else got on the elevator. *She was nervous about the consequences of her actions. She'd been able to live life as though she didn't care while they were apart. What if they were over? What if she'd destroyed everything?*

Zach caught up with her and laughed, "Slow down, Brighton. Why did you take the stairs when there's an elevator?"

"I needed some time to think," she answered as she waited for him to catch up.

"Maybe they're not here yet? Don't read anything into it. I say we go upstairs, have a nice long bubble bath and meet up in the restaurant downstairs when we're done. I'll stay with you tonight if you need me to. As long as I'm around you'll never have to be alone."

That much she knew. He'd proven it time and time again. She swiped her key card. *It didn't work.* Zach took it off her and tried. *Of course, it worked when he did it.* She paused at the door and said, "See you later alligator."

"In a while crocodile," he sang, opening the door to the room next to hers.

She was still smiling about their dorky exchange as she locked the bathroom door and opted for an invigorating shower. She got out, brushed her teeth, fixed herself up and put on clean clothes. *If there was a chance she was going to be dumped, she might as well look good when it happened.* As she stepped out of the washroom, her heart skipped a beat. Frost was sprawled on her bed shirtless, flicking through the channels.

His lips slowly spread into a wry smile. He patted the mattress beside him and baited, "Hey beautiful."

She froze in place. *Maybe he didn't know and she was going to have to confess?*

"Didn't you miss me?" Frost teased, opting to come to her.

She wanted to run over there and leap into his arms, but the fear he would deny her kept her from moving a muscle. In a second, he was standing in front of her with a million questions in his eyes.

"Is there a problem?" he asked as he seductively tucked her damp curls behind her ears. "I've missed you," he disclosed, gazing into her eyes.

She decided to just say the words dangling on the tip of her tongue, "Aren't you mad?"

"About what?" Frost whispered naughtily as he moved her shirt off her shoulder and kissed her exposed skin. "We should just take this off," he provoked as he grabbed her shirt at the waist and lifted it up.

She raised her arms and allowed him to take it off as she confessed, "I can't control myself. I've done things."

"So have I," Frost revealed as he tossed her shirt aside. He laced his fingers through hers and towed her with him to the bed. "Baby, we've already talked about this. With our abilities and duties within the Clan, total physical fidelity is impossible, but I haven't slept with anyone else... Have you?"

"No," Kayn vowed as a surge of emotion brought tears to her eyes.

"You don't have to worry about making mistakes. You don't need to hide any part yourself. I want you just as you are," he whispered as she melted into his arms. They slowly moved back and forth, almost dancing.

"I honestly thought that conversation we had was about you," she divulged. They both started to laugh.

"Ouch, that actually stung," he pretended to be offended but his grin gave it away. Frost chuckled as he undid the top button on her jeans and seduced, "These definitely need to come off."

She bit her bottom lip while swaying her hips doing a sexy striptease as she unzipped her pants. The show ended rather abruptly when she started to laugh. *She really couldn't get her pants off, they were too tight.* Kayn tipped over and bounced on the mattress.

"Froggy, that was the hottest thing I've ever seen," he naughtily taunted. She swatted him. Frost grabbed the ankles of her jeans to help but the jean removal scenario had become far too funny to be sexy. After a few good tugs, he gave up, flopped down beside her and declared, "I can totally still rock your world."

"Oh, can you?" she egged him on.

Frost rolled on top of her and they seductively kissed until she was squirming in her partially removed jeans.

He naughtily suggested, "Let's just leave them like that, it'll be like I have your legs tied."

"Maybe you should tie my hands too?" Kayn provoked.

"You'd like that wouldn't you?" He whispered while nuzzling her neck.

She crossed her wrists above her head and called his bluff, "What are you waiting for?" He started tickling her sides. She was laughing hysterically as the adjoining door opened.

Zach was standing there with Grey, Lexy and Emma. *This was awkward.* Frost didn't miss a beat. He hopped up, sauntered over to the door shirtless wearing only his jeans which were now super tight in obvious places. He held out his hand and greeted the new girl, "You must be Emma. It's a pleasure to meet you."

Emma shook the mischievous immortal's hand as they all gawked at his situation.

He looked down as he realised what they were looking at and nonchalantly shrugged. Frost pointed at Emma's protruding belly and blurted out, "How did that happen?"

Quick witted, Emma pointed at Kayn frantically trying to pull her pants up on the bed and sparred, "It looks like you already know."

Frost looked at Kayn and apologized, "We're going to have to hit pause. We should be down at the restaurant for this conversation."

She could eat. Kayn yanked until she managed to get her pants up.

Frost turned to Zach and questioned, "Has Markus seen this?"

"No, not yet. We obviously didn't know you guys were here," Zach explained.

Frost grabbed his flashing cell off the nightstand and announced, "They're down at the restaurant already." He strolled over, sweetly kissed Kayn's cheek and whispered in her ear, "After dinner I'm going to cut those pants off and make you scream until you lose your voice."

She smiled as he walked away because that was his move. *He loved saying shockingly sexual things and then leaving. He'd been doing that since they met.* Frost started shooting random questions at Emma.

Zach gave her two thumbs up and silently mouthed the words, "Everything is okay?"

She smiled and nodded. *Happy endings were the best.* They piled into the fully mirrored elevator. Kayn was standing in front of Frost as he wrapped his arms around her waist from behind and whispered, "Just as you are."

Her heart swelled as she leaned against him and quietly repeated the words that meant so much, "Just as you are."

As the door opened into the lobby, Emma glanced at Lexy and commented, "You know, I've made it all of the way through this pregnancy without puking."

"I like her," Frost announced as they strolled through the lobby. "The new Ankh are in the restaurant with the others. There's Dean, Samid and… I got you a little something."

With her curiosity peaked, Kayn turned to Frost and teased, "It's not another ring from a vending machine, is it? I already have one of those."

They were all smiling as they entered the pub-style restaurant. The table full of Ankh waved them over. It looked like almost everyone was here and that's when Kayn saw Molly sitting at the end of the table. *They had her back.* Overcome with joy, she dove into Frost's arms and whispered, "Thank you."

He lifted her off the ground and spun her around as he whispered, "Better than a ring?"

Kayn kissed him and whispered back, "You are in so much trouble later."

"I've been in trouble since the day we met," Frost quietly admitted as the rest of their Clan got up in awe and gathered around.

The silence was deafening as Markus walked over and stood in front of Emma. He looked at Kayn in full panic mode as he questioned, "How did this happen? You're sure you took her after her Correction?"

"One hundred percent certain. She told me the lady in the light sent her back," Kayn explained.

Markus looked directly at Kayn and asked, "Is the baby alive?"

Emma laughed as she waved at Markus and said, "You know, you can speak directly to me. I'm standing right here. It's moving right now."

"I'm sorry. That was rude. This is just so unexpected. Can I touch it?" Markus questioned. Emma nodded her consent. He placed his hands on Emma's rounded belly and declared, "I have absolutely no idea how we're going to do this."

The Beginning

BIOGRAPHY

Kim Cormack is the comedic author of an epic dark sci-fi fantasy universe, "The Children Of Ankh." She worked as an Early Childhood Educator in preschool, daycare, and as an aid. She has spent most of her life on Vancouver Island in beautiful British Columbia, Canada. She currently lives in the gorgeous little town of Port Alberni. She's a single mom with two awesome offspring. If you see her back away slowly and toss packages of hot sauce at her until you escape.

All heroes are born out of the ashes that linger after the fire of great tragedy.

Sweet Sleep

Please take a moment to write an honest review. Spread the word so more readers will discover my field of dreams.

TRAGIC FOOLS TEASER

The bliss of sun-kissed skin awakened her. Twitching fingers in velvety sand as a heavenly breeze tickled her spine, Kayn peered up, grinning. *Somebody gave her an immortal time out.* Even with unlimited free passes to the In-between, a surprise trip was jarring until she recalled why she died. *Who killed her this time?* Cross-legged in pristine desert with silky granules trickling through fingers, her memory kicked in, clarifying why she was deceased. *Lexy knocked on her door and took her out of the equation. Their Oracle must have caught Kevin telepathically asking her to warn him before Ankh stole the girl he had a thing for. Her attachment to him was always getting her in trouble. She shouldn't be having conversations with an ex-boyfriend while in bed with her new one. Frost's patience had to be wearing thin. They'd just been separated as punishment for killing Kevin at a banquet. She tossed her ex off a balcony for giving her a clover. It was still fun.* Sensing a presence, Kayn got up, squinting in luminescence.

Ankh's Guardian Azariah sighed, "I'm beginning to think you enjoy being punished."

She didn't know what to say, she kind of did.

"Being part Guardian doesn't mean you can bend rules to your will," the angelic entity reprimanded.

Brushing the sand off her short ivory In-between attire, Kayn responded, "I wasn't going to say anything."

With divine angelic light attaching Clan Ankh's Guardian to the sky, Azariah wandered off, explaining, "That's just it, if he can tap into your mind, you have no say over what he knows."

Keeping pace, strolling the clean slate desert with warm, silken sand underfoot, beneath an azure sky, Kayn thought of a monarch butterfly. An orange and black distraction flitted by as proof she wasn't focusing on what the Guardian was saying.

The angelic entity trailing radiant light scolded, "I'm not talking to hear myself speak, child."

She wasn't a child. Now, a variety of vibrant butterflies were fluttering around. *She couldn't shut her feral imagination down.* Wincing, Kayn apologised, "I'm listening, I swear."

With a clap of her hands, distractions vanished. Smiling, Azariah carried on, "Here is the issue. Ankh needs a Venom before Immortal Testing. As you know, the Third-Tier sped up the timeline in response to the glitch your group used to get out. Currently, Triad is the only Clan with one. Your ex's crush means nothing. Residual mortal sentiment is clouding your judgment."

It was. She couldn't deny it.

BACK IN THE LAND OF THE LIVING, Ankh's Oracle voluntarily stayed with Zach to make sure Kayn remained deceased until their compromised job was finished. Relaxing on the queen-sized bed by Kayn's corpse, Jenna mindlessly flicked channels.

With Kayn's head on his lap, Zach gently stroked her hair, asking, "Do we have to keep killing her? Can't we lock her in a Tomb?"

"The bracelet to block Kevin's connection isn't working. I need to tweak it. He's psychic, and they're linked. Taking her out when we're dealing with Triad may be our only option."

"We all have ties to other Clans, I used to be Triad," Zach implored, meeting Jenna's eyes.

"Aren't you glad we stole you?" Jenna baited as Kayn's chest rose and fell. "Heads up, Handler. She's back."

"Can't we just keep her occupied? She doesn't know where they went," Zach bartered.

"Azariah needs time with her. A Guardian's word is law, take her out," Jenna instructed.

Looping an arm around her neck, he released his grasp as she went limp, muttering, "You're doing it next time."

"Suck it up Zach, you're immortal," Jenna teased.

CONTINUE READING TRAGIC FOOLS

Reading this may inadvertently trigger your Correction. If you survive or have shown great bravery during your demise, you may be given a second chance at life by the Guardians of the In-between. For your soul's protection, you must join one of the three Clans of immortals living on Earth. Clan Ankh, Trinity or Triad will train your partially mortal brain to reboot without a shock response and attach you to your Testing Group, then you will be taken to another world and dropped into Immortal Testing to prove that even after dying thousands of times, you comprehend greater good and would never leave your fallen behind.

You will be returned to Earth to serve an eternity with Tri-Clan, training Correction survivors, maintaining order and protecting the mortal population from themselves. **Welcome to your afterlife. Choose Your Clan.**

COA Universe

Children Of Ankh Series

Sweet Sleep
Enlightenment
Let There Be Dragons
Handlers Of Dragons
Tragic Fools

COA Series

Wild Thing
Wicked Thing
Deplorable Me
Sacrificial Lamb Club

More Titles Coming Soon.

www.ingramcontent.com/pod-product-compliance
Lightning Source LLC
Chambersburg PA
CBHW072114020726
47501CB00003B/815

9 781989 368220